Grace in the South China Sea

AVIOTT JOHN

ISBN-10:1514616807
ISBN-13: 978-1514616802

DEDICATION

To Mhairi
Who made the island possible.

Grace: def:. The exercise of love, kindness or goodwill; disposition to benefit or serve another.

CONTENTS

ACKNOWLEDGMENTS

This is a work of fiction. All people and events in it are products of my imagination. However, Tony and Pawel are two real, wonderful people who live on the island. I am eternally grateful for permission to use their real names. Although much about them has been fictionalized in this book, two facts remain true. Tony's coffee is the best I found in Hong Kong - this includes a US $ 35 cup of Kopi Luwak (civet-cat-processed coffee beans) that I tasted in a city café. And Pawel takes the most exquisite photographs, many of them close-ups of the island's extensive plant, insect and animal life. Pawel's photographs also showcase the beauty and infinite variety of Nature's design. Contact me through my blog at aviott.org if you wish to see some of them. Having two real people in the story made it come alive in my head, and I hope it has the same effect on you as a reader. Whatever your opinion, I hope you get a chance to try a cup of Tony's coffee, the best there is, if you ever visit the island.

I am indebted to the following people for valuable advice, corrections and input. To Mary McGechaen for detailed comments on every aspect of the story and the writing. Mary's feedback helped improve spelling, grammar, hyphenation and dozens of points of style. Ellis Nelson read the MS with great care, pointing out inconsistencies, suggesting alterations and showed me numerous examples of words used in the text that might be incomprehensible to the average US reader. This work has improved considerably in places where I have taken her advice. In others, I ignored her suggestions at my own peril. In this age of ubiquitous internet access, the correct or alternate meanings of words are only a Google or Baidu search away from the average reader. My thanks to Nasir Ahmed for taking time off from the busy schedule of a budding Oxford don to read through the MS. I am also grateful to Emily Ho (author of *Memoirs of an Ice-Cream Lady*) for comments about names of people and places on the island and in Hong Kong. It goes without saying that I am responsible for whatever flaws and shortcomings you find in this book. Finally, eternal credit to my wife Mhairi, whose willingness to uproot herself made the island a reality.

Aviott John
Vienna, November 2015

.

CHAPTER 1

Grace fumbled in her handbag for change and placed her Octopus card on the counter.

"Three hundred dollars, please."

Immediately behind and above her head, the bell that warned latecomers to board the ferry clanged like an oversized alarm clock and reverberated through the zinc-roofed hall. She found three one-hundred dollar bills and pushed them through the small counter opening along with her card. The lady behind the counter held up three fingers in mute query. Grace nodded and got her card back in a trice with the amount added to its electronic wallet.

Grace slapped the card on the electronic sensor mounted on the flat metal panel and stepped through the revolving turnstile into the long waiting hall. As she stepped through, one of the red digital numbers on the display board overhead changed from seventy-nine to seventy-eight, showing the number of vacant seats left on the ferry. At this hour, the Sea Supreme was not quite full. It had a seating capacity of three hundred and fifty. At the far end of the hall, lined on two sides with grey molded plastic chairs, she turned one hundred and eighty degrees down the shallow slipway that led to the gangplank and boarded the ferry. It was a blue and white catamaran with the HKKF spouting whale logo of the Hong Kong and Kowloon Ferry Company adorning its superstructure. The boats were workhorses, reasonably comfortable, seating the passengers on green or brown plastic-covered seats in air-conditioned cabins for the twenty-five minute ride to Victoria harbor. All the ferries had seating on two decks. On some of the boats, an outdoor rear seating deck could be accessed from the upper level cabin. From here, in fine weather, you had unobstructed views of the little islands along the way and the dramatic shoreline on all sides when entering Victoria Harbor.

The air was cold with a typically damp wind blowing in from the sea. It was a mid-April wind that could make one feel cold and hot at the same time. Walking to the ferry pier past the giant Chinese banyan tree with its hanging aerial roots that perhaps gave the harbor its name, Banyan Tree Bay, Grace had shivered in the breeze coming off the sea on that 18-degree morning and walked faster to warm up. By the time she reached the ferry, she felt clammy chills run down her spine as a thin film of perspiration formed on her body. But no matter, she was soon shivering again in the air-conditioned interior of the Sea Supreme. She drew a shawl from her large green shoulder bag, draped it around her shoulders and sat in one of the front rows.

A minute later a giant of a man sat down on an adjacent seat with a shy smile and a sideways glance. She vaguely knew him from a chance encounter weeks earlier at a bar on the island and smiled back. Ever cautious and deliberate in her actions, she acknowledged the greeting only because, despite his intimidating size, he exuded an air of kindness and gentle good humor. Rocked by the soothing undulating waves as the boat throbbed its way to Victoria harbor, Grace promptly fell asleep as usual and awoke refreshed just as the ferry docked at pier four.

The walkways were less crowded at ten o'clock in the morning. This was a city where most people began their working day early. Even the bosses at the top of the economic food chain were in their offices by nine, while the great majority of ordinary workers, the cogs and gear-wheels of Hong Kong, routinely worked sixty to seventy-hour weeks to keep the machinery of this prosperous city in good order.

Grace walked comfortably and silently in flat-heeled, rubber-soled shoes. Her entire outfit was designed for comfort and made few concessions to style. Her black hair, cut severely in a fringe above her eyebrows, ended in a straight line at her collar. The severity of her dark brown eyes was softened by an oval face, though even that, seen in profile, looked square-jawed and unyielding. She wore a maroon dress that fitted her well without being clingy. Of medium height and what a conservative might call well-built, she was the kind of person you'd walk by on the street without a second glance. But if you did happen to take that second glance, you might see a bit of steel in her eyes and some other alloy of tensile metal in the spring of her walk. There was a certain subdued elegance in her stride that spoke of hours of physical labor; maybe in a gym, or maybe not, it was hard to tell, but there was an unmistakable touch of the outdoors about her.

She walked quickly along the elevated walkway and into the chilly air-conditioned halls of the International Finance Centre. Maybe the IFC really was an international finance center. Grace did not know and really did not care. All she saw walking through it were elaborate temples of brand-name consumer goods that left her unmoved. She walked past upmarket designer label stores staffed with rows of androgynous young men and women, seemingly poured from a common mold; mostly Chinese, mostly

Cantonese. The men wore tight-fitting black suits, snowy shirt fronts and long-pointed shoes. The girls or women were also mostly dressed in black; all were young, lean, hungry, patient, lining shop fronts, looking out onto the throngs in the mall, waiting for the occasional customer who might pause in hasty passage to look into the store. They mostly looked mildly bored, all these young men and women, and Grace had often wondered what they did or had the energy to do after the long hours of seemingly futile waiting for customers in the malls.

She walked past the shops with hardly a glance at their contents, but she was aware of faces; of every single oncoming face in the throng. Perhaps a weakness, looking at people instead of things. The welter of faces impinged on her consciousness, on the retina of her inner eye, and each passing face was a little explosion of awareness that quickly overwhelmed her so that she had to hood her eyelids and deliberately soften her piercing gaze so as not to collapse from exhaustion.

She quickly exited the mall at the far side and within minutes was on the escalators that led to the mid-levels area, halfway up to the world's most expensive real estate that was Hong Kong's much vaunted Peak. The escalators were one reason she had arranged the coming appointment for ten-thirty. From six to ten every morning, the escalators moved downhill, then reversed direction for the rest of the day, from ten in the morning until they stopped at midnight. She traversed the series of escalators that brought her up to the mid-levels, ignoring the advertisements for eateries or manicure parlors that beckoned from second and third-floor windows on either side, and the street scenes two floors below. She got off the escalator at Staunton Street and turned right past the bars and restaurants that lined both sides. A few hundred meters further on she entered a tiny lane and pushed open the door of the fourth building on her right. The lift was on the ground floor and after quickly checking the address, she pressed the button for the fifth floor where her first and only client of the day waited.

The door to the flat opened before the buzzer stopped ringing and a worried looking face in thick-rimmed glasses peered out.

"Mrs. Hsiung?"

"Yes, yes," Mrs. Hsiung nodded eagerly. "You must be Grace. Thank you for coming. Thank you. I'm so worried. I'm so worried. I don't know what to do." She was a tiny woman and clung to Grace's shoulder with a smile of welcome and relief that could not hide the anxiety beneath.

"I'll see what I can do for you, Mrs. Hsiung. I hope everything will be alright soon. I'll do my best to help you though I can't promise."

"How much will I have to pay? Do I pay you now?" asked the old lady fearfully.

"Don't worry about money, Mrs. Hsiung. Let me see what I can do to recover what you've lost. Can we sit down for a minute and talk?"

"Yes, yes. I'm sorry. Come in. Come in." She led the way past the tiny hallway into a slightly larger sitting room with four cushioned armchairs ranged in a tight circle around a low table. Grace took in the oil painting that dominated one wall of the room. She recognized it as a painting by Tan Ping, a Chinese artist whose work had recently attained prices of a quarter of a million dollars at auction. American dollars, she remembered, not Hong Kong dollars. Either this was a very wealthy household, or they had had a discerning eye for art, or they had been simply lucky to buy a painting before it became very

5

valuable. Grace did not remark on it, however, and set her large bag down on the floor.

"Now Mrs. Hsiung, tell me about what you've lost." Mrs. Hsiung smiled her nervous smile again.

"Call me Vicky, please." She fingered the double string of pearls around her neck and noticed Grace's glance. "These are not real," she said hastily. "These are imitation. I keep the real ones in a bank safe and don't often take them out."

"Your loss…" Grace said patiently, bringing her back on track.

"Yes, yes. The necklace I lost. I don't know where it could have gone. It could have been stolen, couldn't it? After all, a valuable piece like that… who wouldn't want it?" She stopped and looked for an answer. Grace did not reply, but prompted her with a faintly raised eyebrow to continue. Vicky Hsiung collected herself for a moment and immediately her eyes filled with tears.

"It's such a valuable piece. I can't afford to lose it. It's a bad omen; very, very bad," she sobbed. "One million dollars. My dear late husband gave to me on our twentieth wedding anniversary. And now it's gone. He would never forgive me. I could never forgive myself." Grace sighed inwardly.

"Mrs. Hsiung, Vicky, as I told you on the phone, I need only a physical description of the lost object to work with. I don't need to know the value."

"I know, I know," she sniffed, wiping her nose with a sleeve.

"Do you have a picture or a photograph?" Vicky shook her head.

Grace rummaged in her bag on the floor, then placed it on the table to see better inside. It was a large green bag, a Mary Poppins bag made of imitation leather.

She extracted a number of velvet boxes from it, arranging them on the table in front of her and opening three.

"Now, here are a few varieties of single diamonds in plain gold settings. I use them as samples. Do any of these match the ones in yours?" Vicky shook her head.

"What color were the diamonds in the necklace?" Grace asked.

"You know, they were typical diamonds. You know what diamonds look like, don't you?"

"Yes, I do. But the more I know about them, the better."

"What do you want to know?"

"Vicky, jewelers classify diamonds by what they call the four Cs; cut, color, clarity and carat weight. Now I don't expect you to know all the details of your missing necklace, but the more you can tell me, the easier for me to locate them. For example, what shape were the diamonds and how were they cut? Were the diamonds colorless? If you tell me the necklace cost more than a million Hong Kong dollars, I'm sure they were colorless diamonds. The stronger the color, the lower the value of the stone." Vicky looked impressed by Grace's knowledge.

"I'm sure they were colorless. I mean, I didn't see any color on them. And the necklace cost a little more than a million dollars when Harry bought them ten years ago."

"Tell me, if you can, what the setting and the chain looked like. Were the diamonds mounted in gold, or in platinum?"

"Umm, let me see…"

The discussion lasted for a good hour. Vicky had no photographs to show, except for one taken at a birthday celebration two years earlier and then the necklace was half hidden by the angle of her body and the high collar of her silk cheongsam. She examined Grace's three diamond samples at length. None of them matched her missing necklace, so Grace conjured up images of diamonds of various cuts and quality on the screen of her mobile phone. Vicky finally identified one as being the closest match to the missing diamonds, although hers were much bigger, she said, and cut squarish shaped.

When they were finished, Grace leaned back into a comfortable position in her chair and asked for a glass of water. Vicky brought a glass and placed it on a coaster on the low table. Grace raised her hands, put a finger to her lips before Vicky could say another word and slowly closed her eyes. She listened in the silence for the sound of objects falling, tiny objects falling into unnoticed crevices. Behind her closed eyes, she was in a vast, cavernous space, a black space tinged with red at the edges, and little objects floated into her mind. She visualized again in her mind the diamond necklace whose fragment she had seen in Vicky's photograph. There was a dusty ball-point pen under the dresser in the adjacent bedroom; probably had been there for months. A man's cuff-link had fallen into the U bend beneath the wash basin in the bathroom, but it was of no consequence. She felt her mind straining to see and forced herself to relax. With relaxation came improved clarity of vision and she located a number of small coins that had fallen under a cupboard, again of low value and no consequence.

After nearly twenty minutes of this, Grace swept over the flat in her mind's eye one last time and determined that the missing diamond necklace was not in the flat. She slowly opened her eyes and felt the flutter of nervous exhaustion.

"I'm sorry," she said gently, fearing Vicky's dismayed reaction. "The necklace is not here. It's not in this flat. Maybe not even in this building, although I can't be sure of that. Too many people… too much going on." Vicky looked disappointed but remained composed.

"Will I have to pay, then? How much?"

Grace sighed. She hated dealing with money. Vicky was obviously a wealthy woman, despite being a widow, and could easily afford to pay.

"Nothing," she said on impulse, rising to her feet. "You owe me nothing."

Vicky Hsiung, obviously preparing to bargain, looked at her in open-mouthed surprise. Grace got ready to leave and said nothing. She had her own secret. By her own frugal living standards, she was filthy rich and felt she didn't deserve to have more. It hadn't always been that way.

CHAPTER 2

"Grace. Gracie. Wake up. Your mother's calling you… you'll be late for school." It was Flora, the housemaid, standing at the foot of her bed, holding one foot and trying to shake her awake.

"No, Flora. Leave me alone. I want to sleep," Grace grumbled. She didn't like being called Gracie, but Flora consistently ignored her protests and persisted.

"Gracie, if you don't get up, your mother will get angry…" When Flora was anxious, each of her sentences would end unfinished on a rising note. "Your mother's calling you… she'll get angry…" Most of Flora's anxiety was caused by Grace's mother.

Sarah was a charming, handsome woman with a stubborn streak and she could be very cutting when she didn't get her way. She was tall, as tall as Grace's father Olivier and, when it came to Grace, her only daughter, this stubborn streak became domineering. Grace had inherited some of her mother's character, of course, and so the more Sarah pushed in the direction of obedience and discipline, the more Grace resisted.

Olivier Lam saw what was going on between his wife and daughter, but was helpless to stop it. He put his head down and did what he was best at; being charming all round and making money hand over fist, embedding his business ventures firmly in Malaysia's rapidly developing young tiger economy. These were the boom years of the 1990s and the Asian economic crisis had not yet arrived. That would only happen in 1997.

Olivier heard Flora calling for Grace to get up and knew it was only a matter of minutes before Sarah invaded Grace's room and an argument began. At best the argument ended with ruffled feathers and a few slammed doors, but on bad days it could erupt into a full-blown shouting match which resulted in Grace locking herself in her room and refusing to go to school.

Olivier finished knotting his tie and walked swiftly along the shaded verandah to the door of his daughter's bedroom. It was a Peranakan-style planter's house that had been built in the early 1900s and impeccably renovated so the red tiles glowed in the morning sun and the dark brown polished woodwork managed to look glossy and cool despite the gathering warmth of the early morning. He knocked and quickly entered without waiting for a response.

"Grace," he said urgently, "Get up now. I'll drop you in school if you can be ready in forty-five minutes."

Grace sat up in bed, long hair down to her waist, and sleepy-eyed.

"Okay." Going with her father meant she had an extra fifteen minutes to get ready if she could avoid an argument with her mother. She switched off the aircon, drew back the curtains to let in light and swiftly brushed her hair before going into the bathroom to wash her face and put on her school uniform of freshly ironed white shirt and green skirt that Flora had laid out for her. She put on white socks and black uniform leather shoes, picked up her school bag and quickly skirted the verandah, avoiding her parents' bedroom and the main staircase before tripping down the narrow staircase that was used by the servants, looking out onto the rear of the compound and the kitchen garden. The garden was lovingly tended and watered by their Malay gardener, Bujang, who at that very moment was wrestling two large clusters of manioc roots from the clinging black earth and Grace knew that this was for her mother's favorite dish of steamed tapioca with a fiery red kokum-laced fish curry.

"Buji," she called out to the gardener in Malay. "Get some drumsticks from the tree and give to the cook for this evening."

He grinned with pleasure, large gaps showing between his stained teeth. Bujang the gardener was a solitary old man, and lived alone as befitted his Malay name that meant bachelor, in a tiny hut not too far away from their large compound.

Still looking to avoid her mother, Grace went into the kitchen that led off from the servants staircase and grabbed a plate that Dwi the cook was just about to carry through the batwing double doors into the dining room. She smacked her lips at the two steaming nests of string hoppers on the place.

"This is for me no la?" she sing-songed to Dwi.

"For your father. Give. He's waiting." Dwi tried to take it back but Grace easily evaded her.

"Get him another plate, la. I'm going to eat here. I'm hungry." Dwi bit her lip in exasperation, and resignedly hitched her dark blue patterned sarong a little higher.

"If your father complain, I tell him you." Dwi pointed a finger. Grace ignored her and began to wolf the food down, eating with her fingers. As she ate standing, some of the sweet mixture of coconut milk and palm syrup dribbled down her chin. She licked her lips, savoring the taste as Dwi emerged carrying a fresh plate of steaming hoppers for her father. Dwi raised an arm in passing as though to ward off an attack.

"This plate for your father. If you want more I come back." Grace laughed.

"No Dwi. It was very good, but I have to go now. Can you make steamed drumstick for me tonight? I've asked Buji to cut some from the tree."

"That man will do anything for you," Dwi said as she entered the dining room with the steaming plate in hand.

"Who will do anything for whom?" asked Olivier Lam, who sat at the head of the table, reading a newspaper and sipping from a cup of coffee as he waited for his breakfast.

"Missy," explained Dwi. "Buji do anything for Missy."

"Ah, you mean Grace. What's she doing in the kitchen?"

"She eat your breakfast sah. I make fresh 'gain for you. That why because you wait," Dwi explained.

"Grace, what are you doing in the kitchen? Come sit down here and eat a proper breakfast."

"I've finished Dad." Grace emerged from the kitchen, licking the last of the syrupy coconut milk from her fingers and wiping her chin on the sleeve of her clean white shirt. Olivier looked mildly exasperated.

"Well, at least you're in your uniform." Sarah strode into the room at that moment and stopped short on seeing Grace.

"Ah you're here already. I didn't see you come down."

"I went down the back way to tell Buji to get me some drumsticks for tonight."

"They don't grow fast enough on the tree to keep up with your appetite," snorted Sarah. "Have you finished your geography homework?"

"Let her take responsibility for herself," Olivier interjected before Grace could reply. "She's growing up now and high time she answers directly to her teachers."

"Very well for you to talk," Sarah shot back. "You're not the one who goes to the parent-teacher meetings and has to deal with what they say about your daughter." Olivier knew worse was coming because Sarah had said "your daughter" instead of "our daughter" as she usually did.

"Miss Chaves is a witch who always complains about everybody," said Grace indignantly. "I forgot just one paragraph at the end of the answer and she said I hadn't done my homework. She's a liar."

"Well, I've spoken to your friends' mothers, Rita's and Malini's. They both say Miss Chaves is very fair, and they are both getting good marks in geography."

"Why don't you ask what they got in history and math?" Grace exploded, throwing her school bag down and hating her mother at that moment with every fiber of her thirteen-year-old being.

Sarah, large, purposeful, dressed for work in her design showroom in an elegantly tailored blue silk shirt and dark trousers, stood with arms akimbo and glared at her daughter. Olivier rose hastily to his feet, gulping down the last of breakfast, trying to head off the escalation that he knew was imminent. Sarah was such a practical, efficient woman who handled people amazingly well in her business dealings, but there was definitely a large blind spot as far as her own daughter was concerned.

Olivier was tall for a Chinese, almost one eighty but Sarah was only a couple of centimeters shorter and leaned over Grace. "I don't have to ask anybody anything. I simply asked if you've finished your geography homework. I know you have to hand it in today and Miss Chaves asked me to make sure you did it. That's all I asked."

"Yes, I finished it. I hope you're satisfied." She picked up her bag and flounced out of the dining room onto the verandah and ran to the front porch where Sebastian, their Tamil Christian driver was waiting to drive Olivier to work. As usual, the Jaguar's deep green paint and coachwork gleamed to a high polish as though to match the shine of Sebastian's perpetually sweaty smiling face.

Grace opened the front passenger door, threw her bag in and climbed in the back.

"Are we dropping you in school today, Miss Grace?"

Back in the dining room, Olivier shrugged into the jacket hanging over the back of a chair, straightened his tie and tried to calm his wife.

"Be gentle with her. She's a good girl and she's only thirteen."

"You always take her side against me. That's the real problem," said Sarah furiously. Olivier picked up his folded newspaper.

"Sorry, I have to go. I don't have time for this."

"Yes, go. I'll deal with it as I usually do."

CHAPTER 3

Sarah was in very good humor in the weeks leading up to Grace's fourteenth birthday and readily agreed to help her organize a party for all her school friends. At first Grace was dismayed by her mother's enthusiasm and automatic assumption that Sarah was going to help organize it, but as the day came closer, Grace was secretly glad. Sarah was independently wealthy, her interior design business was flourishing. She knew exactly where to buy things and how much they would cost. And, of course, she paid for them. So come the day, the house was freshly decorated with colorful bunting, festive balloons, there were decorative paper napkins with matching paper plates and disposable cups, cartons and cartons of fruit juices and fizzy drinks, a large, interesting looking piñata had been conjured out of hemp, old clay pots and banana fiber and stuffed with small packets of assorted birthday party takeaways.

Dwi outdid herself in the kitchen and produced mounds of sweets, feather-light cakes and savories. There were Indian milk sweets, samosas, assorted cakes as well as her specialty, a bird-shaped cake decorated with poppy seeds and a filling of stewed jackfruit that was always a big hit.

Sarah had agreed to the party because things were going so well for the family as a whole. Her constant fights with Grace had eased, partly because she took Olivier's advice and began to be less strict with her daughter.

Olivier's charm combined with good luck and business sense had attracted the attention of a couple of tycoons with good connections to the Prime Minister. Although Prime Minister Mahathir Mohammed was not corrupt, there was such a strong personality cult surrounding him that anyone with close personal ties had enormous influence within the corridors of government power. The Prime Minister had a habit of handing large government contracts to people he trusted without going through the usual process of competitive bids. No civil servant dared to question these awards. Many of the Prime Minister's cronies had thus become influential businessmen who now had to fulfill these contracts, granted to them by the Prime Minister as personal favors. One of these political favorites had taken a liking to Olivier, found him trustworthy and efficient. As a result, Olivier got exclusive permits to build for various ministries. Hard-to-obtain licenses flew in his direction and his business expanded enormously. In addition, the official contracts meant that generous lines of bank credit were extended to him at preferential rates. He built offices for various ministries on government land using government money.

Additionally, Olivier's construction firm put up good quality housing stock. These units were Olivier's private initiative, financed by himself, designed by architects he employed. The units, which were well built and good value for money, were snapped up at a handsome premium and left everyone satisfied. Commodities were at an all-time high. Malaysia's economic pie was growing fast in those heady years and Olivier was able to take a generous slice of the pie. He was wise enough to know that his growing wealth was due to the protection of patronage, but at the same time he also knew that his products were good and his dealings were fair, albeit within a framework of protected privilege that did not allow real open competition.

The day of Grace's birthday party was a bright sunny day; small wonder in this part of the world where most days were bright and sunny except for short, sharp tropical showers that came down on a regular basis and kept this land so lush, green and steamy. But that was the unusual thing about the climate in this part of the world, almost at the equator. It was cool in the shade and, provided one didn't move about too much, it was perfectly comfortable with only a fan to circulate the heavy air.

The guests, mostly Grace's classmates and the children of a few family friends, arrived in chauffeur driven cars, but some of them were dropped off by parents. Sarah had stayed at home to welcome them. She closed her design studio for the day and invited parents, mostly mothers, to stay if they wished. The house was big enough for them all. There was a large formal drawing room, hardly ever used, at one end of the large square-built house with a generous verandah running around all four sides. The windows were ornate with outer wooden shutters, the Peranakan style being given to colorful stucco designs on walls and windows. Today all the windows were wide open and long-stemmed ceiling fans stirred the air in the drawing room where Sarah hosted a few of the early arrivals, parents and children.

Grace wore a simple white blouse and navy-blue skirt with black shoes that looked like a variation of her school uniform, and the only festive concession she made was that the blouse was of silk, one that Sarah had urged upon her. The children wore a rainbow of colors to the party; some of the girls in elaborate lacy outfits and one was even in something that resembled a child-bride's wedding dress. There were some children who wore clothes that were similar to Grace's plain outfit. Although the school catered mostly to the children of Kuala Lumpur's upper crust, Sarah had carefully chosen one that admitted a few bright children of less affluent parents who were given financial help by the foundation that ran the school.

Susan Hill was one of Sarah's particular friends, a jolly Englishwoman whose banker husband, Hugh, was perpetually busy in exotic corners of the world, helping affluent Asians of every stripe from all the Southeast Asian tiger economies find secure storage for their burgeoning fortunes at British-run offshore havens; in Jersey, the British Virgin Islands, Cayman, Guernsey, the list went on… Sarah liked Susan because she laughingly mocked their own affluent lifestyle, admitting to its questionable morality.

"You know, when the Americans do it, they're called brash, or brassy and crass. Like they're shoving their expertise in your face. And when the Swiss do it, it's somehow shady, central European and immoral. But when we Brits do it, we're upholding tradition, we're being honorable, helping far-flung outposts of the old Empire to administer and develop their natural assets." Sarah laughed and embraced Susan, the only one among their large circle of acquaintances whom she thought of as a true friend.

"Come and sit under the fan here. Can I get you something to drink?"

"Are you joking?" Susan sank down onto the white sofa with another peal of laughter. Laughter came easily to Susan and her laughter was infectious. Sarah's normally stern face softened into a smile, something that always happened when Susan visited.

"Are you joking?" Susan exclaimed again. "The sun went over the yardarm ages ago. It's past two, child!"

"Silly question," Sarah agreed. "I'll get you a G&T" Flora entered just then carrying a tray with various biscuits and savories. Sarah removed a couple of glossy books from the coffee table to make room for the tray. "Flora, can you make a gin and tonic for Sarah, please?"

"Flora, we'll take two," interjected Susan with another laugh. "I think Sarah deserves one too."

"Oh yes Madam, I'll bring two right away," Flora laughed. It was impossible even for her not to be infected by Susan's good cheer. Meanwhile Gordon, Susan's fourteen-year-old stood impatiently by, waiting to get a word in.

"Mum," he said hastily the first chance he got, "don't forget, I'm going off with Emilio at four-thirty. His dad's picking us up and taking me to the airshow outside town. We might be home late. Don't wait for me."

"I suppose Emilio's dad will drop you home, won't he? All right then. Go find Grace and enjoy your party." After Gordon left, Susan briefly turned serious.

"I think Gordon's a good boy. Hugh always thinks I'm too indulgent with him."

"I don't know about my daughter." Sarah shrugged in uncharacteristic helplessness. "I accuse Olivier of the same thing, of being too indulgent, but his methods seem to be working well with Grace. I'm so frightened of her not turning out right that sometimes I just want to sit and keep telling her of all the ways things could go wrong. She's simply so naive…"

"I know. I know just how you feel," Susan clucked sympathetically. "And that's why…" Flora entered carrying the two glasses of gin and tonic. "…that's why we're going to have a drink together. Sit down here and tell me how your new showroom is doing." She patted the white sofa cover beside her.

The afternoon turned to evening. The light softened. A steady stream of cars dropped children at the front porch. Some of the chauffeurs waited for their charges, and they parked their limousines on the grass verge of the road on both sides of the front gate. They stood in groups while they waited, smoking and chatting in a smatter of Malay and Chinglish with an occasional exclamation in Tamil. A few of the parents who dropped their children stayed to chat with Susan and Sarah in the drawing room. Flora was kept busy serving tea, biscuits and cakes. Around four-thirty there were sounds of revelry from the garden and they sauntered over to observe from the verandah as the piñata was demolished and some of the kids dived for the goodies that fell from the parcel while others assumed lofty disdain and continued to talk to their friends. Sarah could see that Grace seemed to be having a good time and was glad. A year earlier, her thirteenth birthday party had been a disaster. Grace, ill at ease in her home and in front of her friends, had hardly talked to anyone and hated the whole thing. She had been furious with her mother for talking her into having a party and swore that she never in her life would have a birthday party again.

"What a difference one year makes in the life of a teen-ager," she remarked, as they stood on the verandah and watched their children taking turns to flail blindfolded at the piñata.

"Sarah, you really have a talent for organization. No wonder your design showroom is doing so well." Susan sighed. "I really must be going." Sarah heard the reluctance in Susan's voice.

"Gordon's not going to be home till much later. And Hugh, I assume, is out of town working in someplace exotic. Why don't you have dinner with us? Olivier will be home late today, so we won't wait for him. It's only you and me then."

"Oh, alright then. Twist my arm. With Claire in University, the house seems so empty when Hugh is away."

"Good," said Sarah, reaching out to touch her friend's arm. "I'll tell Flora to make sure your chauffeur gets something to eat."

CHAPTER 4

The line of limousines and the knot of chauffeurs had disappeared by six-thirty. Susan's black Daimler reversed into the driveway. The chauffeur left his black peaked cap on the passenger seat and went round to the back of the house where he sat on a bench outside the kitchen door. Dwi brought a heaped plate of food out from the kitchen and sat beside him. They chatted in Malay as he ate. Meanwhile Susan and Sarah walked to and fro in the garden, clearing the alcohol-induced fuzziness at the edge of their brains, deep in conversation. At the edge of her consciousness Sarah had the fleeting thought that she hadn't seen or heard any sign of Grace since the piñata demolition two hours earlier, but shrugged the thought away. She must be somewhere around, or has gone to her room. Anyway, the subsequent conversation with Susan drove all thought of Grace from her mind.

Susan's conversation turned unexpectedly serious to reveal a deep wound beneath the cheerful exterior.

"You're the first person I've talked to about it. I can't go on with Hugh like this. It has to stop." Sarah was shocked and sad for her friend. She stood still in the middle of the lawn when Susan broke the news.

"Oh my dear!" she exclaimed, hugging her tight. "I never knew... I didn't have the slightest inkling…"

"I'm a good liar," Susan said sadly. "I even lied successfully to myself. I closed my eyes and refused to believe anything bad about Hugh, refused to see all the signs that were in plain sight. I suppose I can't blame Hugh though."

"Oh shut up," said Sarah fiercely, hugging her friend again. "I won't have you blaming yourself. I'm so disappointed in Hugh." They walked and talked for more than two hours. It was completely dark and past eight when they re-entered the smaller living room that was normally used by the family. It was adjacent to the dining room. Flora had turned the lights on earlier and, unasked, laid out a full flask of coffee with a jug of milk, and a container of biscuits. Sarah motioned Susan to one of the sofa chairs and went to the kitchen to ask Dwi to serve dinner for two. There was no sign of Olivier and she assumed he was going to be very late.

Susan and Sarah dawdled two hours over dinner, talking about life's uncertainties, their spouses, the way things turn out, and about how one's greatest fears are never realized but trouble erupts from a totally unexpected direction. They drank water with the meal. Susan's confession had sobered them and they did not drink wine at dinner as they usually did. It was ten when Susan pulled herself together and reluctantly left, mainly because she felt bad about keeping the chauffeur waiting.

Sarah was in a melancholy mood after Susan left. There was still no word from, or sign of Olivier and so she readied herself for bed. She went to the kitchen first, where Dwi had finished scrubbing and cleaning and putting away leftovers in innumerable little plastic containers in the industrial-size refrigerator in the kitchen. Having grown up in a thrifty household herself, this was the quality she most appreciated in Dwi. The diminutive Malay woman in her pastel blouses and colorful sarongs never wasted a morsel of food that was prepared in her kitchen. On days like today Sarah knew, when there inevitably was too much food left over to be eaten in the household, many of those plastic containers would wander to the outskirts of Kuala Lumpur and be distributed to Dwi's friends and family. This was something Sarah and Olivier had explicitly allowed at the time of her interview for the job over a decade ago. She poked her head into the kitchen.

"Thank you for today. Dwi. You did a lot of work."

"It's alright Mum. I've left some food covered for Sir and Missy in the dining room."

"You mean, Missy's gone to bed without eating?"

"Don't know Mum." Dwi glanced at the kitchen clock. "She went up to her room at seven."

"Maybe she ate too much at her party. I'll check her room before I go to bed. Good night Dwi."

"Goodnight Mum."

Sarah looked in on Grace on her way to bed. The lights were off and there was no reply when she softly knocked on her door. She opened the door a crack and made out the outline of a still form on the bed.

"Maybe she really is exhausted after her party," Sarah thought, softly closing the door behind her. Sarah slept heavily that night and was only vaguely aware of her husband quietly creeping into their double bed around midnight.

"Mmmm. How was it?" she asked, drifting off to sleep again and not hearing his murmured reply.

The phone, when it rang in the small hours of the morning, did not wake them up the first time. It rang again a few minutes later and in Sarah's dream it was a fire engine clanging. She thought the house was on fire and struggled to open her eyes. There was no smoke, only Olivier heavily sitting up in bed and fumbling for the receiver.

" Hullo. Who is that?" Olivier was annoyed. A practical joke? "Do you know what time it is?" There was a polite voice at the other end. A voice with authority. This was no practical joke. Sarah was awake by now and sitting up in bed. She turned on the light beside her bed and thought incongruously that Olivier's smooth, hairless back still retained its youthful outlines and he had weathered his forty-six years much better than she had. And then she thought with a pang of sorrow of her friend Susan.

Olivier's back straightened and suddenly Sarah was wide awake and alert. A premonition? She couldn't explain the dagger of fear that pierced her side like physical pain, but it was real.

"Who is it?" she asked, clutching the back of his shoulder. She noticed her watch lying next to her bed. It was two o'clock in the morning.

CHAPTER 5

They were at the hospital in twenty minutes. Sarah's heart was in her mouth as Olivier drove with reckless speed. They raced up the steps to the emergency room and had to cool their heels for fifteen minutes while the nurse went to fetch the doctor who was in the intensive care unit. While they waited, they looked at each other in dismayed disbelief, speaking in hushed tones. Olivier looked at his wife in puzzlement.

"Did you know Grace had gone out?"

"I didn't see her after the party. She didn't come down for dinner. I thought she was in her room sleeping."

"And you didn't check?"

"Of course I did. I opened her door and thought I saw her sleeping."

"You thought you saw?"

"Yes. I didn't want to disturb her in case she was asleep." Olivier frowned at this, but thankfully said nothing to make her nightmare worse.

When the doctor emerged from the intensive care unit, they discovered that their daughter had been in a high-speed car crash, that the young man driving the car had been killed, and the driver's younger brother who was in the front passenger seat was seriously injured and might be paralyzed for life. The young woman in the back seat had got off relatively lightly, with two crushed ribs, two broken bones in her right arm, and lacerations to her face from some metal object that had been lying beside her on the back seat of the car. Fortunately, the scars on her face, if any remained, could be easily treated by a plastic surgeon. Both Sarah and Olivier were shaking in disbelief as they listened.

"Whose car was it? Who was driving?" The doctor was a young Indian and he looked at them incredulously.

"You mean you don't know who your daughter was out with?" He seemed to look accusingly at Sarah as he said it, or perhaps it was her imagination. In any case, she felt a need to refute the accusation, real or implied.

"We mean we don't know what happened. We didn't know she was out. As far as we knew, she was sleeping in her own bed at eight. We want to see her. Can we go in now?"

"No. Her injuries have been tended to. I've given her sedatives and her condition is stable. You can see her tomorrow."

"Even if she's sleeping, could we look in on her please?" He was about to refuse, but Sarah, knowing how the Indian psyche, even male chauvinists, worshipped motherhood, quickly added, "This is only a mother's wish." As she expected, he grudgingly agreed to the request, instructing a nurse to accompany them. They glimpsed their daughter through a round glass pane in the door of the ICU and when they turned back there were two policemen waiting to speak to them.

Despite Grace's injuries and month long stay in the hospital, Sarah was furious with her when she learned the whole story. Olivier was inclined to be more forgiving.

"After all, she just went along for the ride. Her bad judgment was only in getting into the car with her classmate, Aktar. The real villain in this story is Aktar's older brother and he's dead now. Aktar has learned a lesson he will remember all his life, and I'm thankful Grace is healing." Nevertheless, Sarah persisted.

"We must send her to a school where there's more discipline. Perhaps a boarding school in England. You studied in one, and look at how disciplined and well you've turned out." Olivier shot a glance at her, searching for a trace of irony and finding none. Despite the seriousness of the discussion, Olivier laughed.

"The discipline you so admire was beaten into me by my Cantonese parents, not by a British boarding school. They penny pinched and saved the earnings of their little takeaway restaurant in Toronto's Chinatown to afford us children the education we wanted, bless them. They were wonderful parents, but the children of today can't be brought up like that. Society has changed. We're simply too rich. Our children wouldn't understand, our friends wouldn't understand, and Grace would be totally isolated socially… from her friends and her peers."

"Exactly. We're too rich for her own good, and it's known here. That's why we have to send her away. To a boarding school where she'll be strictly disciplined like we were."

They walked out of the hospital, hand in hand. Sarah realized they had not walked together or held hands for months, for years perhaps. Where had time gone while they rushed about building up careers, participating in Malaysia's economic boom? The heady sense of excitement, of growing affluence; where had it led them? They'd had no time to think about themselves, really, immersed as they were in constant activity. Partly it was their upbringing and mental makeup which regarded slowing down as wasting time. They chided themselves inwardly for it. To slow down was to be lazy. Sarah gripped Olivier's hand tightly, loving this man whom she had met as a shy young fellow-traveller on a flight to Singapore twenty years ago. Maybe this accident that had happened to Grace was one of life's punctuation marks; a significant event that announced itself with every birth, death, wedding, illness, trauma, accident or natural disaster.

Sarah visualized all these events as life's commas, quote marks, and colons. At the end of every life sentence of course, came a full stop. And after that? After the full stop came the big question mark, Hard and unalloyed like Captain Hook's hand of polished steel, but she never worried about that. That question was something to be answered when time came and it was foolish to waste life worrying beforehand.

Sarah felt a surge of happiness as she held hands with Olivier and walked out of the hospital, stricken with a parallel sense of guilt for feeling happy while her only daughter was in intensive care. But her tender feelings for her husband persisted even after they reached home where Dwi and Flora were anxiously waiting up, each wanting to know how their "Missy" and "Gracie" was.

It was ironic, Sarah thought afterwards, that it was the two women of the household help who showed symptoms typical of a mother's concern about Grace's well-being while Olivier and she went up to their bedroom and made passionate love to each other with a tenderness they had not felt in years.

If Grace had been distant with her mother earlier, that distance seemed to have doubled after her return home from two and a half weeks in hospital. She was able to walk without help now although her face was still bandaged. The lacerations would have to heal completely before she underwent minor plastic surgery to remove the scars on her right cheek. Grace was self-conscious about the scars and preferred to keep the bandages on for as long as possible. School and lessons went on while she was recuperating. Both Gordon and Malini came often to see her. Gordon had obviously inherited his mother's innate sense of fairness. He was indignant when he heard unfounded rumors spreading around the school about the accident and Grace's role in it. With her continued absence from school, the rumors became wilder and he could do nothing to stop them.

He began to regularly bring school homework assignments to the hospital. He continued this service after Grace came home and so Susan was also a frequent visitor, sometimes driving him over after their supper and sitting in the smaller living room talking to Sarah while Gordon went upstairs to Grace's room. They usually stayed for half an hour at a time, and this was too short for Susan to confide more to Sarah about her marital problems, but nevertheless it was clearly a pleasure for both to meet like this and to their mutual surprise, their friendship deepened to an extent that, if they ever reflected on it, they would have realized that each was the best friend that the other had. Olivier sensed the depth of the bond, the unspoken understanding between the two women and thankfully was not jealous. He was happy to retire to the study or a comfortable armchair in one of the other rooms and read a book or the newspaper he never found time to read these days. On rare occasions he made phone calls related to his business, but he too had been compelled to reassess his life after Grace's accident and had decided to slow down and devote more time to his family.

It came as a shock to Olivier several months later, towards the end of Grace's school year, when Sarah announced that they should send their daughter to a boarding school in England. It would do Grace a world of good. She had discussed the idea at length with Susan, who had recommended Greensleeves, the boarding school where her own older daughter Claire had studied. Olivier was dismayed by the decision and felt that Sarah had undercut his own role as Grace's father by simply announcing it.

"Nothing's been decided yet," replied Sarah soothingly to Olivier's outspoken objection to the plan.

"Why don't we ask Grace what she thinks." To Olivier's surprise, Grace readily agreed when asked.

"Are you sure about this?" Olivier asked his daughter as they sat together around the dining table after dinner.

"How can I be sure about it, Dad, when I've never been to England and never been to a boarding school?" asked Grace, disconcertingly wise.

"Exactly. So how can you know?"

"It's just that… after the accident a lot of people look at me in a funny way. I don't feel comfortable here anymore."

"Give it a few more months. They'll forget about it."

"No they won't." Grace shook her head firmly. "They think I took drugs that night, and it's only your influence with the government that I wasn't punished or didn't go to jail."

"Nonsense," said Olivier warmly. "You didn't take drugs and the accident wasn't your fault, so you weren't punished."

"I know that. You know that. But people simply believe what they want to believe and I can't do anything about it. I can't go and talk to them about it if they don't ask and pretend they don't want to know. They look away when they see me coming."

"She's right, you know," said Sarah. "She has no way of defending herself. I've talked to Susan about it and she's talked to Gordon about what happens in school. He says it's very unfair to Grace but that's the way people are reacting to the incident."

"Running away is no solution."

"Grace is not running away from anything. We're only sending her off to get a good education in a place where she hopefully has space to grow."

Olivier looked at his daughter helplessly, sad that she would go away and when she returned he would have missed the rest of her childhood. She would return to the family all grown up and with experiences he was no part of. But he knew that Sarah had set her mind on it, and Grace was convinced it was the best thing for her, so he flung out his arms, gathering his wife and daughter in a tight embrace, wondering if another whole year would pass and Grace would be sixteen before he did the same again. Fate was kind and gave him no inkling of what was in store for his family.

The school year passed quickly. It was Grace's last year in Kuala Lumpur and for her the days were a blur where she tried to just get through each day like a weary traveller hurrying over a mountain pass to see the promised land. The only school friend she saw something of was Gordon. Their friendship had grown in parallel with that of their mothers. Theirs was a comfortable relationship, with not much hormonal interference between them. It wasn't as if they both were asexual. They were both normal, full-blooded young people, but somehow they saw each other as brother and sister or truly good friends without a trace of sexual desire or innuendo to complicate their relationship.

Olivier was busier than ever, inspecting ever larger construction projects with his chief engineer. He employed a team of engineers and building contractors now. He tried his best to find good people he could delegate to, so that he did not have to look after too many details himself. But he was also conscientious and it was not easy to find employees who paid attention to detail as he himself did, so for some projects it was hard to let go. He was home late very often although he knew that Grace would soon leave for England and that he would miss her youthful presence in the house even if they didn't interact all that much together.

Sarah too was living her life in limbo, as though waiting for a one-legged man to drop a second shoe, waiting for life to resume normality again after Grace left for boarding school, but hating the thought of her leaving.

And so all three of them lived the weeks before Grace's departure in a state of suspended animation; all of them busy with their daily lives, but equally stuck with the helpless feeling that they were waiting in an antechamber for real life to happen.

Grace swept through her exams and emerged like the winner of a long-distance race, flushed and triumphant, and indeed she passed all her subjects with higher marks than she'd ever achieved before. Her admission to Greensleeves was already secure but her good marks meant that she would be admitted to a higher grade than was initially promised. Olivier took sad comfort in the thought that Grace would now return home a year earlier than planned, but it would still mean he would miss the rest of his daughter's teen years.

"Will you have time to come with us?" Sarah asked when Olivier returned home late one evening. She and Grace had eaten their dinner much earlier and it was past eleven. Grace had already gone up to bed and Sarah sat at the table, keeping her husband company as he wearily ate a few mouthfuls. She saw how tired he was and pushed a glass of red wine towards him.

"Here! Have some. It's very good and goes well with Dwi's soufflé"

"Come with you where?" She laid a hand softly on his outstretched left hand.

"Grace starts school in England eight weeks from now." He looked up at her as though in physical pain but said nothing and her heart went out to him.

"I'll take her there and settle her in. You don't have to worry about it. You're so busy."

"You know something?"

"What?"

"I've been thinking. It's not right to be so busy I don't have time for my family. This new chief engineer Rajkumar seems to be a good fellow. I'll let him look after all the projects for the next eight weeks. Let's go together, have a real holiday with Grace and after she's settled in school, maybe we can have a second honeymoon before we come back home."

CHAPTER 6

Olivier's problems began two years after Grace went to boarding school. She was doing surprisingly well academically, although she systematically stonewalled her parents' questions about her happiness. Olivier was vaguely troubled as soon as he read a headline one day in the New Straits Times. It was only a reported rumor in the newspaper. But in a country where important decisions were dependent on one strong leader, such rumors were not to be taken lightly. However, there was nothing Olivier could do, so he kept his head down and worked as efficiently as before. The rumor was that a big financier named Ananda Kumaratunga had fallen out of favor with the Prime Minister. The little rumor gathered strength over the succeeding months. For Olivier, it was like being in the path of a tsunami with no higher ground to run to.

Olivier had no direct connection with Ananda Kumaratunga, but the latter was a godfather of one of Olivier's own benefactors. It appeared that, as a friend of the Prime Minister, Ananda Kumaratunga had been granted exemption from stock market rules that had enabled him to privatize state companies. Once he fell out of the Prime Minister's favor, the blanket of privilege fell away, and some of these takeovers were seen to be illegal. One of the takeovers in question was a large tract of government land that Olivier had developed for the ministry of defense. The case went on for several years. Ananda Kumaratunga fled to comfortable exile at a large estate in the United States to escape the Prime Minister's displeasure. Olivier's benefactor was next in line for ersatz punishment. He passed the buck and put the blame on Olivier. Olivier's fate was sealed by two sheets of paper, a forged document with an authentic signature, Olivier's own, on it.

The fourth year after Grace's departure from Malaysia, Olivier suddenly found himself fighting to clear his name and save his fortune. The battle took a heavy toll on him, but despite all his troubles, he never failed to write a long, affectionate weekly email to his daughter. He never wrote a word about his problems. It was Sarah who finally hinted at it in a letter to her daughter. By this time, Grace was already in her final year of a Bachelor's Degree in Accounting at Leeds University.

"Dear Dad,

Sarah wrote to me about the problems you're going through. You remember when I had that stupid accident seven years ago, just before my fourteenth birthday? Afterwards, so many of my classmates stopped being my friends because they believed I'd done something bad. It was only a rumor. No one asked to hear my side of the story, but they believed what they wanted to believe. Gordon was the only one who stood by me and I'm glad he is still a close friend. He asks about you and Sarah whenever he comes to see me in Leeds from Southampton where he is studying to be a civil engineer. I'm always happy to see him and we try to meet two or three times a year. But don't get any ideas about us. We're just friends and I think he has a girlfriend although I've never met her.

I still remember that wonderful holiday we had together when you and Sarah took me to boarding school in England. It was the best holiday I've ever had and I remember it with pleasure. Not a week went by when I didn't think about it. I hated boarding school, but never told you both because you thought you were doing the best for me. I totally understand that and don't want this confession to cause you any pain now. But the two-week holiday we spent together on that Greek island was absolutely the best time of my years growing up. There were simply no barriers between us. I felt grown up and I felt I was with two of my best friends who happened to be my parents. And sometimes I cried at night because I didn't know why I was leaving my two best friends and going to live for the next four years in a cold, damp country among a bunch of emotionally stunted girls who never say what they think.

From what I understood in Sarah's letter, it sounds like you're going through the same thing now that I did then. Dad, I'm so lucky to have you and Sarah as parents. You stood by me when I was going through a teenage nightmare and now I feel so helpless and far away while you go through your trial, equally undeserved. I'm sure the commission of inquiry will find nothing wrong and your name will be cleared soon. I'm coming home in two months, as soon as my exams are over and then I hope to be of use to you. If you need help, I'll work for you. Otherwise I'll find a job and do whatever it takes to help clear your name. You and Sarah are very strong and you've both taught me to be strong. We are a family and we'll fight this together.

What news of Susan? Give her my love if you see her and tell her I'll be seeing Gordon for a quick celebration after I finish my exams and before I return to Malaysia. Your loving daughter, Grace."

Olivier put the letter down and removed the reading glasses to rub his eyes which had become a little misted after reading Grace's letter. The reading glasses were a cheap store-bought pair that Sarah had brought home only two weeks earlier. Olivier prided himself on his good eyesight. He was fifty-three now and the strain of the trial and of not working was beginning to show. He grew tired easily and when he was tired his eyes couldn't focus as well or as quickly as they used to. Sarah had noticed his difficulty reading as he sat in the drawing room and pored over the pages of material, preparing with his lawyer for the commission of inquiry that was to begin its work in a week from now.

"The charges are all nonsense, of course," he had said to Bednarz at their first meeting two months ago.

"Of course," Bednarz had nodded matter-of-factly. "But they have to be taken seriously. A negative outcome can mean imprisonment and the end of your career. That is the reality, so we can't afford to be complacent."

"I've collected everything I can think of that we might need for the defense." Olivier indicated the huge stack of cardboard boxes piled up behind him in the living room. I had everything brought over from the office as soon as I first had an inkling of the charges against me."

"Very wise." Bednarz nodded approvingly. "But I must warn you. In politically motivated cases like this one, our biggest enemies can be the ones who declare public support for us. So we have to keep a low profile at this time and try not to let the newspapers get wind of it."

"Too late for that. I've been asked for interviews already by two different papers, one English and one Malay."

"Too bad. Then let's sort through the papers and see what we've got."

Bednarz was the high-profile civil lawyer Olivier had hired to defend him before at the commission of inquiry. Sarah had seen the man's fees and wrinkled her nose at the huge figure.

"This is only a commission of inquiry. Not a court trial. Do we really need such a high-profile lawyer?"

"I'm afraid we do." Olivier sighed. "This is a trial. Don't kid yourself. This is a trial, made all the worse by being labeled a commission of inquiry"

Working for days at a stretch with Bednarz, reading through the piles of documents, not being sure of the exact charges against him, all this was a great strain and Olivier began to rub his tired eyes while reading, sometimes had trouble focusing them on the print. Sarah worried about him, worried about his eyesight, worried about their finances. Most of the construction work had had to stop while the inquiry was going on. This meant that Olivier could not pay his engineers. His building contractors, who had their own roster of employees, could not afford to keep their workers idle, so they moved to other jobs with other firms. Although these workers were not on Olivier's payroll, there were penalty clauses in the agreements with the contractors and so sums of money had to be paid out. Olivier initially intended to keep his team of engineers together, but after two months of no income and regular salaries flowing out of the company's coffers, as well as Bednarz's substantial fees, the accountant had handed in his resignation saying he had found a better job elsewhere.

Olivier knew this was not true. The accountant had simply been the first to see that the firm was hemorrhaging money and, with a politically motivated inquiry, there was no potential solution in sight. There was initially the reassurance of income from Sarah's successful interior design consultancy; but in a city like Kuala Lumpur, in a country dominated by one powerful and charismatic political leader, society tends to resemble a small village community. Sarah's business dried up within a matter of weeks as news of Olivier's problems spread through the capital. After all, many of Sarah's wealthiest customers were beholden to the same people who had now abandoned or turned against Olivier.

Grace came home three months later. Sarah drove out to the airport to meet her. The flight was on time and Grace bounded through the arrival hall to meet her mother.

"Is Dad here?"

"No, he couldn't come. But you'll see him at home. How did your exams go?"

They tossed the luggage into the back of the car and Sarah drove the long way home, ostensibly to show her some changes that had happened in Kuala Lumpur since Grace's last visit three years ago, but in reality to prepare her for the changes that had happened to her father since then.

"This temple was completed last year and there's a new highway which goes almost directly from here to our house. The house needs some repairs but we've both been so busy and have kept putting it off. And the garden looks a bit neglected as well."

"Buji…"

"Buji's grown old. Nobody knows how old he really is. Your Dad and I guess he's somewhere between sixty and eighty, but we could be ten years off either side…"

"Dear Buji. I hope he remembers me."

"Of course he does. I personally think he's hanging on to life until you come back again." Sarah changed lanes deftly with one eye on the road ahead. Grace's eyes filled with tears of guilt and shame, remembering Buji's loving devotion to her as a child; a neglected grandfatherly figure at the periphery of her existence; someone she had tolerated, whose devotion she'd carelessly accepted without really knowing anything about him. Sarah now broached the real reason for the unsolicited drive around the city before going home.

"When did you hear from Dad last?" she asked, seemingly a careless question.

"Two months ago," Grace replied instantly. "I guessed he was overworked, because previously his emails were regular as clockwork, every two weeks and more often if it was to answer one of my questions… usually when I asked for money…" Sarah laughed.

"Ever thrifty. He couldn't leave such details to me, even when my design studio was doing well and making almost as much profit as his construction firm."

"It did?" Grace couldn't hide her astonishment.

"Yes. I'm talking about profit, mind, not turnover. The construction company's turnover was huge, but so were expenses. Salaries had to be paid, materials bought, subcontractors also incurred expenses, and Dad won contracts because he bid low on every project, sacrificing profit margins. But he never compromised on quality."

"Couldn't he have made higher bids?"

"Yes, but he never would. He didn't want to disappoint the people whose political patronage gave him all these contracts."

"But isn't that the system? I thought it was political protection that enabled him to make all these huge profits." Sarah shot a surprised look at her daughter.

"That's the way things usually work, but your father wasn't like that. He was extremely conscientious with the government's money and any public building he put up is instantly recognizable for its quality. He barely broke even with these government projects, and all of our real profits came from units sold in his many housing projects."

"And now?" Grace noticed Sarah's face cloud involuntarily at her question.

"The commission of inquiry, the freezing of the construction company's assets, terminating the contracts of most of his employees, the financial worries, they've all taken a heavy toll on your father."

Grace subsided into troubled silence for the rest of the journey home. As the car drew into the gravel driveway, she noticed at once that the house looked a bit the worse for wear but the garden looked as well-tended as ever. Sarah stopped the car under the porte cochère, pushed a button on the panel and the trunk lid moved up, obscuring her view to the rear of the car. She saw Grace get out on the passenger side to take her suitcase and then give a curious strangled cry. She didn't know what had happened until she rushed round the back and saw Buji lift Grace's two suitcases seemingly effortlessly, one in each frail hand. Grace stood by, seemingly in shock, cradling a bunch of arum lilies. Apparently Buji had been waiting for the car and had thrust the flowers into her hand as soon as she got out. Now, obviously embarrassed by his own temerity and her visible emotion, he grabbed her suitcases with superhuman strength and fled round the side to take them into the house through the kitchen.

As they entered through the front door Dwi, obviously alerted to Grace's arrival by the clatter of Buji carrying Grace's suitcases up the rear staircase, rushed into the living room. "Missy!" she exclaimed and, slowing to a decorous stop, clasped her hands in front of her face in greeting, her face radiant with welcome. Sarah took these effusive greetings in her stride but Grace, conditioned as she was by seven years in England to the vast interpersonal distance between people, was overwhelmed again. Much to the astonishment of all three of them, she hugged the diminutive Malay cook, who hardly reached up to her shoulders, and burst into tears. Dwi extricated herself, thoroughly embarrassed.

"Sorry Missy. Sorry." she stammered. "I no want make you cry."

"No, no, Dwi. You didn't do anything wrong. It's so good to see you." Sarah relieved their mutual embarrassment by giving Dwi instructions for dinner.

"Come on now, I'll take you up to see your father." This was the first inkling Grace had that Olivier was confined to bed. She followed Sarah upstairs and hesitated at the door, momentarily unwilling to confront what she might see. Sarah went in ahead of her.

"Grace is here." she announced cheerfully. Olivier sat up in bed with arms held out in anticipated greeting and noted her hesitation.

"Come here Grace," he commanded and for a brief moment she was his little girl again but even as she submitted to his embrace, she knew that she had lost something forever.

"Dad! So good to see you." She studied his face openly. He looked well and she told him so, pretending not to notice the slight tremor in his right hand when it lay briefly on her shoulder. Perhaps the tremor was caused by pent-up emotion, but she doubted that.

"I'm sorry, Dad," she whispered. "I've been away too long, but I'm home now, and I'm here to stay."

CHAPTER 7

It was just past noon when Grace left Vicky Hsiung's flat. The sun had gathered strength during her two hours indoors and she broke into a sweat as she walked quickly down the hill. The hole-in-the-wall eating places on either side of the street were beginning to fill with early lunchtime customers. It was only mid-April and the fierce humid heat of summer was still a few weeks away, so plenty of tourists and locals thronged the streets, looking for bargains in the many shops selling everything under the sun. She traversed Stanley Street, running parallel to the hillside, lined with stationery shops and several that sold electronic goods of all kinds. At the end of Stanley Street, she walked quickly along the narrow sidewalk down the steep road that brought her face to face with the grand temple of Konarak. This was what Grace had thought, the first time she'd seen the enormous building that took up an entire block, clad in white and black glass, with the name of an Italian designer emblazoned across the side. Of course, this temple was only one of many in the city and every day, thousands of tourists, mostly from mainland China, came to worship here. They bought luxury articles regardless of high prices, flush with cash, often paying out of suitcases full of currency brought from the mainland.

The passage through the various air-conditioned temples provided Grace with welcome relief from the humid heat. Two blocks further on, she shivered in the unnaturally cool comfort of yet another marble pharaonic palace, rode an escalator to the first floor and emerged through a glass door onto a walkway that took her all the way back to the central piers. She passed the general post office on her right and continued along the walkway, oblivious to the gigantic half-chewed apple on her left, and the brand new giant wheel on her right. There was a party of some sort going on at the base of the wheel. Loud rock music played, drowning the sound of jack hammers, rivet guns and pile drivers that was a constant in this city.

Hong Kong was locked in a decades-long struggle with another Asian city-state, Singapore, to be the most irresistible center of commerce, the most inviting tourist destination and the largest shipping port; in Asia and the world. Both of them had been long eclipsed by Shanghai, but the two cities were so busy competing that they hadn't realized this yet, because China was still a dictatorship while Hong Kong and Singapore were ostensibly bastions of free trade and commerce.

Most outsiders were unaware of the truth, Grace thought, just as she herself had been before coming here. Behind the glittering facades of Hong Kong lurked a few immensely wealthy individuals who had cornered the real estate and capital markets, and used this asymmetric power to systematically increase their wealth. These Hong Kong super-rich were undoubtedly talented individuals, many of whom had come up the hard way. But now they were typical profiteers, rent-seekers in economic parlance, using political connections and manipulation of the rules to grow even richer. Thus the bulk of Hong Kong's free trade was merely competition between these dozen-odd tycoons who vied with each other to open the next glittering mall or auction the next lot of three hundred apartments in the next residential tower. Their competition against each other did serve to raise standards of service, but it was nothing like a truly open market. Singapore's model was quite different politically, but similar to Hong Kong in others. Here too, wealth and power were concentrated in the hands of a few, legitimacy being granted by close connections to the ruling elite.

Grace knew that everything she bought from the Wellcome supermarket chain fed the coffers of Jardine Matheson, a notoriously opaque trading house. On the other hand, if she shopped at ParknShop, every purchase was a ka-ching into the coffers of Hong Kong's wealthiest tycoon, Li Ka-shing. Every aspirin bought from a Mannings chain store fed Jardine's Keswick family. On the other hand, if she bought her drugs at one of the ubiquitous Watsons branches, it was again a contribution to Li Ka-shing. One of the first things Grace had heard on arriving in Hong Kong was the local nickname of the Jardine Matheson headquarters building, perhaps an indicator of their local popularity. The building with its distinctive round windows had earned the sobriquet 'the House with a Thousand Arseholes.' The list of local monopolies went on; in buses, petrol, concrete...

Once Grace came to this realization after a few months in the city, she began to have tremendous appreciation for the ordinary people of Hong Kong. It was their hard work and enterprise that truly fuelled the wealth of this city. This was also the reason Grace had moved to a small, neighboring rural island a few weeks after her arrival in Hong Kong six months earlier.

She descended to street level from the walkway, short of the entrance to the iconic Star ferry, and walked left along the tiled sidewalk, glad for the shading overhead and the afternoon sea breeze blowing in from the harbor. She walked the few hundred meters to pier four, glad she was leaving the bustle of the city and returning to her rural haven. The Sea Sprite waited at the pier, a twin sister of the Sea Superior. She boarded quickly and since the sun was not too hot, climbed the stairs to the upper deck and along the aisle to the door that gave out onto the open rear deck. She chose a corner seat and leaned back to enjoy the harbor view of the skyline. Hong Kong at the moment was her favorite city in the world, but mainly because she could make quick short visits, living as she did on a tropical island paradise just thirty minutes away by ferry.

Half an hour later she disembarked at the island's pier and strolled down the main street of the town. Past the knot of early retirees sitting around a metal table in front of an unwatched television set showing a Cantopop musical. The table was adorned with a white table cloth and dozens of empty cans of the eminently drinkable local beer. Past the two large seafood restaurants, each set with dozens of round family-sized, lazy susan turntables, overlooking the small harbor and the dozen or so fishing boats riding at anchor. A couple of fishermen paddled out to their boats, squatting on rafts of driftwood or styrofoam strips lashed together.

She passed the giant Chinese banyan, its hanging aerial roots neatly trimmed like a fringe above head height over the concrete path. A black kite circled overhead and swooped down to pick something that a fisherwoman tossed over the side of her boat. Meanwhile the two squatting paddlers climbed into their own boat and began to arrange the nets. One of them started the outboard and balanced easily, with one foot on the tiller, maneuvering between the other boats and heading out to cast their nets into the waters around the headland. Grace stood for a minute and took in the idyllic scene with pleasure; the small harbor, the low waterfront shops, the clusters of houses that rose up the hillsides of the interior, none of them more than three stories high.

She passed the grocery story where a queue of shoppers stood before the elderly owner who tallied her customers' purchases with lightning speed while a young assistant shoved them into plastic bags.

"Sahm sap yi mun," she murmured, seamlessly taking in a fifty dollar note and handing back eighteen in change. Grace bought two avocadoes and continued on her way past the Szechuan restaurant where she sometimes dropped by of an evening to eat her favorite dish. She passed a sprinkling of other bars and restaurants where one could always stop for a drink or a chat. There was Tony's coffee place at the entrance to the Prime Bar, and the Waterfront Cafe, with its friendly staff who served delicious Indian food and offered seats with superb views of the small harbor and the innumerable ferries and boats that crossed the western channel on their way to Victoria Harbor.

She literally ran into the old woman who came out of a narrow side lane, cradling a bundle in her arms. The old woman walked unseeing past Grace without a word of greeting or apology. Grace recognized her. She was a local hermit by the name of Beulah. Since cars were not allowed on the island, everyone walked or cycled and most long-term residents knew each other by sight if not personally. The only motorized transports were narrow village vehicles, basically motorized carts on four wheels, that transported goods up and down the island's winding paths. Beulah was reputedly a harmless eccentric who lived alone somewhere on the island. Grace lengthened her stride and caught up. The old lady lived not far from Grace's house, outside the next village, and normally always gave her a cheery wave in passing with a good morning greeting of Josan. There was clear distress now, in the curve of her shoulder and in the hurried staggering walk.

"Beulah," Grace called gently, not knowing what to say. She spoke little Cantonese and did not know if Beulah spoke English at all. Beulah walked on, staring into the distance, leaning forward, slightly off balance with each quick, staggering step.

"Beulah!" She called a little louder and reached out to touch the old lady's shoulder. Beulah shuddered and stopped in mid-stride, looking at Grace as though she'd seen a ghost. Grace was thoroughly alarmed now. Two in the afternoon and there were few people about, mostly tourists walking through the narrow main street of town, heading for the beach twenty minutes further on, or for the next harbor town, one hour away by the twisting path across the green hills.

Beulah said something in Cantonese. Grace recognized the word "*gau*." It could mean either dog or nine. She looked down at the bundle the old lady was carrying and thought she could make out a small form and the tip of a paw peeping out from under the cloth. Of course, she must have come from the vet's practice on the side street; the old lady's dog must have died. She had noticed the dog on earlier encounters. It had looked rather young, a feisty, cheerful little white and tan mongrel with a broad chest, short legs and a very waggerly tail. Such a loss always hit old people hard, she thought sympathetically. Often their only companions. Although here on the island, most old people had family networks to fall back on. There were no old age pensions in Hong Kong although the government had debated it for years and had even commissioned academic groups at the University to study the question and help decide whether the social benefits would justify the cost of such a program.

"How did your dog die?" she asked sympathetically and was answered by another flood of Cantonese. Seeing Grace's blank face, she stopped dead in the middle of the street.

"Doodle die."

"Doodle?"

In answer Beulah thrust the bundle forward. Grace took the bundle in an unthinking reflex movement. She felt claws rasp against her skin. The dark cloth covering suddenly fell away and she started as Doodle's dead body swung down against her arm. A black, swollen tongue and two sightless eyes stared up at her. She staggered back, momentarily repulsed by the gruesome sight. Beulah leapt forward and took Doodle's body back with fierce, possessive pride and grief. Grace covered it again with the cloth that had fallen to the ground. Beulah moved on and Grace fell into stride beside her, determined not to be put off by the woman's anger that had more to do, she instinctively knew, with bereavement than resentment of her company.

"Can I do something to help you?" she asked after they had gone on wordlessly for a few minutes. Beulah shook her head, a tiny gesture that Grace might have missed if she hadn't been looking at her.

After a while Grace noticed that the woman was flagging and said, "May I carry Doodle for a while? It was such a good dog," using the impersonal pronoun since she wasn't sure of Doodle's sex.

Beulah stopped suddenly and turned. Grace held out her arms as though to receive a tray and the older woman delicately transferred the little body. They had already walked up the main road past Grace's apartment in the neighboring village. Grace wondered where Beulah lived. As though in answer, the old woman turned off the main street, up a narrow path to the left. The path climbed rapidly and the old lady, relieved of her burden, walked with surprising speed. Grace considered herself very fit but had a hard time keeping up. Trees and bushes growing profusely on either side of the path had been neatly trimmed back by unknown hands and the path itself had recently been swept clear of leaves.

They came to a bend in the path, another steep rise, and suddenly were over the hump of a hill. A breathtaking view unfolded. They were at the top of a steep cliff whose sides were overgrown with small bushes. At the foot of the cliff was a small bay with a sandy beach. From here, it looked as though a narrow path ran down the cliff side to the beach, but otherwise the only approach was from the sea. A small boat had been pulled up high above the water onto the rocks and covered with a blue and white tarpaulin. Even from this height, Grace could see that the tarpaulin had been lashed down with rope and additionally weighted with rocks to keep it in place. Was this Beulah's boat, Grace wondered? Is this how she made a sparse living?

She did not speak, trusting her instinct. Now, in this place with this grieving woman, was not the time for words. Grace hoped that her silent presence might assuage this woman's loneliness and grief, if only for a short while. A bit further on was a little cottage in a small clearing. Two jackfruit trees grew at the edge of the clearing and the light in this space was green from all the tall bushes and trees around it. The sound of cicadas was deafening and the chirping of birds everywhere, all loud and unseen. In the background to all this noise, was a dull murmur and after a minute Grace realized it was the sound of the sea and the surf on the rocks far below, all but drowned out by the raucous forest concert.

The cottage door was unlocked. A pair of worn black plastic sandals was neatly placed outside the door. Beulah shucked her soft cloth-topped shoes, depressed the door handle with an elbow and entered. Grace followed, not expecting an invitation to enter, but instinctively knowing her presence was not unwelcome. It was a single room with a wooden bed in one corner. A colorful red dragon-print bed cover was draped over the mattress. The bed cover was ripped at one end and the dragon's tail drooped onto the cement floor. A plain wooden table with two rough wooden chairs completed the furnishing of the room. Grace had noticed a fair-sized outhouse or a garden shed at the fringe of the clearing and guessed that was the toilet. Several articles of clothing hung from nails driven into a horizontally mounted wooden post along one wall. Several more articles of clothing hung from a line strung across the yard.

Grace now handed the little body to the old lady. Beulah stood at the wooden table and motioned with her chin at the dragon print bedspread. Grace whipped it off the bed, revealing a threadbare cotton sheet over a paper thin mattress and an equally thin pillow. Everything was worn but clean. She folded the bedspread in two and draped it over the table. Beulah gently laid her bundle down on it and stood with bowed head. Grace stood by uncertainly for a minute. The old lady's hunched shoulders and bowed head were the epitome of dejection. Grace was overcome by a wave of deep compassion and put her arms around the stooped shoulders. Beulah began to shake with dry sobs and Grace silently held her, stroking the back of her shoulder from time to time. She was willing to do anything for this poor woman at this moment, but did not know what else to say or do. After a long while Beulah turned, freeing herself from Grace's embrace.

"Thank you," she murmured, motioning Grace to one of the two chairs.

"How old was Doodle?" Grace felt bold enough to ask.

"Young dog. Very young. Baby." said Beulah.

"Oh, I'm sorry. Was he sick?"

"No. No sick." Beulah waved her hands emphatically. "No sick." There was puzzlement in her tone.

"No sick?" Grace grimaced, held her stomach and wrinkled her eyebrows in an imitation of discomfort.

"No sick. Die." Beulah drew two staggering stick fingers over the surface of the table like a drunken man walking. "Doodle come in. Sick. I carry to doctor. Die"

Grace was concerned now. If she understood right, Doodle had been in good health and, for unknown reasons, entered the hut staggering and died on his way to the vet. When placing the body on the table, she had seen that Doodle was a he. The immediate thought that came to mind was that the dog had been bitten by a poisonous snake, of which there were plenty on this island. Grace had skimmed through a book once of the flora and fauna of Hong Kong and its surrounding two hundred-odd islands. She had been alarmed to learn that out of twenty different kinds of snakes on land and water, eight were poisonous. After a few days of living and walking around the island, her alarm had dissipated. Snakes were shy creatures and rarely threatened human lives. On the other hand animals, especially smaller dogs and cats, were at risk if they encountered one. One of Grace's neighbors had mentioned, during a backyard chat, that her cat had been caught by a wandering Burmese python that entered her back garden one night. She had heard the mortal squeals of the cat just in time to see the snake glide under the gate, back into the surrounding bush. It was the way of the wild, Grace thought. Nothing to be done, although she sympathized with the old woman and her grief.

"Snakes," she thought, patting Beulah's shoulder. "Fortunately they almost never attack humans, unless they are cornered or unless one steps on one by accident." Grace must have unconsciously thought out aloud, because Beulah turned suddenly with a fierce glint in her eye.

"No snake," she said, shaking her forefinger vigorously. "Doctor say poison. No snake."

"Poison? How can he know it was poison?" Beulah's vocabulary was not up to the task of explaining how she knew.

"Doctor say poison," she insisted. "Poison." Beulah's lips twisted savagely. "Doodle murder." Grace stiffened in shock at the vehemence and the twisted lips.

CHAPTER 8

An hour later Grace descended the steep path, leaving behind the small cottage with its breathtaking view of the sea and the steep cliff. She was troubled by Beulah's accusation directed at the world-at-large, or perhaps she had someone specific in mind. In any case, Grace hardly got another word out of the woman. Grace had refused an offer of tea and shared a cup of water with Beulah before patting her on the shoulder and leaving with a few commiserating words.

She was still close to the cottage, walking downhill when she heard loud Cantopop music from behind a thicket of trees and wondered who might be playing it. There was no discernible path through the bushes, so she hesitated for a moment, worrying about snakes. Most snakes are nocturnal creatures, she reasoned, and today she was wearing rubber-soled shoes that she had donned for her visit to the client in the city. Although not as good as the ankle length hiking boots she wore when venturing in the bush, they were nevertheless more protection than her usual open sandals, so she cautiously parted the bushes, treading carefully, looking down at the ground to see where she was stepping.

She stepped abruptly into a clearing with several wooden boxes mounted at waist level on poles. A tall, thin figure in a faded T-shirt, knee-length shorts and rubber sandals was bent over one of the boxes with his back to her. Of course! Beehives and a beekeeper in the middle of a forest. How like this island to find small enterprise seemingly in the middle of nowhere!

Grace must have made some sound, for the music stopped and the man whipped his head round. She raised both hands in apology.

"Sorry, I didn't mean to startle you." The face lit up with a smile and Grace noted with surprise the wispy beard, rimless glasses and Cantonese features. Seeing the figure from behind, Grace had assumed from the person's height that the beekeeper was a *gweilo*.

"Hello, are you here to buy honey?" he asked in unaccented English.

"No. I heard the music and came to investigate."

"Ah, the music! I don't care much for it, but the bees like Cantopop."

"What?" He laughed at her surprise.

"Yes, it's true."

"You sound American," Grace said at a tangent.

"Pu-leese," he protested with a mock groan. "I'm Canadian."

"And you've come all the way here to entertain bees on an island in the South China Sea with Cantopop?" she asked cheekily. He nodded, looking so earnest she had to smile.

"Yes. They produce twice as much honey now. I had a small farm and raised cows in Canada. Tried different kinds of music on them. They gave a lot more milk listening to Beethoven and Mozart than to rock or pop. So when I moved here, I tried the same music on the bees. They didn't like it. Tried Russian composers, western pop and Italian opera too. No luck. And then I hit on this pop music. They love it. These are Cantonese bees alright."

"And now you can retire rich with all the gold the bees produce for you," Grace laughed, feeling instantly comfortable with this man. He smiled at her.

"I'm retired already. This is just something to do. So you want to buy some honey?"

"Sure," she said, realizing that because of her trip to the city, she still had her large handbag and money with her. She bought a glass jar of honey, paid and was about to leave through the bushes the way she had come when he pointed to a trail to the right.

"You'll find it easier to go back to your path this way. Do you always dress like this to go walking in the woods?"

"No, I don't." She hesitated a moment. "D'you know Beulah?"

"Beulah? I don't think I do. Why do you ask?"

"An elderly lady who lives alone up the hill along the path back there."

"Oh, the one with the mongrel puppy? I've seen her. Her name's Beulah?" Grace nodded.

"Poor thing. Her puppy Doodle died. Beulah thinks he was poisoned."

"Poisoned? Why would anyone do that?"

"I know. There's no reason. He was such a friendly dog. But that's what she thinks. She's totally grief-stricken, poor thing." He digested the news thoughtfully for a moment, then stuck out his hand.

"I'm Raymond. Raymond Chan."

"Grace Lam." she replied and they both laughed, together recognizing the absurdity of their situation. Two people, both of Chinese extraction, with no other language in common except English. They stood for a few more minutes in a preliminary exchange of personal information and realized that even had they known the Chinese spoken by their respective grandparents, they might not have understood each other. Raymond's family were Hokkien Chinese speakers who had settled in Toronto, while Olivier's parents had spoken Cantonese. It was only under the communist regime in Mainland China that Putonghua, or Mandarin Chinese, the language of Beijing, spread as a common language throughout the country. They nodded their good-byes.

"Did Beulah say why she thinks her dog was poisoned?" Grace shook her head.

"Well. I'll keep a look out for her now. Let me know if I can ever do something for her."

Grace was smiling to herself as she left Raymond, but a few paces on, the smile left her as she recalled Beulah's grief.

"Poor thing," she thought again. "It isn't nice to grow old alone and then have one's only living companion taken away so suddenly."

She walked back down the steep path and turned right, following the coast to the village where she lived near the main street. She saw a familiar stocky figure ahead of her walking his dog. She knew him only by sight but again knew who he was. He was the only vet in the village. He was a retired Englishman who loved animals and had a private practice on the main road of the village three evenings a week. She had often seen him with his dog, a friendly black labrador who always came to sniff at her heels when she walked by. She had often slowed down to allow this and the vet had occasionally nodded acknowledgement.

His name was Richard Croydon. At the Island Bar once she had heard someone say he had been veterinary officer in charge of the Happy Valley Race Course during the last two decades of British colonial administration. He had fallen in love with Hong Kong, had married a Cantonese woman and had permanently settled down on this island, despite fears prevalent at the time about the changes that Mainland Chinese rule might bring to the island. Hundreds, if not thousands, of Hong Kong natives had had similar fears, hence the extensive diaspora from here in the cities of North America, Europe and Australia. Richard Croydon had dared to stay, with the assurance that his British passport would enable himself and his family to relocate to some affordable small town in England should the change of administration prove to be unbearable.

As things turned out, the Chinese government had largely honored its promise not to interfere with the administration of Hong Kong. In the decade immediately after the handover, China had still needed the entrepreneurial skills and financial know-how of this island mini-state. By 2005, Hong Kong's status had been eclipsed by other powerhouses in the roaring Chinese economy; most important of these were the four cities directly under Central government rule - Shanghai, Beijing, Chongqing and Tianjin. These four cities now had more than enough expertise in the modern dark arts of international banking, trade and finance to no longer need Hong Kong's assistance. However, Hong Kong and neighboring Macau were convenient playgrounds for the newly rich and privileged of China, so the continued existence of these enclaves was tolerated, albeit with an increasing watchfulness that native Hong Kongers were beginning to find suffocating. All this led to the paradoxical result that the presence of the former colonial masters, of *gweilos* like Richard, was more than welcomed by the local population as a tenuous guarantee of continued freedoms, of perpetuation of the "one country, two systems" agreement between China and the Special Administrative Regions, as Hong Kong and Macau were known.

Grace lengthened her stride and tried to catch up, but he was walking too fast. Maybe another time, she thought. She walked into the village, stopping at the grocery store run by the grandmotherly type who always waved to her in passing, and bought half a kilo of cherry tomatoes. She would use them to make a salad with the avocadoes she had already bought. The thought of food made her realize it was past two in the afternoon and she was very hungry.

A black labrador snuffled at her heels in a friendly way as she turned to leave. Grace looked down in surprise. It was the vet's dog. Seeing Richard's dog at this juncture was no coincidence. Grace did not believe in coincidences. The vet was nowhere in sight. Grace snapped her fingers and the dog trotted after her. She walked to the little lane from which Beulah had emerged less than two hours earlier, hesitated at the vet's door, then pressed the buzzer.

Richard's wife opened the door. The questioning look at Grace turned into a smile when she saw the dog. "Come in Bruno. You've been wandering again." To Grace she said, "Thank you. He does this all the time, but usually returns on his own... Are you new here? Would you like to come in?"

Grace nodded and slipped in. "Only for a minute," she said, seeing the vet standing at the door to the examination room. Richard was not looking at her so she took a moment to examine him. His hair was almost all gone. What remained curled in wisps around his ears and formed a halo around the top of his head. His eyebrows were bleached by the sun to be almost invisible. His features were unremarkable. Seen from a distance he had appeared overweight, but up close she could see that he was still powerfully built and there was strength in the shape of his wide shoulders.

"I'm Emma Croydon." Mrs. Croydon was holding out a hand.

"Grace Lam," she said, taking the proffered hand. "I'm fairly new to the island. I've been here a few weeks."

"Welcome to our little island. We're a small community during the week, and on weekends an overcrowded tourist hotspot." Emma smiled ruefully.

"I'm learning to avoid the weekend crowds," said Grace. "Could I ask you... I've just come from the cottage of an old lady named Beulah. Do you know her?"

"She keeps to herself, though I've known her for years. She comes to see Richard occasionally."

"Yes, I know." Grace turned to Richard. "She thinks someone killed her dog. How did it die? Could it have been poisoned?" Richard looked away and did not reply. Grace felt foolish. Emma seemed to read her face and repeated the question.

"Could Doodle have been poisoned?" she asked her husband.

"Doodle... umm. Yes."

"So you think Beulah is right? That someone deliberately poisoned her dog?" Grace asked.

"I said poisoned. I know nothing about deliberate. Accidental poisonings happen all the time."

"How can you be sure it was poison?"

"Paraquat, or some such pesticide. Classical symptoms. Renal failure, massive fluid buildup in the lungs. Terrible death, convulsions and spasms, but must have been a high dose, at least a couple of teaspoonfuls, so he didn't suffer too much." This was more information than Grace expected. She turned to face him and he looked her in the face for the first time.

"Who are you?" The tone was not unfriendly.

'I'm Grace Lam. I live on this island."

"Been here long?"

"About six months."

"What are you to the old lady?"

"A neighbor of sorts, I suppose. I never spoke to her till today."

He nodded and turned back to his consulting room. Grace smiled apologetically at Emma and followed him in. She was increasingly beginning to rely on her intuition and knew that he was neither ally nor foe. He was simply an animal lover who made the common mistake of thinking of human beings as something apart from the animal world instead of being part of it. Of course, the large majority of human beings made the reverse mistake; of thinking of themselves as being above the animal kingdom rather than part of it. She brushed the thought aside and decided this man would become her ally.

"So is there any truth in what Beulah believes?" He replied at length without answering the question.

"Among humans, especially rural populations in developing countries, pesticides are a major means of suicide. Paraquat and its ilk are cheap, easily available and small doses kill effectively. As I said earlier, two or three teaspoons are enough. Not a method I would choose, but I suppose beggars can't be choosers."

Grace looked sharply at him for traces of sarcasm, contempt or irony and found none. He was merely being himself, talking about people without the passion that he reputedly reserved for animals.

"Could the dog have poisoned itself? Eaten poison not intended for it, I mean."

Richard dismissed the question with a shrug and outspread arms, but made no other reply. They stared at each other for a while in silence, curiosity in her glance and mild incomprehension in his. Bruno licked her hand and Grace suddenly remembered she was very hungry.

CHAPTER 9

Once back in her little flat, Grace made herself a
salad with half the tomatoes, one of the avocadoes,
generous lugs of olive oil, a dash of Worcester sauce,
adding pepper and salt to taste. While this was going on,
she had sliced most of a baguette into sections and toasted
it in a pan with a chunk of homemade garlic butter. When
all was done, she laid the table on her balcony for one and
set the food down on it, tasting as she walked. It was
delicious. She had nothing else planned for the day, so
decided to treat herself to a glass of Australian white wine
that a neighbor had given her; from the Margaret River
basin, fine wine country, she had been assured. You must
go there someday. Someday! she thought as she broke open
the bottle and tasted. It was really fine wine, and she
decided she would plan a trip there in the near future. One
of the advantages of being a multicultural brat was that she
had friends and acquaintances everywhere, and felt at home
in most parts of the world. Her mother Sarah on the other
hand always worried, mired in her nineteenth century
outlook on the world. Grace, you're over thirty now and
still single! If you don't look out, you'll find yourself high
and dry and slowly turn into a brittle, waspish spinster.
Sarah was a one to talk, Grace thought. Sarah had married
relatively young for love, become a mother, run her own
business and now there she was, in a crumbling old family

home in Kerala, becoming exactly what she feared her daughter would become; a brittle, waspish old woman.

She thought of Olivier with a touch of sadness, missing her father, nearly nine years gone and there was still an ache in her heart when she thought of him. The move to this island had done her good, though. There were so many new impressions, and it was soothing to be surrounded by nature in a second floor flat that looked down over a hill slope with thick vegetation, including a couple of giant paper bark trees, a lychee tree, and a Taiwan acacia with sickle shaped leaves that bore tiny yellow flowers in the spring. There was a cacophony of birds every morning to wake up to. She had had visiting cards printed and put up posters on the fence along the ferry pier to spread the word of her services as a diviner of lost objects. The initial trickle of phone calls of enquiry had become a regular stream, with one in five calls resulting in an invitation to find a missing person or object. After six months the trips into Hong Kong were at least once a week, sometimes more often. It was mostly wealthy widows like Vicky Hsiung at first, calling to find lost objects misplaced in tiny overfull apartments, but after a few successes word got around and most of the calls came through personal referrals rather than because of the posters and flyers she had distributed around the city. It did not hurt that she was very casual about money, and if the client showed the slightest reluctance to pay, Grace waived the fee completely. Bad business practice she knew, but that was one of the advantages of being independently wealthy. Whoever would have imagined her, Grace, a rich single girl at thirty-three, with a bank balance of over four million US dollars.

First came the sadness of bereavement, she thought, and then the money flowed in. She would gladly forfeit all her wealth to have her father back. But that was life, and there was no connection between the bereavement and the wealth. None at all. Except, perhaps, that the sadness of bereavement had heightened her sensitivity to life and brought out in her the gift; the gift that was the source of her wealth. Life was strange. Life made unexpected turns. There was truth in those clichés. When she returned from University in England, she had had no idea what was coming. Olivier had looked tired and ill, but he was still very young. The end had come with express train speed, his financial ruin roaring along on tracks parallel to his deteriorating health. Sarah and Grace had stood by and watched helplessly, powerless to influence the succession of events. Sarah's own design consultancy had failed around the same time as Olivier's business. The city of Kuala Lumpur was a small village, really, and Sarah's business was irreparably damaged by association with her husband's downfall.

Grace had watched bitterly as KL's rich and famous came in droves to her father's funeral. They stood in shiny suits beside their sleekly adorned wives and mouthed platitudes about how it was men like Olivier who were responsible for Malaysia's economic success. She knew that these men were just as dependent on political patronage as Olivier had been. That was the system. But she also knew that her father had been scrupulously honest, had delivered great value for money in his high quality constructions. These monuments to his hard work dotted the city and would serve as his legacy for decades to come. The thought was small comfort though. She still hated the fat cats who had withdrawn their patronage and made him the scapegoat for their own felonies.

She poured herself another glass of wine and allowed her mind to wander through the years since Olivier's death, revisiting events she had not thought much about since. She and Sarah had rented a small flat and lived together in Kuala Lumpur. She had worked for five years, as a private secretary to a property magnate. She had worked hard and gained his trust. She was paid well, and Sarah still had some savings from their affluent years, so they lived in reasonable comfort and financial security. There came a time when Grace was allowed to make a few important decisions on her employer's behalf. Mr. Anwariah was a reasonably good employer and she was prepared to continue here till she knew what she wanted to do with the rest of her life. She had liked her boss, although she knew nothing of him personally, except that he was married and had three children.

Then the incident. She had been working late one night in the office. He had come in staggering drunk and made a pass at her. She fended him off successfully. Grace was no prude, but after agonizing all night, decided there was no future for her in this job. Her decision proved right, for the next day Mr. Anwariah came early to work and wordlessly handed her a check for several thousand ringgit, amounting to three months notice, severance pay and accumulated benefits.

In a world of coincidences, another one. The week that Grace quit her job, Sarah's eighty-eight year-old mother wrote to say she could no longer manage alone in her crumbling 'tharavad,' the grand ancestral family home in Kerala that had been all but abandoned by Sarah and her siblings.

"Poor Amachi! All alone in the big house .I have to go and help her. D'you mind?" Sarah, plagued by guilt, asked Grace. "And now you've just lost your job. Maybe I shouldn't go." Sarah, torn between mother and daughter, uncharacteristically unable to make up her mind.

"Don't worry about me," Grace had said with a confidence she did not feel. "I'm going to..." this was a decision that came into her mind on the spur of the moment, "...I'm going to use my savings, I have more than twenty thousand dollars worth, including severance pay, to take a break and travel for a year." Seeing the doubt on Sarah's face, "Go." she urged. "It'll do you good, and Amachi needs you."

Still undecided, Sarah had called her brother Ranjan, an oncologist in California, for advice. Ranjan, perpetually busy, with a six-figure income and no time to spend it, was short with her.

"For heaven's sake, go and look after Ammachi, Sarah. With Olivier gone, what's keeping you in KL?"

"There's Grace..."

"Grace is a capable young woman." Ranjan had met her only once, briefly, flying into Kuala Lumpur for two days to attend Olivier's funeral. He hardly knew her. He was given to decisive remarks, perhaps a reason for his financial success.

"She will manage. And if the family house needs repairs, let me know. I'll send the money."

Grace had been twenty-six when she set off on her year of travel and Sarah relocated to her mother's house in a remote corner of Kerala. At the end of a year spent mostly wandering around small towns in southern Europe and a few memorable weeks trekking along the Lycian way, exploring Greek ruins in the mountains and along the Mediterranean coast of Turkey, Grace had ended her travels, visiting her mother in Kerala.

Sarah had adapted remarkably well to life in the old *tharavad*. Her sketchy knowledge of Malayalam had improved considerably, although she still could read it only haltingly. However, Amachi's lively factotum, Nirmala, lived on the premises, was absolutely devoted to Amachi and the family, and could always be relied upon for translations, helpful suggestions, or running errands as needed.

"Did you see many memorable places? Anything special about where you've been?" Sarah asked.

"Loads," said Grace. "I can't even begin. So many beautiful places in the world where I could just settle down and live for ever. But I can't, because there's always something new and exciting around the next corner." Sarah laughed at that.

"I was just the same. But you know, coming here, and living with Amachi has given me a different perspective. She's lived all her life in this house and couldn't dream of living anywhere else, even when she was a young woman."

"How is Amachi?"

"I'm glad I came when I did. Her mind was very clear last year, but in the past few months her memory is fading fast. She often doesn't recognize people now. Come and say hello to her."

The old house was more beautiful than Grace remembered. On her two earlier childhood visits, she had hated the rambling house, its dark interiors with mysterious insects that scurried in distant corners, the steps that creaked as she climbed up to the loft, the heavy four-poster beds with upright supports at the corners, the mosquito nets that hung on them, the sense of being closed in as she slept. The bed was made of dark rosewood, timber that had grown plentifully here in Amachi's childhood, but by now Kerala's rich teak and rosewood forests had been virtually cleared out. Coffee, rubber and tea had been planted in their stead.

The house was built as a two-story four-square with an inner courtyard that was open to the sky. A net had been put up to cover the opening and keep birds from flying into the kitchen. The courtyards and the broad verandahs were the place where Sarah and her two siblings had spent most of their time, growing up, going to school. And then they had left. Ranjan to a medical college in Manipal, five hundred kilometers north, up the coast through the hills of the Western Ghats. Sarah, who was good at numbers, went to a college in Madras to study commerce and emerged with a Bachelor's degree three years later. Ranjan was ambitious and spent all his summer vacations doing various unpaid internships so, after going to university, Sarah rarely met her brother and they grew apart. There was a third sibling, Georgie, who was never mentioned. Georgie had been the apple of his mother's eye and, Sarah later told Grace, 'the really brilliant one among the three of us.'

Sarah asked Nirmala to take Grace's suitcase up to her old room in the loft and led her daughter across the four-square, through a corridor past the kitchen to a spacious rear verandah in the shade of a giant mango tree. Amachi lay curled up in a broad wicker chair. She wore a simple white blouse and a *mundu* tied in the traditional way. Despite the heat of the afternoon, she had a thin blanket spread on her lap and she was chewing on something. She was still alert despite her age, sitting up and turning her head as she heard their footsteps.

"Nirmala-eh," she began in a sing-song voice. "Oh, it's you. Who's this with you?"

"Amachi, this is Grace, my daughter. You remember her, don't you?"

"I remember a little girl with two pigtails. I don't know this person. Why is her hair so short?" This

71

conversation was in Malayalam and Grace did not understand.

"She's asking why your hair is so short, and what happened to your pigtails," Sarah explained. Hearing this exchange, Amachi switched to labored English, speaking unnecessarily loudly to make herself better understood. She had lost some of the lower front teeth so she whistled as she spoke.

"I know English. Why didn't you come and see me before? So many years, you've all left me alone, my girl. My granddaughter was a little girl with long hair. Now a big girl with short hair walks in and says she is my granddaughter. How am I to know who you are?"

Grace was tongue-tied at Amachi's sudden indignation and looked helplessly at her mother. Sarah's response was swift and tart.

"Oh, Amachi. Stop it. The poor girl walks into the house and you begin to attack her. First of all, I introduced her as your granddaughter. Don't chase her away before you even get to know her." Amachi smiled a mischievous smile, as though she enjoyed the scolding.

"Come, come, Gracie *molae*." She patted the chair beside her. "Sit down and tell me about yourself."

After this rocky start, Grace found herself immensely enjoying the next half hour of conversation with her grandmother who had a lively sense of humor. But then, disconcertingly, Amachi began ordering her to close the gate before the cows came in and ate all the flowers. Sarah who had stood by silently till then, bent down and patted her mother's hand.

"It's four o'clock Amachi. Time for your tea and biscuits. I'll tell Nirmala to bring them." She motioned Grace away. "That's what I told you earlier," she explained softly. "Her mind wanders. She thought she was talking to your grand-aunt Gracie, who died twenty years ago."

"What happened to your brother Georgie? Why do you never talk about him?"

This was much later in the evening after an early dinner of fish head curry served by Nirmala with brown rice, a green papaya *thoren*, yoghurt and jackfruit chips. They were sitting in comfortable cane chairs on the red-tiled front verandah and watched the silky, sultry evening light soften and then, as with the noiseless fall of a curtain, night fell. Something swooped and fluttered under the champaka tree in the front garden. Sarah was silent.

"What happened to Georgie?" Grace asked again.

"I haven't thought of him for a long time… he was such a lovely boy… three years older than me, five years older than Ranjan. Amachi loved him more than any of us, but we weren't jealous. He was simply too clever, larger than life, even as a ten year-old, I remember, he held his own in conversation with adults and spoke to them as an equal, very unusual in a traditional Kerala household in those days. He made them laugh. He was always top of his class and then, around fifteen, something went terribly wrong. He began to drink, he disappeared for days at a time, no one knows where. There were no drugs in those days, as far as I know… but he was on something. And then one day, they brought him home dead. He drowned in the river, they said." Sarah sighed.

"So it's no secret. We don't talk about him because there's nothing to say, really."

"What a terrible waste," said Grace.

"Maybe we should have talked about it, nevertheless. But we never did. Amachi refused to speak about him and closed up when I asked her. Maybe that's why Ranjan and I both moved away and more or less stopped talking to each other as well." After a long silence, she said. "What really saved me was meeting your father on a flight to Singapore at the age of twenty-three." Grace said nothing.

"And what about you, Grace?" Grace shrugged in the dark.

"There's nothing about me you don't know. Except…" she stopped.

"Except what?" Grace shrugged again.

"Oh, it's nothing. Nothing worth talking about."

"Except… and then a nothing, usually means there's a something," said Sarah with inimitable circular logic. Grace tried to dismiss the subject but Sarah was persistent.

"It's just that, over the past year, ever since Dad died, really, I've been feeling these occasional tremors," she finally confessed.

"What kind of tremors? Chills? Flushes? Fever?"

"Nothing like that. I can't explain. Sometimes it's like I feel a minor earthquake, sometimes a quiet unease. I look around and no one near me senses anything different."

"Have you been to a doctor?"

"I went to several while I was travelling and there was never anything. They probably thought I was a hypochondriac. Maybe I am. Anyway, during the two weeks I spent in California with uncle Ranjan, I mentioned it to him and he referred me to several of his colleagues. They did a battery of tests. Blood tests, MRI scans, CAT scans, the works, you know what he's like…" Sarah nodded.

"And…"

"And nothing. There's nothing wrong, all the tests said. But I still feel it. I felt it strongly today when I arrived here."

"You miss your father very much, don't you? I do. Every single day." Grace shook her head.

"I miss Dad, but I know my tremors are nothing to do with that. They happen when I'm not even thinking of him, or completely engrossed in something else."

"*Entha kunjae, irrutath irrikunnu?*" It was Nirmala, aghast that they were sitting in the dark.

"The light will attract insects Nirmala. Leave us in the dark. Is Amachi asleep?"

"Amachi is sitting up in bed and listening to the radio. Says she can't sleep."

"You go to bed now. I'll go and look in on Amachi shortly." Nirmala turned to leave. "And Nirmala, I want you to take Grace to Amachi's vaidyan tomorrow morning."

"*Entha molae?*" Nirmala looked at Grace, her concern visible in the glimmer of light from the adjacent room. Grace looked puzzled.

"It's nothing," Sarah assured her. "I'll tell you tomorrow."

The next day, after a breakfast of *puttu,* steamed plantains with *pani* and the remains of the previous day's fish head curry, Nirmala appeared in the dining room wearing a white silk blouse and a freshly ironed blue checked lungi. Sarah raised her eyebrows and Nirmala blushed.

"The *vaidyan,*" she said. "Don't you want me to take Grace to the *vaidyan?*"

"Yes. But I just realised the *vaidyan* doesn't speak English. How will Grace talk to him? Maybe I should go."

"No *kochamma.* I know English. I'll translate for Grace-mol. Amachi wants you to give her a bath. She's been waiting since six in the morning."

So Grace walked out into the morning heat at nine. It was already burning. Grace wore a hat, but Nirmala seemed unconcerned. Her hair was combed, oiled to a high gloss and plaited thick down to her waist. Grace was reluctant to see the physician, but Sarah was insistent and in the end she gave in, driven as much by her curiosity to see an Ayurvedic practitioner as anything else.

They walked along the grass verge of a red dirt road lined on either side by dark laterite blocks whose porous surfaces and blackened moss-grown edges reminded her of the walls of Angkor Thom that she had visited on a school trip many years ago. As they walked, Nirmala pointed out sights, practicing her English along the way.

"School bus," she said, as a careening van full of singing children sped by, and then "autorickshaw," for a three wheeler that slowed down as it passed them. There were three occupants in the back, but the driver slowed down, looking curiously at Grace.

"*Ithara Chinakarthi?*"

"*Poda!*" Nirmala replied with a contemptuous wave of her arm. "Idiot," she said indignantly for Grace's benefit.

"What did he say?"

"He call you Chinese."

"Well my father was Chinese you know, and I do look like him."

"Your mother is Kerala. You are home here," said Nirmala emphatically, dismissing the topic with finality.

"How much further?" Grace was pouring with sweat. They had left the road, crossed two emerald paddy fields walking along their earthen bunds and were now on a dirt path lined with large leaved bushes that grew to head height. Grace recognized them as tapioca. Further on a creeper grew over a low wall. It was covered with white flowers that gave off a familiar, heady scent.

"Queen of the night," Nirmala explained, plucking a few flowers and pushing them into her hair. "*Vaidyan* next door only," she assured, seeing Grace wipe a red face on her sleeve.

"Where did you learn English?"

"Studied Malayalam medium school only," Nirmala confessed. "Then learn English from radio and friend to take job in Gelf. Two year."

"Guelph? You worked in Canada?"

"No, no. Middle East. Gelf."

"Ah. Where? In Dubai?"

"No. Cooking for Indian family in Oman. But I earn money two year and come back. Here only much better. Kerala God's own country, you know. I stay here look after my old mother, your mother and Amachi." Grace reached out on impulse and touched Nirmala's long hair.

"Thank you for looking after Amachi and my mother." Nirmala looked surprised and pleased.

"*Vaidyan's* house," she said, pointing ahead.

CHAPTER 10

The *vaidyan's* house was a small brick structure with red tiles and thick vegetation all around. It was a simple box with yellow painted walls, but the overhanging profusion of pink and white bougainvillea gave it an elegant, cool and attractive appearance. A large bush grew beside the front door. On it hung pink bell-like fruit that Grace had never seen before. The *vaidyan* was sitting on the red-tiled verandah in a wooden grandfather chair with a woven cane back and long arms that unfolded outwards to become footrests.

He rested a glass of tea, held in his right hand, on his bare stomach as he lay reclined with his feet up. He lowered his feet and stood up as they entered the gate. He was lean, of medium height, had a thick shock of unruly white hair, and wore a simple white dhoti. He leaned towards the open front door of the house.

"*Kunjae*! Beena!" he shouted into its dark interior in Malayalam. "Bring me a shirt and two cups of chai. We have visitors."

A tall girl in blue jeans and white shirt emerged from the interior. She had thick, unruly hair, just like her father's, except it was still black. The resemblance was unmistakable. She carried a faded blue shirt that she gave to her father. She nodded at Nirmala, gave Grace a curious, friendly smile and disappeared again.

"*Irikku, irikku.*" He motioned them to two wooden chairs on the verandah, pulling on the shirt.

"Sit, sit," he said to Grace. Nirmala preferred to lean, half-sitting on the broad red cement balustrade.

"This is Grace, Sarama-kochama's daughter," said Nirmala by way of introduction. "She speaks only English. I'm here to translate for her." The *vaidyan* laughed.

"I speak Ingleesh. But you tell me if I don't understand." He motioned Grace to draw her chair closer. "What is wrong *molae?*"

Grace had been skeptical about the visit till then, but she took an instant liking to the man and his gentle demeanor, so she began to explain her symptoms. The *vaidyan* held up his hand to stop her. "I don't want to know symptoms. Tell me who you are first."

"I told you, *vaidiyan sar-e.* This is Sarama-kochama's daughter." said Nirmala. Beena emerged with two cups of tea for the guests.

"*Molae,* you sit here," said the vaidyan tp his daughter in English. "Explain to Grace what I want." Beena spoke excellent English and quickly explained that her father needed to know more about his patients before considering symptoms or a diagnosis.

"Where do I start?" asked Grace, puzzled. "My whole life story?"

"Yes," Beena smiled. "A ten minute version will do. My father will ask you for details if he wants to know more."

So Grace told him the story of her life, of her happy childhood, of not really belonging either in Malaysia or in boarding school and University in England. The shock of her father's death, the strange newness of her mother's life in Kerala, her one-year of extensive travel, the inexplicable internal tremors she had felt after the death of her father, faintly at first, but with increasing intensity during the past year of travel. From time to time the *vaidyan* looked to Beena for explanation of a word and sometimes he looked courteously to Nirmala for a translation. Grace felt so comfortable talking that she went on for nearly an hour. At the end he smiled and stretched out a hand to her.

"I'm not sure. But I think you're very lucky. I think you have a gift. We will try and find out what that is. Give me your hand." Unsure of what to expect, Grace leaned forward and held out her right hand. He placed three fingertips on the inside of her wrist, leaned back and closed his eyes. After five minutes, her shoulders began to tire.

"Pull your chair closer and rest your elbow on your knee," Beena advised. Another fifteen minutes of sitting there, having her wrist silently held by a man who seemed to be asleep. Grace began to think this was a waste of time.

"I'm not simbly holding your hand." The *vaidyan* seemed to read her thoughts, spoke suddenly, making her jump. "Your pulse tells me everything. Give me your other hand." Ten minutes later Grace was getting tired of the whole exercise again. He suddenly released her hand, opened his eyes and sat back.

"*Nadi vijnan.*" he said enigmatically. Seeing Grace's wrinkled eyebrow, he explained. "Pulse diagnosis. *Nadi*, river. Pulse flows like a river all over the body. *Vignan*, knowledge. Knowledge of the river of life. I studied pulse for four years." He held up three fingertips. "Each of these detects a different *dosha.*" He pointed to his fingers and Beena quickly expanded.

"Forefinger, *vatha*, middle finger, *pitha* and ring finger, *kapha.*" Grace had read of the three *doshas* that denote the balance of humors in the human body in Ayurvedic medicine.

"*Vata* is like a cobra," the *vaidyan* explained, pointing to his forefinger. "The middle finger feels *Pitha*. It is like jumping frog. And the *kapha* finger pulse is swan. A *Hamsa*."

"Life teaches," he was speaking to the ceiling now. "We have to learn why we are here. Sometimes we don't learn, so differend people go differend ways." he made butterflies in the air with both hands. He saw that Grace's glass of tea was empty. "Do you want more tea?"

"No. thank you."

"Beena," he said something to his daughter in Malayalam. She disappeared into the house and came back with what looked like a wooden Y of a catapult with no rubber or sling attached. The *vaidyan* pointed wordlessly to Grace.

"What should I do?" Grace asked, taking one end of the forked wood.

The *vaidyan* spoke to his daughter again in Malayalam. She stepped off the porch, plucked one of the pink bell-like fruit and handed it to Grace.

"Go for a walk." He pointed to the west. "Go alone. Walk for at least twenty minutes, then come back here and tell me if anything has happened." Grace rose, fruit in hand and put the forked stick down on the chair.

"No, no, no. You take the stick with you. The fruit is only for refreshment only. I saw you were curious about it. It is called *Chambeka* in Malayalam. I don't know the Engleesh name. Very good for thirst. You go." Grace looked uncertainly at Nirmala who rose to accompany her.

"Rose apple," Beena said.

"What?"

"The fruit in your hand," Beena pointed. "Its English name is rose apple."

Meanwhile, "*Avadae irikku,*" her father said sternly to Nirmala in Malayalam. "Sit down, Nirmala. Grace, you must walk alone. You have a gift. It will be easier to find if you are alone. The *chambeka* is for refreshment only."

Grace walked in the direction indicated, feeling foolish and a little resentful. At first she thought of walking home to Sarah to complain of a wasted morning, but she was not sure of the way back. There was intense green all around; the emerald flashes of paddy fields interspersed with the dark green of forest, the lighter green of banana tree groves and fields of tapioca. Brown, curving trunks of coconut trees everywhere amidst the green and the air was heavy with moisture, the humming of thousands of unseen insects and the rising kawoo, kawoo, kawoo calls of an unseen bird. It was close to noon and she walked in the dappled shade of jackfruit, mango, tamarind, soap trees and coconut palms. She bit into the *chambeka* and the juice ran down her chin. It was tart and sweet at the same time. She swung the wooden stick loosely held in one hand. She considered throwing the stick away, looking back to make sure she was out of sight of the *vaidyan's* house. To her surprise, she found she had walked a considerable distance and was almost at the top of a low hill. Looking at her watch, she found that she had been walking for twenty-five minutes already. She finished the last of the fruit and decided to turn back when the cleft stick fell out of her hand. She bent to pick it up, almost by accident grasping one end of the fork in each hand. She felt a familiar mild vibration go through her body and the stick bent downwards of its own volition. She tightened her grip on the stick and bits of bark flayed off the stick and dug into her palms. She stood there immobile for a moment, the stick juddering in her hands, pulling downwards like a live thing. Then with a sigh she released one end of the stick and stepped back as it hung limply in her other hand.

She walked back to the *vaidyan's* house, finding her way without thinking about it, guided by a newfound instinct. Sitting on the verandah of the house waiting for her return, the *vaidyan* saw her first, immediately noting the change in her carriage and step.

"*Beena molae, Nirmalae, kando.* Look." He beamed with pleasure. "She's found her gift."

It was past one by the time they returned to the *tharavad,* Nirmala hurrying along in front. She was excited at the discovery of Grace's gift but also worried about leaving Amachi alone for so long. Her worry was only a little bit diminished by what the *vaidyan* told her while they waited for Grace's return.

"It's getting late for Amachi. I should get back," Nirmala had fretted, looking anxiously down the path where Grace had disappeared.

"Don't worry about Amachi, Nirmala," the *vaidyan* had told her. "You are a good woman and have looked after Amachi well. She has very little time left. Now her daughter has come back to be with her. Let Saramma take the responsibility now."

Despite this reassurance Nirmala, from force of habit, worried that it would get late for Amachi's lunch, delaying her afternoon nap and throwing her entire routine out of kilter. Once that happened, it was difficult to re-establish her daily routine again. Grace had caught a bit of Nirmala's concern and they both hurried home now, the former's face flushed with the heat, exertion and excitement.

CHAPTER 11

Entering the compound through the sagging gate down the straight driveway to the house they both stopped short in surprise. Sarah was walking to and fro in the garden with an extremely tall white man in tow. Sarah waved as they entered and beckoned them over.

"Come and meet Hans van Houten," she said. "My daughter Grace. And this is Nirmala who really manages the household."

Grace shook the proffered hand while Nirmala blushed in embarrassment and bobbed her head in awkward curtsey. Noting her embarrassment, van Houten nodded a friendly hello to her. Meanwhile Sarah had noted Grace's wide-eyed curiosity at meeting this stranger here in the depths of Kerala, far from the usual tourist haunts along the coast or the traditional backwaters. Grace's immediate thought was that Sarah had advertised the property for sale and this was their first prospective customer.

"Grace, I know you only arrived yesterday and the place is new to you as well, but can you walk Hans around the property and show him what there is to see. Meanwhile, Nirmala, come and help me get the visitor's bedroom ready." Nirmala seemed equally puzzled at the presence of the stranger.

"*Kochammae,* what about Amachi's lunch?" she asked in Malayalam.

"All taken care of. You were away at the *vaidyan's* much longer than I expected. Amachi's had her lunch and is already asleep. She was very tired today, she said."

Grace hadn't walked around the grounds since arriving, but had a vague memory from childhood visits. They walked down the driveway that led to the disused garage beside the house. Hans was interested in everything and asked innumerable questions, which spared the need for polite conversation. Grace remembered things she had forgotten she knew, so when asked, she was able to tell him, this is a soap tree, that's a jackfruit and these bushes are tapioca plants. She picked up a few soap nuts from the ground beneath the tree and he put them into the pocket of his beige sleeveless safari jacket to try them out later. He exclaimed at the size of the jackfruit and she made a mental note to ask Nirmala to buy some from the market since the ones on the tree did not yet look ripe. Hans wanted to know how tapioca was cooked and eaten.

"I'm sure you'll taste some. How long are you staying here?"

"I've booked for a week," said Hans, giving her a first inkling of why he was here. "Your mother said the guest room is free for the whole week." Grace almost laughed loud at that. Trust Sarah to leap into a business venture with supreme self-confidence and no preparation. Well, Grace herself had no intention to remain here and be part of it, although she had no idea what to do with the rest of her life.

So Grace entertained Sarah's first guest, explaining to him how the giant, edible roots of the tapioca were harvested and cooked. Some varieties contain significant amounts of cyanidic compounds, so the poison has to be removed by boiling once, throwing out all the water and boiling again with fresh water to make it edible.

They walked round to the rear of the house and the well that supplied them with water. She recognized the water pump in its tin-roofed housing and explained the working of the biogas digester that provided the kitchen with methane for cooking, surprising herself with details recollected from childhood visits. There was a small fruit garden with mango and papaya trees.

"How did you hear about this place?" she asked as they walked back to the house at the end of the tour.

"I was staying at the Malabar Hotel in Cochin, a very fine hotel by the way, and I asked someone there to recommend a quiet place very far from crowds, and he gave me your mother's phone number."

They had a late lunch in the rarely used large dining room with its heavy dark rosewood table and matching chairs.

"Your stay here is to be an authentic Kerala experience," said Sarah as they sat down to their meal. "So we don't use any cutlery apart from these wooden serving spoons. You'll have to eat with your fingers; you can wash your hands over there," indicating the ledge with a row of brass pots filled with water.

"I like to eat with my hands, that's why God gave us them," said Hans gamely, as he struggled to follow Sarah's example to mix rice with fish curry and bring the food to his mouth before the grains and drops of curry slipped through his fingers.

"So what did the *vaidyan* say?" Sarah wanted to know. Grace shrugged.

"He said there's nothing wrong with me."

"And it took him so long to find out. You were gone for four hours."

"He discovered I have a special gift. That's what's caused the tremors."

"What kind of a gift?"

"Sort of, like, water witching."

"A diviner? You, a diviner?"

"Why not?" Grace reacted, stung by her mother's critical disbelief. She had thought nothing of her gift until this moment. Now she defended her right to own this gift and be a part of it.

"It's simply that you're so practical and ordinary…"

"Thank you very much."

"I'm sorry Grace. I don't mean to belittle you. But you've shown no particular sensitivity to…" Sarah struggled for words to express the thought inoffensively "…to natural phenomena or the world around you…" Meanwhile they noticed that Hans had stopped his struggle to pick up food and gone perfectly still. They both put aside their argument to look at him.

"You can find water?" He turned to Grace. Grace shrugged again.

"I suppose so. There was some kind of a reaction. The *vaidyan*, that's the Ayurvedic physician, thought that was the reason for my tremors."

"What tremors?" Grace really did not feel like explaining, but he was obviously very concerned and interested. So she explained what had happened that morning. Hans correctly interpreted Sarah's skeptical glance at him.

"I'm sorry to ask your daughter these questions, Sarah. But I'm not merely being inquisitive. This is such an amazing coincidence."

"Coincidence?. How?"

"I visited Israel on my way here. I went to see someone there, but was unable to meet him."

"What has this to do with Grace's new-found gift?"

"Well, you see, the man I went to see was Uri Geller."

Grace's face remained blank, but Sarah's ears perked up. "Geller, the spoon-bender? The clock stopper?" Sarah asked. "I haven't heard of him in decades."

"The same." Hans nodded. "The rumor is that Uri Geller earned millions working for various oil companies and now lives in retirement in Israel."

To Grace's embarrassment, Sarah almost quivered with curiosity. "Was he a diviner too?" Hans nodded again.

"And he could find oil?"

"We don't know. There are only rumors. Apparently Atlantic-Richfield paid him millions to tell them where to drill."

"But if he was successful, why make a secret of it?" Sarah was very skeptical.

"The rumor also goes that he was sworn to secrecy; not allowed to say that he was employed by an oil firm at all."

"Why?" Grace chimed in.

"Two reasons. One, if he was successful, they didn't want him poached by another company. Second, more important, all oil companies have large teams of petroleum geologists who work very hard to study underground strata and tell them where to drill. Even if a company has a sure-fire way of knowing exactly where to drill, they'd still need geologists to help them analyze the sediment types they were drilling through and help in case of blowouts."

"So?" Sarah prompting again.

"According to the US Geological Survey, for example, the kind of place where they employ a large number of our kind of guys, water dowsers appear to be successful because there's underground water nearly everywhere. In other words, geologists believe that a diviner's ability to find water is mere coincidence, that belief in this method is superstition."

"I felt the rod tugging at my hand. It was like a live thing…" Hans held up a hand to stop Grace's protest.

"I believe you… that's why I'm interested to know more."

"*Kochamae*, something wrong with the food?" Nirmala put her head in the door and saw they weren't eating. "Food not ok?" Grace nodded hastily and pushed the dish of fried colocacia to Hans. "All delicious, Nirmala, Grace said.

They spoke of other things during the rest of the meal. Grace successfully steered the topic of conversation away from herself and asked Hans about himself. He had travelled a great deal and seemed to have visited most of the places she had been to on her year of travel, so they exchanged notes, and she found herself warming to him. Sarah spoke little for the rest of the meal and seemed lost in her own thoughts.

Hans refused the offer of coffee after the meal and spent the afternoon walking about the extensive grounds and the garden with a pair of small but powerful field glasses trying to spot birds. He was quite excited to hear a deep throated call from one of the trees, a mango tree that grew at the edge of the compound. Nirmala was passing by on her way to the market and he asked what the bird was called.

"*Ooppan*," she said. "Malayalam name *Ooppan*." He thanked her and stood motionless beneath the tree for a few minutes till he spotted the large purple-black bird with brown wings. He came back to the shade of the front verandah and thumbed through a copy of Salim Ali's book of South Indian birds for a long while.

"Crow Pheasant," he said to himself, pleased. "Greater Coucal or Crow Pheasant." Shortly after, he disappeared in the direction of the haystack armed with field glasses and the book of birds and did not reappear till it was almost dark. Meanwhile, Grace sat with her mother under a ceiling fan on the verandah and drank a cup of tea.

"I didn't know till Hans appeared that you're taking in guests."

"Well now you know," Sarah said with some asperity. "He's the first. The very first. I need money to renovate this place if I'm to make a go of it. As it is, I'd be completely lost without Nirmala."

"And you? What are you going to do for a living?" Sarah asked quietly. Grace shrugged in reply. "I don't know."

"Grace! You're twenty-six. You don't have a job."

"I'll find something," she assured her mother with a confidence she did not feel. "I'll find something."

Hans's presence was a welcome distraction for Grace in the days that followed. The man took a keen interest in anything and everything he saw. Seeing the familiar surroundings through his eyes, she began to see that Sarah's guest house scheme had a real chance of success. Which brought her to her own predicament. What was she going to do? How would she earn a living and where did she want to live?

Unexpectedly, the answer emerged from the woodwork after a casual conversation with Hans the following week. Grace told him one evening about her symptoms of unease following the death of her father. She had initially put it down to grief, but the symptoms had persisted even when she was not thinking about him.

"So you had no idea of your capability before the ayurvedic doctor suggested it?"

"No, I didn't. But once I knew, the surge of feeling and intuition was very powerful." Hans looked at her thoughtfully. "What do you, as an engineer, think of this capacity to divine water?" she asked.

"Why do you ask?"

"Well. At dinner that first night, you mentioned that geologists don't think much of it. And my mother is very skeptical. She thinks I'm quite useless and worries that I'll be a financial burden to her."

"And you? Do you worry as well?"

"Yes. Quite a bit," Grace admitted. It was as much an admission to herself as to him.

"Tomorrow is my last day here. Are you free in the morning?"

"Yes. Why?"

"I've just had an idea. Come for a long walk with me. Perhaps you can show me what you can do."

They walked out into the lush green countryside the next morning, Grace with her cleft stick and Hans wearing thick-soled walking shoes, his usual beige sleeveless safari jacket and carrying binoculars. They had walked less than ten minutes before Grace stopped and said, "I feel something. I think there's water here."

She grasped the stick with both hands and walked a few paces to her left. The stick began to bend downwards. Hans reached out and held her hand, trying to pull it upward. He could feel the resistance, the powerful downward pressure. He straightened up and there was a smile in his eyes.

"Maybe I have a job for you," he said. "Let's go back."

"You know where I work, don't you?" Hans asked Sarah later as they sat together at lunch.

"Yes, for a big oil company. Why?"

"You can say it's a big company. Rotterdam Oil drills for oil and produces it in more than fifty countries around the world." Sarah said nothing, but looked at him expectantly.

"Now, about Grace's gift…" Hans began.

"You think she can help your company find oil? I thought your geologists didn't believe in this sort of thing."

"No they don't. But I do. And I can perhaps convince our board of directors as well."

"Wouldn't the geologists be happy to have someone who can confirm their own guesses?" asked Grace shrewdly. "They never know for sure, do they?"

"Good question," Hans admitted. "And logical thinking. But the world doesn't work that way." He blew out a lower lip in a parody of frustration. "People aren't logical, don't ask me why. Even science-driven fellows like our geologists have their pride and they'd walk out on us if they knew that you, for example," pointing to Grace, "were to be employed by Rotterdam Oil to tell us where to drill." Grace and Sarah looked at him speechless.

"I didn't mean to put it so bluntly, but perhaps it's better this way. Now you know why I'm interested in your water dowsing capabilities or otherwise."

"What are you offering my daughter?" Sarah asked, seeing that Grace was silent.

"A job with Rotterdam Oil. I can't guarantee anything until it's cleared with our executive director. If it's approved, on paper you'll be my personal assistant,." He looked earnestly at Grace. "All above board and proper. You'll be paid economy class airfare to Rotterdam. Your starting salary will be that of an administrative assistant.

"How much is that?" Sarah asked again, seeing Grace was silent.

"Around thirty thousand Euros a year."

"Will she be able to live on that?"

"It's a reasonable starting salary. And she'll travel to places around the world where we have drilling options, expenses paid. She will scout the areas and pinpoint where to drill. We'll evaluate the accuracy of your hunches, see how well they overlap with geologists' recommendations. If your hunches are accurate, there will be bonus payments for oil struck at the first attempt."

"How much will she get?" Sarah asked suspiciously after a slight pause, seeing that Grace had not reacted at all. Impossible to know what that child was thinking. Why doesn't she say something? Sarah in silent exasperation.

"Drilling oil wells is an expensive and risky business," said Hans in his slow, methodical voice. "You see, companies like Rotterdam Oil, we subcontract the drilling jobs to specialist firms. There are several, not widely known to the general public but they're household names in the oil business; Transocean, Diamond Offshore, or Noble, for instance. We recently switched to a new outfit called Subterrain that charges less than the average, around three hundred thousand dollars a day."

"And how long does the average well take to drill?" Sarah asked again, glancing sideways at her mute daughter, trying to will Grace to become involved in the conversation or somehow indicate interest in Hans's offer.

"There is no such thing as an average well," Hans smiled. "That's what makes our business so exciting and challenging. Great risks and great rewards."

"I don't mean to be rude, but you haven't answered both my questions. How long can it take to dig a well and what can Grace expect to earn in bonuses?"

"Sarah!" Grace interjected for the first time, appalled at her mother's rude directness. Hans held up a hand.

"Grace, I appreciate your mother's questions. I was being evasive, because I have no definite answers." To Sarah he said. "I intend to propose that Grace be paid a couple of percent of the cost of each successful oil strike at locations pinpointed by her. Assuming it takes ten days to drill the well that's, maybe, thirty thousand dollars per well."

"Why dollars? I thought you mentioned a salary in euros."

"Her salary in Rotterdam will be paid in euros," said Hans. "Internationally, in the oil business, we deal in dollars, so bonuses, if any, will be paid in dollars. By the way, I can't guarantee anything until I put it to the board. We've not done this before."

Around ten wells per year, thought Sarah to herself, that's three hundred thousand. Provided Grace's hunches were correct. And if not? Would they take it out of her pay? She smiled to herself at the absurdity of the thought.

Grace misinterpreted Sarah's smile, thinking her mother saw a six-figure income dancing in the air. She knew Sarah worried about how to finance the extensive renovations that the old *tharavad* needed. She also knew Uncle Ranjan had offered to cover the cost of all renovations, could well afford it but Sarah, sensibly enough, did not want him involved.

Ranjan had already agreed Sarah was to be the sole inheritor of the property. He had made his life in California and did not want any part of the family home in Kerala. But owning ancestral property was a very emotional matter. Hearts and minds often changed as one grew older, so Sarah had refused his offer of money. Grace was another matter. Grace was Sarah's own daughter and would naturally inherit when Sarah died. All these thoughts were running through Grace's head, so she remained silent. She was not even thinking of Hans's offer. Of whether she wanted the job or not.

"So around ten days per well? Three million dollars?" Sarah was speaking her thoughts out loud.

"Ten days, three weeks, a month...Three million, ten million, twenty million," was Hans's reply. "There's no way of knowing in advance how much and how long."

"So if Grace successfully points you to a drilling site, she could earn up to five hundred thousand dollars per well?" Sarah couldn't keep the incredulity from her voice.

"No, sorry. I should have told you earlier. There will be a cap on what she can earn per well even if successful."

Nirmala brought in a dessert of tapioca pudding, saying the taxi had arrived to take Hans on the two-hour drive to Cochin airport.

After lunch Grace and Sarah stood on the verandah and waved goodbye as Hans climbed into the white Tata van and disappeared in a spray of gravel. Grace sat down in a wicker basket chair suspended from the ceiling while Sarah disappeared inside the house.

"Well?" Sarah challenged later, appearing in the doorway behind her. Grace revolved meditatively in the air, pretending not to understand.

"Well what?"

"Aren't you going to say anything about Hans's offer? Why did you let me answer for you?"

"I didn't ask you to answer for me." Sarah didn't do rage, otherwise she would have been speechless with rage. Instead she merely went speechless with annoyance.

"You assumed I'd want the job. You didn't ask me."

"Grace! You're twenty-six! You have no job, no income. You've been travelling for a year and presumably have used up all your savings. Do you expect me to support you? I can't. Why do you think I'm taking in paying guests?"

"And so you'd love me to take Hans's offer, whether I want it or not. Because you need the money!" Grace knew she was being childish and mean even as she spoke, but the words were out and she wasn't in a mood to take them back. Sarah bit her lip and stepped back into the house, turning on her heel and heading to Amachi's room to see what she wanted.

Grace watched her mother go, angry at herself, angry at Sarah. She didn't want to earn a huge salary helping a big fat corporation grow even richer The year of travel had truly changed her. She had seen many beautiful corners of the earth, seen bits of the planet in all its natural glory. She had also seen the ravages inflicted by the hand of man. She had seen bleak denuded landscapes, entire ecosystems destroyed, whole forests felled, seen with her own eyes littered beaches and plastic-polluted ocean waters.

But on the other hand, she didn't want to go back to working for another Anwariah either. One of the things she had hoped to do while staying with her mother was to try and make sense of the welter of emotions, impressions, the jumbled kaleidoscope of images in her brain, try to bring them to some sense of order and then decide where to go next. She was not avaricious. She knew she was capable of simple living and did not demand much from life. But freedom and independence were paramount and she would never sell her soul for a job, however lucrative.

Sell her soul? Surely that was being unnecessarily melodramatic! Perhaps. But she was determined to take only worthwhile employment, work at something that would make a positive contribution to the world. What, she was not sure. But she knew there was more to life than simply earning a living. And she knew she would know the right thing when she found it. And meanwhile, she could hear Sarah's voice in the back of her head. You need to have something to do while you're trying to find the right thing to do, said the Sarah in her head with irrefutable logic. It could takes weeks, months or years... and you'll still need to earn a living.

She was sunk in thought, knees to her chest and feet drawn up to the seat, the wicker chair like a cocoon spinning gently in the air. Sarah continued her tight-lipped silence in Grace's presence the next day. Grace tried to think about what she really wanted to do, but there was no resolution in her mind, and so her thoughts churned in useless frustration.

Grace could see that Sarah was rather anxious, both on her behalf and also because of the shaky financial position Sarah herself was in, having rejected Ranjan's offer to finance repairs. Nirmala had pointed out that much of the timber work had been attacked by white ants, and this needed urgent attention before the rot spread to other parts of the building. So it was a welcome relief when a letter finally arrived from Holland with a job offer as personal assistant to Hans van Houten.

CHAPTER 12

Three months later Grace arrived in Rotterdam for the first time. It was a fine day in late spring on the 29th of May, her twenty-sixth birthday. She was met by a company representative and taken to a hotel in the center of the city, overlooking the River Maas where a room had been booked. It was three in the afternoon and Grace had nothing to do till her appointment with Hans van Houten at nine the next morning. She had slept well on her connecting flight from the Middle East, so after a quick shower and change, she decided to celebrate her birthday with a breath of fresh air before treating herself to a fine dinner at the New York Hotel's reputed in-house restaurant. It was six and getting dark by the time she came back to the hotel, having refreshed herself with a long walk along the banks of the Maas, admiring the stunning architecture of the skyline, but unable to find the picturesque canals with boats and lined with old houses that she had hoped to see.

As she approached the desk and asked for her room key, "A gentleman has been waiting to see you," said the girl. Grace turned and gasped as she was enveloped in a bear hug by a tall man.

"Happy birthday, Grace," said Hans, stepping back and releasing her.

He wore a broad smile. Grace stood silent, uncertain what his presence at her hotel implied. He understood her confusion and quickly stepped aside to introduce two equally tall woman who stood a little behind him.

"My wife Jutta, and daughter Miep," he said proudly.

Grace laughed with relief as apprehensions fell away and the two women, understanding, laughed with her. Hans stood by and watched with a bemused smile as the three of them exchanged pleasantries.

"Such a pleasant surprise to see you. It's kind of you to welcome me like this."

"We didn't come here simply to welcome you," interrupted Hans with mock seriousness. "I was working at home, preparing my talk to introduce you to two board members, and then I looked at your CV to refresh my memory. I saw your date of birth and raised my eyebrows when I realized it's today. Jutta noticed, asked what's up, and I told her. Miep heard, and then I had no peace at all.

"Paus, you can't leave her all alone in a strange city on her birthday," she says. And Jutta says, "Really Hans, how could you not notice?" So I called your room. There was no reply so we decided to take a chance and come here. And now we're taking you out for dinner."

It would have been churlish to refuse and Grace was truly delighted not to spend her birthday alone in a strange city. Despite her misgivings about the oil industry and working for a large corporation, she was beginning to enjoy the trip to Rotterdam. Maybe this wasn't a bad place to work after all and Sarah was right. It had been a good decision to accept this job.

Chapter 13

Grace finished the avocado and tomato salad, mopping up the last traces of olive oil with the remaining garlic bread. The wine from the Margaret River had lived up to its reputation,. Fruity, modestly eloquent, dry, but left a lingering residual sweetness on the tongue, she thought, in parody of expert reviews. A good wine. A good year. She allowed herself another glass.

The next morning she had nothing to do, so lay awake in bed and read a book till the doorbell rang at ten. It was the Filipino maid who worked for and lived with a family nearby. She was a slender, smiling thing who looked eighteen, but in actual fact she was married, thirty years old, a mother of three whose own family lived back home on an outlying island far from Manila city. The three children were being looked after by her husband, who was unemployed. Estrella was aptly named, a real star, the sole breadwinner of the family who managed on the earnings she sent back to the Philippines from Hong Kong. Her employers, fortunately, were kind to her, allowing her much more than the statutory time off work. This was not always the case. According to the law, house maids were to work not more than eight hours a day, have Sundays off and have a secluded private area, if not a room of their own, to which they could retire. In practice, many of them worked ten hours a day or more, and were compelled to provide personal services that went beyond normally accepted definitions of domestic help. Estrella's employers also turned a blind eye to her working outside their home in her spare time, which was against the law, so she was able to earn extra money doing housework for Grace. She came twice a week and stayed for two hours each time.

Grace was thoroughly impressed by Estrella's perpetual smile and constant good humor.

"Good morning Mum." Estrella bounced in, wearing a blue T-shirt that said I LOVE BANTAY SREI in red letters, and a pair of knee-length white shorts, both of which Grace had given her. She surveyed the few dishes in the kitchen, left over from Grace's late afternoon lunch the previous day. Opening the fridge, she saw that the dish of Lechon Kawali she had cooked on her previous visit was still untouched.

"You didn't like the food Mum?" Grace was apologetic.

"No Estrella. I tasted it and loved it. But I was out yesterday. I bought avocadoes on my way home and they were just right, so I had a late lunch of that. Sorry. And then I wasn't hungry at dinner. But your pan fried pork is delicious and I'll have it for lunch today."

Estrella was mollified and then was a whirlwind of activity for the next hour and a half, leaving Grace's apartment spotlessly tidy and the plants watered. Meanwhile, Grace looked at her watch, saw it was almost eleven and decided to treat herself to a good cup of coffee.

She dressed quickly, saying goodbye to Estrella who had a key to the apartment and would lock up when she was finished. She hurried down the path to the road that led through the center of the main village where Tony had set up his morning coffee trade.

Tony was a self-taught master barista who set up temporary shop in a bar on the main street. He was there every morning, rain or shine, from five-thirty to eleven. Over time, he had become an island institution and many

of the office workers and teachers who hurried to catch
their morning ferry to the big island of Hong Kong slowed
down to pick up a cup as they passed by. Tony knew each
of his many regulars by name, their taste in coffee, whether
they took sugar and if yes, how many lumps.

With the passing of time, Tony came to know more
about his customers than simply their coffee preferences.
He had vast knowledge of the minor foibles of each and a
shrewd idea of what made individuals tick. He also could
be relied upon for timely weather warnings.

"David," he might say to a lightly dressed customer.
"There's a cold weather warning for this evening and a
hurricane heading towards us from the Phillipines. Might
rain for the next two three days." And David might grab
his coffee and hurry on his way or, if he had time, nip back
home to fetch his rain gear.

Grace had come to rely on Tony for local news and
a caffeine fix several times a week. A fount of information
about local personalities although he was discreet and never
gossiped maliciously. On this morning Grace had woken
up thinking of Beulah and decided to find out what Tony
knew about her. So she hurried down the main road
leading to the ferry pier and found him getting ready to
pack up his coffee machines at ten minutes to eleven.

"You're just in time, Grace," he smiled at her. "The
usual?" Tony bought coffee from various sources, mostly
directly from suppliers in Latin America and roasted them
carefully himself in small quantities.

"What's the weather going to be like today?" she
asked while her cup was brewing. He cocked his head at
the ceiling as though looking at the sky, thinking about the
weather forecast he had heard.

"It's going to get a lot warmer in the next few days.
You'll need to have your aircon on tonight. Summer's been

late coming, but it's here finally. Not looking forward to it."
He sweated profusely and hated the summer. Grace always
looked cool and comfortable and didn't mind the heat even
if she didn't like it. Tony set her cup on the counter and
Grace hitched herself onto one of the high bar stools.

"I'm going to sit here and drink my coffee but don't
let me stop you." She knew he was very punctual about
clearing the counter by eleven o'clock when the bar owner
usually arrived to prepare for his business for the day. Tony
emptied his fresh water containers and unplugged the three
coffee makers on the counter, each machine dedicated to
one of the three blends he offered every day. Today the
offerings were Guatemala, Brazil and a "Tony's special"
blend. He took the coffee signs down, loading the
machines onto a handcart.

"D'you know Beulah?" Grace nonchalantly took a
sip of coffee. He stopped and gave her a keen look.

"Poor lady. Her dog died yesterday, I hear," he
murmured. So he knew already. Nothing much that
happened on this island escaped him although he didn't
talk about it.

"I ran into her coming out of the vet. She was
distraught. She thinks it was deliberately poisoned." Tony
said nothing and continued loading the handcart.

"D'you think it might at all be possible?" Grace
persisted. "Who would want to harm the old lady's pet? He
was such a good dog and never hurt anyone." Tony
glanced briefly at her and again said nothing. Grace decided
to ask directly.

"D'you think anyone here might do it?" Tony
stopped loading the cart and straightened up. The answer
was a long time coming.

"A few years ago, there was a pack of wild dogs that
roamed around near the abandoned village on the other

side of this island. They were quite ferocious and attacked other dogs that went too close to their territory. Finally, last year they attacked a tourist who was out for a walk. He managed to fight them off with a stick and he wasn't hurt, but he complained to the police. So a dog-catcher was sent to round them up and put them down. They were rounded up and taken to the island ferry pier in cages to be shipped off to whichever place. And then there was trouble."

"What kind of trouble?"

"There's a *gweilo* lady, an animal lover, who it appears has been feeding stray dogs for many years. She now appeared on the pier as their champion and demanded that they be set free. She was very fierce and authoritative in defense of the dogs. The dog catcher was a young man who was very uncertain of his rights and responsibilities. His argument was that he was merely following orders. After much argument and a phone call to his superiors who didn't back him up, he just gave in. The dogs were transported back in their cages and released at the village where they had been picked up."

"So some island citizen who'd been threatened by the dogs decided to poison them?"

"Some of the villagers were very angry at the *gweilo* lady. They are the original inhabitants of this island and they don't like it that some foreigners who come to live here behave as if they make the rules."

"Do they dislike dogs in general?"

"No. Not at all. They have dogs of their own, and some of them have been attacked by these wild dogs, so they are angry at the woman for feeding them."

"So then what happened? Did everything quiet down?"

"More or less. And then the wild dogs disappeared. I've not heard of a problem here for two or three years now."

"Somebody poisoned them?" Tony shrugged.

"Maybe. No one knows. The *gweilo* lady complained to the police that the dogs had disappeared. She had found one dead body. It had died of poisoning. But since she was not an owner, the police refused to make a case of its death and the others' disappearance."

"Hmmm. So there've been no poisonings since?"

"Not that I know of."

Grace thoughtfully finished the last of her coffee and strolled back to her flat. The sun was very hot now, so she walked slowly, enjoying the respite afforded by shaded sections of the path. She stopped at a roadside stand and bought some chicken kebabs for lunch with steaming saté sauce in a plastic bag.

Estrella was on the point of locking up and leaving when Grace returned. She saw the chicken kebabs Grace was carrying and smiled.

"Oh, I think I'll go and buy some for my lunch."

"Yes, please do that, Estrella. You should treat yourself, you know. You do so much for other people."

Estrella blushed and hurried away. Grace watched her go, certain that she wouldn't allow herself even a small snack like that. The Thai lady who cooked the skewers charged twenty Hong Kong dollars for three pieces. Elsewhere they cost double that. But Estrella sent every penny she saved to her family back home. It had taken Grace a few weeks to suss out all this information in informal chats with her while she cleaned. Once she realized this, she had doubled Estrella's wage. Estrella had protested at first.

"No, that's too much Mum." But Grace had been firm.

"I insist. If you don't want it, you can give it away, but this is what you'll earn in future."

Estrella was silent after that, but she still blushed when she was paid, so now Grace simply left the money in an envelope on the table to be picked up on her way out. This seemed to have made it easier somehow and avoided the awkward moments.

There was cold rice in the fridge. The chicken was still warm, so Grace made herself a pot of weak jasmine tea as a heat and thirst killer and ate the kebabs with the cold rice. After she ate, she took the pot and a mug to one of the two armchairs and sipped jasmine tea with her computer on her lap and did a search for "poisoned dogs on Hong Kong's Outlying Islands." She was surprised by the number of articles that came up. First was a long article in the South China Morning Post, fairly recent, about a spate of dog poisonings in Hong Kong's outlying islands.

Police are investigating a new wave of suspected dog poisonings on Hong Kong's outlying islands, which have seen five dogs die in agony since December. Two dogs have died of suspected poisoning since Friday, one on Lamma Island and the other on Peng Chau. They follow the deaths of three other pets on Lamma last month. Long-suffering dog owners on the island say over 100 canine deaths there have gone unpunished in the last ten years.

A petition and open letter, released by owners in the wake of the suspected poisoning deaths of three more dogs last month, have garnered more than 700 signatures in three weeks. After several months of repeated requests from residents, Lamma police finally revealed that 17 cases of suspected poisoning of Lamma dogs have been logged since January 2011.

While owners have long lost faith in local police, it is understood

Senior Inspector Joyce Wong Siu-man of Lamma police apologised for the perceived mishandling of dog poisoning cases in a face-to-face meeting last week with concerned residents. Locals have posted bilingual posters urging owners to keep pets on leashes and in muzzles, and are mounting regular patrols to search for poisoned bait.

Some psycho has spent years poisoning dogs in Hong Kong, went another headline. She clicked on the link and read:

Dog owners on Lamma Island, Hong Kong, have been terrorized for the past several years by a mysterious serial dog-poisoner who has claimed more than 100 canine victims. Scores of dogs have died after eating foods laced with toxic amounts of weedkiller, left intentionally for the animals to find.

Surely not true! A hundred dead dogs on just one island in the past few years? She looked up a link to an article in the South China Morning Post. She read a long article about dog poisoning in Hong Kong, beginning in the 1980s.

Timeout had a detailed account, dated nearly a year ago, which related three recent incidents of dog poisoning and then went on to write...*If these three stories sound familiar, it's because they were reported with some prominence in the local media. And then – nothing. That's the second part of the story: outrage followed by inaction. Over the past 20 years, hundreds of dogs have been deliberately poisoned in Hong Kong. A serial dog killer on Bowen Road has poisoned more than 200 canines, while at least 100 have fallen prey on Lamma. Hong Kong clearly has a poisonous problem.*

She read several more articles, less cogently written, a few of them anguished rambles by people whose beloved pets had been hurt but survived. They threatened dire punishments to the despicable cur if they ever laid hands on him. The perpetrator was always assumed to be male. One even suggested terminal punishment for the killer if caught; the death penalty, death by hanging or death by paraquat poisoning.

Grace stopped reading after an hour. Each additional article only repeated the same information in different words with little new to go on. It was nearly two-thirty, so she decided to have a short siesta, then go for a swim and drop in on Beulah on her way back.

Chapter 14

Grace woke refreshed after a half hour nap. She packed bathing suit, towel and swimming goggles into the favorite green canvas shoulder bag, slipped on a comfortable pair of beige Skechers and stepped out into the still, hot and sunny afternoon. Judging by the sun it was around four. She stepped onto the winding path that led to Lo So Shing beach. It was a half hour walk from the island's main village called Banyan Tree Bay. This was the town, village really, with the most frequent ferry connections from Hong Kong, with one to three ferries running every hour, from 6 a.m. till midnight, depending on the time of day. The path rose and fell, steeply at times, so that, although only around three kilometers distant from her home, it was a good workout and her white T-shirt and the back of her beige shorts were soon soaked with patches of sweat.

She loved the walk and listened to the twittering of birds as she went. In the thick undergrowth were numbers of little red-cheeked bulbuls with their trademark jaunty tufts that looked like pompadours. Most common were spotted doves with their deep cries and noisy flapping wings, a wonder, really, how they managed to flourish, they looked so inept and unfit to survive with their mechanically bobbing heads and their stupid pigeon-toed walk. In the background, were their more elegant forest cousins, the emerald doves. These were much more discreet, and rarely seen, but Grace heard them, the same deep cooing as the spotted doves, hidden somewhere in the undergrowth. Common magpies flitted across her path, dipping their saucy, long black and white tails. Bulbuls twittered, sparrows shrieked and doves cooed, while high above circled raptors on sharp-eyed lookout for small rodents, one eye on fishing boats near the shore where they could expect an easy meal of low-value catch tossed overboard.

There was one point on the exposed brow of a hill that she always looked forward to reaching, high enough to see eye to eye with majestically circling black kites. Sometimes she heard their screaming, whistling call close at hand, kirrreee, kirrreee, kirrreee and shivers ran down her spine; there was something unfettered, wild and free in the cry, so that she longed to spread out wings and join them. It was moments like these that she felt a wild fierceness in her heart. She was blessed and invincible and could do anything she wanted, although she was still marking time, waiting to discover her passion, waiting to discover what she was on this earth to do. She had a role to play somewhere. She did not know what, and sometimes the waiting unnerved her.

Although it was comforting to know she had enough money to look after material wants for the rest of her life, she wondered if this cushion also shielded her from the abrasive experiences she perhaps needed in order to uncover her true talents. And the loneliness that crept into her soul from time to time was like an insidious, living thing that could even creep under the armor of affluence.

She crossed the crest of the hill. There were no kites in the air today. She had once, just once in all those months, come face to face with a full-grown sea eagle eating something off a rock, recalling the mutual shock of the close encounter and then the eagle had lazily flapped away, taking its magnificent presence with it, leaving behind a sense of loss.

A long, slow swim at the beach dispelled the melancholy mood that had overtaken her at the crest of the hill. The breathtaking chill of the water was refreshing after the heat of the sun. There were not many people in the water, but the shark nets were out and there was a young lifeguard on duty, bare-chested, twin mirrors hiding his eyes, idly surveying the beach with headphones plugged into both ears, knees pumping to an unheard beat. Coming out of the water, she rubbed herself dry and sat on the tile steps looking out over the water and the curve of the bay. Further down the bayshore, two men stood knee deep in water, balancing on rocks at the promontory with long fishing rods. They were obviously having success and soon they packed up their rods and began their journey back, skipping from rock to rock until they reached dry sand.

Grace was hungry, having only eaten the small chicken kebabs and leftover rice that day. She did not want to cook, and the thought of a meal of fried squid accompanied by cold beer at the Szechuan restaurant in the village made her walk faster. It was much cooler now, although the sun was still out. She came to the little turnoff before her house and hesitated, remembering her intention to go and see Beulah. She thought for a moment, then turned right and trudged up the path, wondering if she would find the old lady at home, wondering if she might be intruding. She crested the hill and held her breath with renewed delight at the spectacular million dollar view from Beulah's ramshackle cottage, all the more impressive now as the sun went down over the sea, romantically highlighting dozens of tiny fishing boats and, further out over the water, the long line of ships berthed in the roads to Hong Kong's harbor and the East Lamma Channel. This channel was the deepest of Hong Kong's waterways, used by the biggest ships to reach the Pearl River delta and the giant berthing docks of Shenzen and Guangdong. From here, much of China's manufacturing was loaded onto container ships bound for ports all over the world. Hard to believe that this beautiful waterway was one of the busiest shipping lanes in the world.

Her peaceful contemplation of the seascape was disrupted by a shrill cry and the sound of breaking wood. She turned back toward the clearing and saw that the door of Beulah's shack was open. Some premonition stopped her headlong rush forward and she darted to the bushes beside the shack and looked in through a side window.

Two men wearing identical tight-fitting black sweatshirts, white slacks and sneakers stood with their backs to the window, facing Beulah who had fallen back on her bed. A chair lay upended beside them on the floor and one of the men held a broken chair leg in his hand. As Grace watched, he brandished it menacingly at Beulah and shouted something in Cantonese.

Beulah looked back, unafraid and seemingly calm. Grace unthinkingly strained forward to hear the answer which she, of course, did not understand. Beulah saw Grace's face at the window. Her eyes widened involuntarily and she shook her head in warning. Grace ducked and crept to the rear of the cottage just in time, thankful for the soft-soled Skechers she wore. A muffled oath and quick footsteps as one of the men emerged from the cottage and looked round the side to see what Beulah had seen. Finding nothing, he struck the side wall of the cottage a heavy blow and Grace, crouching in the bushes at the rear, thought, had she moved a few seconds later, it might well have been her own skull that the chair leg splintered against.

Inside the cottage the interrogation continued. Grace was afraid, but wondered whether she could conscionably remain in hiding while Beulah was in danger. Loud voices of the two men interspersed with occasional replies in the old lady's voice, still sounding firm and unafraid. Despite her fear, Grace decided she had to intervene. She crept all the way round the back to the other side of the cottage, not sure what she was going to do. She sprinted across the clearing back to the path, then turned around and re-entered the clearing with a noisy greeting.

"Beulah," she shouted cheerfully in English. "I have something for you."

She had the feeble hope that using English might save her. The two men were well-dressed and did not look like local thugs. If they were Hong Kong criminals, what were they doing here and what did they want with a poor old woman like Beulah? Grace composed her face and looked outwardly calm. She only hoped they wouldn't hear the thumping of her heart and the uncontrollable tremor of her right hand that she tried to hide by gripping the shoulder strap of her green canvas bag with the wet swimming things. The two men emerged from the cottage, challenging, arms akimbo, glowering at her. Grace paid them not the slightest attention.

"Beulah," she called again, injecting as much of a cheerful note as she could. When there was no reply, she looked innocently at the nearer of the two men.

"Beulah?" she asked. The man turned his head back as Beulah appeared. Grace proffered the canvas bag with her wet swimming things, hoping the men would not examine it.

"I have something for you," she said, walking past the two men and entering the cottage. Beulah looked at her wide-eyed and silent. Grace turned back and looked at the two men.

"Are your friends staying?" One of the men spoke sharply. Beulah's reply was gentle, conciliatory. The two turned and left, swift and silent as cats in their matching white designer sneakers. The women stood at the door of the hut watching them go. When they were gone, Beulah shook her head and gently ran a hand down Grace's cheek in a wordless gesture of thanks.

"And what was all that about?" asked Grace.

Beulah did not reply. She went to the kitchen end of the single room, lighted a stove attached to a blue gas cylinder by a rubber pipe and began to heat water in a saucepan. She waited till the water boiled, then dropped some leaves into the pan and let it simmer for a minute. In the meantime, she searched the ledge behind the stove, frowning, looking for clean mugs. Both were chipped, so she selected the better one, filled it with tea from the saucepan and gave it to Grace, motioning her to the remaining unbroken chair. Grace sat down, blowing noisily on the cup to cool the tea and decided to wait for Beulah to speak. Beulah leaned against a corner of the table, glancing out of the window with her heavy lidded eyes and nodding to herself as though she had come to a decision.

"What is it Beulah?" Grace asked very quietly. Beulah shook her head in reply.

"Were they triads? Did the visit have something to do with Doodle?"

Beulah's eyes widened with grief and glistened at the mention of Doodle's name but she still said nothing, lips compressed, her face composed and impassive. Grace waited in silence till the tea cooled, finished the cup and stood up. Beulah leaned on the table, unspeaking, looking out of the window. Certain now that she wouldn't get anything out of the old lady, Grace set the empty mug on the table and put an arm around the old woman's shoulders, giving it a squeeze.

"Do you know where I live?" she asked.

Beulah looked blank, so she searched in the canvas bag for her wallet and extracted one of her business cards. It was printed both in Chinese and English with her address, email and telephone number. Grace Lam, the card said. Water Divining, Lost Objects found, ESP. She hoped Beulah might reconsider after reading the Chinese translation of her professional qualifications.

Chapter 15

Grace got home, showered to wash the sea sand off her body and changed into a favorite dress. It was an African print, a heady mix of colors; blues, greens, yellows, reds and flaming orange that enveloped her whole body and lightened her severe appearance so that she seemed to be a bundle of movement that screamed reggae! dancing! instead of her customary serious self. She smiled at the memory of the street market in the Niger delta where she had bought the dress three years ago, and the irresistible charm of the enormous lady in a wide-sleeved boubou who had sold it to her. The oil-soaked Niger Delta and its resource curse! She had visited the area often until she quit her job with Rotterdam Oil a little over a year ago. It already seemed like a distant past; another life.

She wore a colorful pair of matching espadrilles, bought at a street market in Mong Kok, to go with the dress, then headed down to the village of Banyan Tree Bay to have dinner at her favorite Szechuan restaurant. The outdoor seating area of the restaurant, facing the harbor, was almost empty and the smiling gap-toothed waiter turned on the large pedestal fan as soon as he saw her approach. A lot of air escaped from between missing teeth and it was often hard to understand when he spoke, but the smile of welcome was unmistakable. He set the menu down with a flourish.

"To darink," he asked. "Usual?"

"Yes," she nodded. "Tsing Tao, small."

"Today we serve spe..al."

Not sure if this was a question, she nodded anyway. He reappeared in a minute with the familiar green bottle of chilled beer, but carried a round-bottomed porcelain bowl instead of the usual glass tumbler.

"This is the way to drink beer in China," he said, setting it down.

Grace ordered food and sipped at her beer, cupping the bowl in her hand, admiring the red-streaked sunset over the harbor outside, the darkening silhouettes of fishing boats and a tall-masted schooner. The sun was now low enough to slip beneath the edges of the awning and the tables glowed red. To her dazzled eyes, the other customers appeared only as dark outlines. She gave a start of surprise when a voice sounded at her elbow.

"Hello Grace. You're here alone? Would you like to join us?" It was Raymond.

"Us?" Grace peered through the contrasting light to see who was at the table.

"My wife, Dawn." explained Raymond. "Come and meet her."

Grace picked up her beer and followed him to their table. Dawn was big-boned, blond, outdoorsy, from Banff in Canada, much more talkative than Raymond. From her Grace learned soon enough that Raymond and she had met in Lake Louise, just half an hour's drive away from the town where she was born. Raymond was a software engineer on a ski holiday from Toronto. She was then a world class downhill skier in training with the rest of the Canadian racing team. Lake Louise, Grace learned, was the first stop on the World Cup ski racing circuit, and the only one in Canada.

"So you must be a good skier too," said Grace to Raymond, "if you met on the slopes." Both Dawn and Raymond went into a helpless fit of laughter.

"Well, he is a passable skier now," Dawn chuckled.

"So what happened? You've made me curious now."

"The first time I saw him, he was screaming on the mountainside."

"No, no, no! Not that story again!" Raymond interjected laughing. Then to Grace, "I'll wait till she finishes and I'll give you the real version."

"Go on. You tell her then," Dawn conceded. They both began to laugh again, while Grace waited to hear the story.

"It was like this," Raymond said. "My Toronto firm supplied some of the equipment used for electronic timers at the world cup ski races on Lake Louise. I had nothing to do with it. It was handled by another division. I happened to be on a skiing holiday there around the same time as the international ski circus came to town. One night I get a frantic call from our Toronto office. Can I help out? It's urgent. Something's malfunctioning and our chief technician's had an accident and is in hospital. So I go down there the night before the races and see that a circuit is damaged, I have no tools and no spares, the race is only sixteen hours away, with dozens of international television crews covering events.

"I screamed in frustration, knowing I might not make it on time. I look up and she's there laughing at me, asking what's the matter? Nothing to you, I say, but I've got to get this fixed before the race trials tomorrow. It means a lot to me, she says, I'm racing here. Came up with the others to inspect the course. Can I help? I think, okay, she doesn't mean it, so I list the tools and parts I need. Right, she says, and before I can protest, she shoots off down the mountain like the downhill racer she is and returns forty-five minutes later with a huge bag of tools, everything I could possibly want. And she has an Austrian technician from a firm called Kapsch in tow. So we have the whole thing finished in an hour.

"By the time we've finished the job, I'm totally in love with this strange woman who brought the tools and skied off to join the rest of her team. I catch a glimpse of her the next day, and then meet her on the slopes, but she's always surrounded by team-mates, coaches, masseurs and reporters, so I'm too shy to ask her out."

"But not the Austrian guy. Anton, Toni." Dawn continued, smiling at the memory.

"He was very fast, chatted me up the next day. Wanted me to go to dinner with him after the downhills were over and we had a couple of days off. I liked him, but I was in training and too busy to think of things like that. He was persistent, though, so I said, okay. But only if you promise to bring that other guy along, I told him. The guy who screamed"

"Yup," Raymond nodded, taking over the telling of a well-rehearsed tale. "Imagine my surprise when Toni comes looking for me. He says he searched every hotel in town, that's how badly he wanted to go out with Dawn." Dawn blushed.

"It was nothing. Only a temporary infatuation of his. Testosterone at work."

"So anyway," Raymond continued. "We go out for dinner, the three of us. Anton and she are chatting away about skiing and travel and all the things they've done. She knows Austria well because of the ski races and even speaks a bit of German. I'm sitting there tongue-tied and shy, loving this energetic, brawny woman. I love the way she holds her knife and fork, I love the way she eats, I love the way she moves her hands and waves them when she talks. I'm not eating much, glad they're talking because it gives me time to watch her."

"Toni completely monopolized me and the conversation." Dawn continued.

"From time to time I'd steal a glance at Raymond and notice he's hardly eaten, seems to be watching me, I can't believe it, with a wistful look in his eyes, as though I were someone he knew long ago. Towards the end of dinner I have to make him talk, so I say the first thing that comes to my mind. You're so quiet, Raymond. How about another shout to liven up things?" They both break into peals of laughter, doubling Grace's curiosity to know what comes next.

"And then?" Grace prompts because they are both still laughing, holding hands across the table.

"I thought I had no chance against fast-talking Toni, so I did the only thing I could think of to attract her attention. Right there, in the middle of that busy restaurant, I set my fork down and screamed as loud as I could. Toni was so startled he spilt his wine all over Dawn's dress. The entire dining room went deathly still. Dawn was gob-smacked for a moment and then burst out laughing. She laughed till she cried."

"So that's how we met," Dawn said. "We exchanged addresses, and then for the next two years we never met but I got postcards from him wherever I was. After the third or fourth postcard, I began to retaliate."

"Yes," Raymond smiled. "Dawn sent cards from Austria, Italy, Colorado, Slovenia… wherever the races were run.

"By this time," said Dawn, "I was getting tired of the nomadic life, the rigorous training, the risks… I mean, I didn't mind the risks if I were winning medals, but I couldn't break into the top ten. I had a few thankless placings between eleven and twenty-five, you know… and when you're racing you cut corners, you have to take just as many risks as the winners, but get none of the rewards. So after three years of this, I felt the wear and tear in my bones, on my knees. By this time, Raymond and I were serious about each other and we talked together."

"I didn't want Dawn to end up a racing invalid," Raymond nodded. "So I persuaded her to give it up." Afterwards they had married and settled in Toronto where she had worked as a fitness consultant to corporate executives.

Grace was spell-bound by Dawn's narrative. Here she was, sitting in a restaurant on a tropical island, eating delicious seafood on a cool evening, learning about the fascinating world of competitive downhill ski racing. She was a bit of a conservative who didn't form friendships easily. Dawn's touching story and their obvious devotion to each other put her completely at ease in their company and soon they had ordered a second round of food. They ordered pork with crunchy haricot beans and fried noodles with prawns and then, because everything tasted so good, a bottle of white wine to share. When the waiter came round again, Grace listened with envy as Raymond spoke to him in Cantonese.

"Were you born in Toronto?" Raymond nodded yes.

"And you learned Cantonese there?"

"Yes. From my grandparents who came from the Mainland in the eighties to join us. They spoke nothing else and so I had to learn a little to talk to them. Comes in useful now." Grace nodded thoughtfully.

"So you know a little bit more about Hong Kong than the average foreigner who stays here for any length of time?" Raymond nodded cautiously.

"Perhaps. Why do you ask?" Grace considered for a moment, deciding not to say anything about Beulah.

"Because I saw two thuggish men on the island today." She described the two men, giving the impression it had been a harmless encounter along one of the island paths.

"Were they tattooed?" was Raymond's first question.

"They both wore long-sleeved sweatshirts. I couldn't see much of their bodies. But maybe, yes. I think I noticed a bit of a mark on one man's hand."

"Nowadays tattoos have become a fashion statement, but in the old days, I'm talking about my grandparents' time in China, tattoos were a sure sign of triads. The name Triads, by the way, was given by British authorities in Hong Kong, because of some of the typical imagery in their tattoos."

"Have they always been around?" Grace took another sip of wine.

"They were called Tongs in Canada, weren't they?" Dawn asked. Raymond nodded.

"Early Chinese immigrants were resented for their willingness to work for lower wages than Americans, and they were often discriminated against, called Chinks and worse. So they formed societies, based on place of origin in China, mainly from Fujian and Canton, to look after their own interests."

"My father's family came to San Francisco in the early twentieth century," Grace said. "And then moved to Toronto in the 1950s. My father was born there."

"You from Toronto? I didn't know that."

"No, I'm not from Toronto. My father was. I was born in Malaysia, but have lived outside most of my life. So I'm not sure where I belong." A note of melancholy had unsuspectingly crept into Grace's voice. Dawn noted it and clinked her wine glass in commiseration.

"Go back another century and my family were immigrants too. Now we call ourselves Canadians, and the descendants of the original inhabitants are called people of the First Nations."

"The Tongs were not secret societies originally, neither were they criminal. Tong simply means 'hall' or meeting place. The rise of the Tongs as criminal organizations was mainly in the second half of the twentieth century."

"Like the triads in Hong Kong?" Raymond shook his head.

"Not exactly. Both Tongs and Triads have their origins in the traditions of southern Chinese secret societies that originated to fight the Qing dynasty; the dynasty that ultimately ruled China for nearly three hundred years till the early nineteen hundreds."

"Were they intent on taking power themselves?" Dawn wanted to know.

"No. They had the wish, early on, to restore the Ming dynasty to power. After a couple of centuries, it became a chronic battle against central authority which ultimately resulted in the era of China's rule by warlords, the entrance of western powers into this chaotic mix, the opium wars, and subsequently, Mao's China." Grace poured out the last of the wine into the three glasses, eager to bring the conversation back to the triads.

"So, the triads were first a political organization and then became criminals?" Raymond shrugged.

"Maybe. If you have a bunch of people with martial skills added to military capabilities and no central authority, some of them will invariably turn to crime to enrich themselves. Initially, they were all rebels against the Qing dynasty, so this explains the need for a shadowy organization with a tradition of secrecy. They developed elaborate rituals to ensure loyalty, initiation ceremonies with thirty-six oaths and so on. Nowadays, few gangs follow these rituals and apparently are even embarrassed by them."

"How do you know so much about them?" Grace was curious.

"Martial arts films," Raymond grinned. "This is common knowledge if you've seen as many as I have; both Hollywood and Canton have played a part in my education."

"I don't know what you see in them, films I mean." said Dawn.

"The movies are mostly fantasy, of course, although some of the actors are exceptionally talented artistes. My only experience of real-world triads came second-hand through a friend of mine in Toronto's Chinatown."

"What happened?" Grace asked.

"His father owned a restaurant in Chinatown and apparently crossed a powerful gangster. Maybe he refused to pay protection money, I really don't know. But his restaurant was firebombed. The first was a small warning fire. The second time it was a big one that gutted the whole building."

"What happened then?"

"The family left the city and retired to live out in the country. The sons moved to other professions. One of them was my friend who worked as an accountant in my electronics firm."

Grace was silent for a moment. It was dark now, quite cool and damp with the breeze blowing over the water. She reached into her bag for a thick blue cable knit fisherman's sweater and shrugged it on. The pier was still brightly lit up with the yellow lights of an approaching ferry in the distance. It was a small, round-bottomed boat that looked like a tugboat with a high superstructure. The last ferry from Aberdeen and Pak Kok at eight-thirty, Grace thought. She still wanted to know more about the triads.

"What about the triads in Hong Kong?"

"They were basically left to their own devices by the British in the old walled city of Kowloon."

"Really? When was that? I thought the British enforced law and order here." Dawn was disbelieving.

"Oh, in the early fifties when my parents lived here, they didn't. Don't forget, Mao's China was next door and Hong Kong was flooded with thousands of refugees who were all allowed in with few questions asked. This was the world of Suzie Wong, if you've seen the film."

Grace nodded, and Dawn said, "No, but I want to see it, since we're living here now."

"And in Hong Kong today?" Grace persisted, her afternoon's encounter foremost in her mind.

"In Hong Kong today…" Raymond thought for a while. "A year ago a former newspaper editor named Kevin Lau was walking in Hong Kong when a man jumped off a motorbike and slashed him in the back with a meat cleaver. Police say that it was a typical triad assassination attempt, only this time the man survived. British police cracked down on triad gangs about a decade before Hong Kong's handover to China, so they went underground and, just like the Mafia, tried to grow legitimate businesses. The level of street crime has dropped and today Hong Kong is one of the world's safest cities for law-abiding citizens."

"But?" asked Grace, downing the last of her wine. Raymond smiled.

"Yes. But. Anyone who indulges in illegal activity is probably contributing to triad prosperity."

"What kind of illegal activity?"

"Gambling is prohibited in Hong Kong, as in all of Mainland China. Except for the horse races run by the

Jockey Club. Macau is the only Chinese territory where gambling is allowed. The Chinese rightly have a reputation of being a nation of gamblers, which is why the casinos of Macau have eclipsed Las Vegas. They now have a turnover seven times higher."

"What?" said Dawn, while Grace's jaw dropped in disbelief.

"Check for yourself. This seven-fold number is already two years old. It may be much higher by now."

"So they run illegal gambling in Hong Kong?"

"Yes, most of the *mah-jong* parlors. If you walk up the next street right here in this village, past the Tin Hau temple next door to us, you'll hear voices and the click of tiles. That's a house run by the triads on this island, but you won't know unless you're looking for it. The local police leave them strictly alone. There's no prostitution on this island, but in Hong Kong most of the shady massage parlors and prostitution are controlled by the triads. As is the drug trade."

Seeing that all three wine glasses were empty, Raymond held up the empty bottle with a questioning look. Grace shook her head.

"I've had enough for today. But thank you for inviting me over. It's really been such a pleasure talking to you both. Raymond, I'm looking forward to a first taste of your honey at breakfast tomorrow." Grace said goodbyes and walked home in the dark. After six months on the island she was totally unafraid of snakes, trusting their instinctive avoidance of human presence.

Living the island life with no need for a daily office commute had its advantages. Although an early riser by nature, Grace could afford to sleep late if she wished to. Tonight she was full of the new information Raymond had given her about triads. It was only nine thirty by the time she reached her house and climbed the narrow stairs to her second floor flat. She had the entire floor to herself as well as the terrace above it. The terrace covered the floor area of the house and half of it had an illegal structure, a gazebo, that was useful shelter for the potted plants she tended. She took her laptop up to the cane armchair in the shelter of the gazebo, tucked her feet on the cushion underneath her and began to search the internet for more information on the triads. Reading through recent reports in various newspapers, she found that the police had largely broken up the power of the triads with the help of an extensive network of informers known as ghosts. The police action had effectively broken up the traditional large organizations into many smaller ones, some of these becoming independent centers of action and thus harder to infiltrate.

It was reported that some gangs had even forged ties with Mexican gangsters, the Sinaloa cartel among others. The triads profited from their cross-border trade, receiving cocaine for distribution networks in China. Most importantly, they gained access to the Mexican cartel's people smuggling pipelines and were able to open lucrative routes for Asian nationals to illegally enter the US. The Mexicans got something in return. It was relatively easy to buy chemicals in the less-regulated Chinese market. Thus they were able to manufacture and supply the North American market with amphetamines, with little or no risk, since the drugs were not marketed locally.

Another unexpected result of the police crackdown was that triads moved to other countries and thus ended up more broad-based and resilient. The more Grace read, the more disturbed she became. She had scratched the surface of a problem, she realized, out of concern for Beulah, and was uncovering some of the rot that lay beneath the surface. She turned off her laptop and lay back on the darkened terrace with her eyes closed, thinking about everything she had read and heard that day. There were few stars in the sky and no moon out tonight.

There had been a spate of dog killings on Lamma island in the past two years. Nearly one hundred dogs had been killed, many of them strays. The incidents of dog poisoning had started on Hong Kong island a couple of years earlier. That seemed to have died down, so police attributed the first series of Hong Kong poisonings to an unknown single, deranged individual who had either died or lost interest in the game.

The Lamma Island canine poisonings were originally thought to be the work of locals who resented the presence of foreigners on their island. Dog owners were mostly *gweilos,* but there was an increasing number of locals who owned dogs and cared for them, so this theory was a bit shaky. The most plausible explanation so far was that the island poisonings were the work of someone who was targeting the feral dogs on the island and that family pets chanced on the poisoned bait without the knowledge of their owners.

But Beulah's dog was a puzzle. Beulah had been so certain that Doodle had been deliberately poisoned. Grace had thought she was merely distraught, but after the afternoon's incident, she was sure Beulah knew something she had not talked about. Perhaps she had unwittingly gotten involved with criminals. And whether Beulah liked it or not, Grace intended to find out how and help her.

Chapter 16

Grace was walking along a winding path in the woods at midday. It was dark under the trees and then she came out of the shade into a patch of blinding sunlight. A giant Burmese python lay coiled in the sun. Pythons were the top predators in this neck of the woods and feared no one. But despite lack of fear, even pythons steered clear of humans, the planet's top predator. She was surprised when the snake raised its head from amidst its coils to look at her, but did not move. Grace moved to the side of the path and warily edged past. She let out a sigh of relief and relaxed once she had passed the huge snake and continued her walk. She had bought one of those fitness tracking watches and had set it to beep after a daily minimum of eight kilometers and now, serpent or no serpent, she was a slave to the infernal device.

A faint noise make her turn her head and she saw that the snake was slithering along right behind her, all six meters of it. She screamed and began to run, looking back often to check where it was. It glided along the path, effortlessly keeping up. The path grew steep and she pounded along, lungs bursting with the effort of sprinting uphill. Still right behind her. Far ahead she saw what looked like several dusty brown ropes spread across the path. As she drew closer, she made out faint white rings at intervals on the ropes and malevolent glittering eyes at the end of each. Banded kraits! What was going on?

She made to leap off the path into the woods and noticed writhing bands of green, living vines, among the carpet of dried leaves that lined the forest floor. Bamboo pit vipers! Grace was more fearful of poison than the python's muscular coils. Panicked and panting, she turned to face the python, which dissolved into an image of the two muscular men in black sweatshirts and immaculate white trousers. They advanced on her. Instead of a hand, one of the men had a python's head with gaping jaws. The jaws advanced toward her, ready to strike, and in that instant Beulah appeared.

She wore loose black peasant pajamas and a bamboo sun hat with a wide brim. In her hands she carried a cleft stick, similar to the one Grace used for water divining, but thinner and with a narrower Y. Beulah caught the snake's head with the cleft end and effortlessly twisted it until the thug's arm broke with a loud crack. Beulah turned and began to frantically sweep the path of advancing kraits with the long end of the stick. She threw them off the end of her stick into the bushes. The kraits' bodies writhed and coiled as they flew through the air. One of them snagged on the end of her stick and flew backwards toward Grace at the end of a swing. It landed on her head and Grace fell with a cry of terror, unable to breathe.

She was drenched in sweat and the feeling of terror persisted for a few minutes after she awoke. Thoroughly shaken, she turned on the reading lamp, got out of bed and went to the kitchen for a glass of water. What was that all about? she asked herself, repeating the question she had asked in her dream. She had never set much store by dreams and usually slept soundly at night. She had read in a science magazine that everyone had dreams while asleep, without exception. If so, then she was one of those who was never troubled by dreams and remembered nothing on waking. Perhaps the encounter with the two thugs at Beulah's cottage had shaken her more than she realized.

She sat back in bed sipping the water. Grace felt exhausted. A sudden wave of loneliness overtook her. She missed her father. She even missed Sarah, although she had never felt close to her. Sarah was too self-sufficient. Sarah always knew what Grace should do and naturally Grace bent over backwards to do the opposite. That was the problem of having a strong woman as a mother. It became hard to do the right thing for yourself when you were told to do it!

There was another dimension to her loneliness, one that she did not often acknowledge, even to herself. This was a deep, three-dimensional ache in her loins, three-dimensional to her because, apart from sexual hunger, it was also a yearning for companionship and comfort. Companionship, comfort, congress, the three C's missing from her life she laughed at herself. When she was younger, she had had affairs with various men, especially during her University years. She had liked some and though several of the men liked her, she had never found a person who deeply fulfilled all three of her C's. Maybe she was deluding herself, and she only had herself to blame for being alone. But she was in her thirties and at an age where she no longer wished to experiment. A chance phrase the *vaidyan* had used in another context had stuck in her mind. Talking about her talents, he had assured her.

"*Molae*. You have found a gift." Her ability to divine water. "But maybe you have more than one. You will know when the time comes."

That single sentence had resonated much more than he perhaps intended. But when it came to sex and relationships, Grace had decided she would know when the right partner arrived and until then, was prepared to live a celibate life.

Now these dreams! Pushing thoughts of sex aside, her mind went back to her nightmare and how Beulah appeared as the rescuer in the dream rather than the rescued. She leaned back and closed her eyes. After five years of successfully helping Rotterdam Oil find places to drill, she had left a lucrative job, sickened by the environmental devastation she had unleashed and the violence done to the earth. Perhaps that devastation was the price of progress. But she no longer wanted to be part of it. After leaving the oil company, she had tried to reinvent herself and discovered that if she was very quiet and inwardly still, she had the ability to visualize hidden shiny objects. It was not a sure thing, but was successful frequently enough to convince herself. And so she had started a second career here on the Island. There was plenty of water here and no need of diviners, but Hong Kong was a rich society and rich people had lots of precious objects to lose.

After six months practicing this profession, Grace was beginning to believe in her own ability. It was uncanny. She could sense things, sometimes they were merely shapes, at the edge of her consciousness. Mostly she did not know what they were, but when she had a client and concentrated on finding a single solid object, the shapes seemed to coalesce into identifiable outlines. Concentration was perhaps the wrong word for what she did. It was more like *unconcentration*, focusing awareness without using her mind. After much trial and error, she had learned to enter some altered state of consciousness, a bit like meditation, where she was able to switch off her thoughts.

It helped if the objects were shiny because they announced themselves as pinpricks of light in the dark recesses of her mind. At other times, the awareness of objects was like some kind of directional acoustic signal in her head that pointed her at what she was searching for. She never knew what activated it, had no control over it. And this was the hard part of the learning. The real skill was to foster awareness without trying. It was a classic Catch-22. If she tried too hard the intuition disappeared completely. She had to get a handle on her frustration, cultivate patience, and also the deep knowledge that she was not really in charge of the process here, was simply a medium.

That had been the hardest part, cultivating the humility needed to be effective, learning to efface herself from the problem, so that she was not in the picture herself, but merely a fly on the wall. She tried this now, recovering from the terror of her nightmare. She closed her eyes, looked inward again and pictured the scene at Beulah's cottage. She slowed down the film in her head and the picture immediately lost all detail. She sighed, relaxed completely and let her mind go blank. Memory faded.

She was underwater, in an ocean, breathing normally in the water while little fish swam all around. She floated out of the water into the air, marveling at the bioluminescence that exploded on the surface of the sea around her emerging body. She drifted upwards, and as she drifted, heard a desperate panting, scrabbling sound. Someone scrambling up a steep path. The climber made involuntary little moaning sounds, whether of terror or exertion was impossible to tell. The image began to fade and Grace's floating body lost substance.

Grace came back to herself with a start. She was suddenly cold, feeling the dampness of the nightgown that was soaked with the sweat from the nightmare. The memory of the phosphorescence she had just seen left her quietly exhilarated. There was something familiar about the cliff side though. Maybe she'd seen the place on one of her long walks through the island, but could not pinpoint where it was. She took off her nightgown, wiped her damp skin down with it, tossed it aside and got into bed naked. She slept dreamlessly for the rest of the night and awoke feeling more refreshed than she had in ages.

The next day was a Friday. Again a day without appointments. Grace opened her fridge in the morning intending to take milk for a cup of tea when she noticed the dish with Estrella's Lechon Kawali. This was a dish that had taken Estrella over an hour to prepare. She had first boiled the pork belly with cloves, garlic, bay leaf and peppercorns, adding salt, soy sauce and cane vinegar to the mix. She had brought this mix in a covered dish to Grace.

"Leave this in your fridge overnight, Mum," Estrella had told her. "I've already cut it up into pieces for frying. When you're ready, fry this in hot oil. I hope you'll like it."

My lunch today, Grace thought, deciding to go for an early morning walk, before swinging round through the woods to the pier and then stopping off for a coffee on her way back. Her phone rang just as she was stepping out of the house. It was Dawn, a bit breathless with excitement, words in a rush.

"Grace, I hope I didn't wake you up. My neighbor called early this morning and she's totally distraught. Her dog's been missing since last night. I know he might turn up on his own, but I thought of you and your ability to find lost objects. D'you think you could help her? She's afraid he might have been bitten by a snake and lying in the woods somewhere needing help."

"I'm not sure. I've never done this before. But I'd be glad to try. I was just stepping out for a coffee. I'll come right on by." She took directions from Dawn. They lived on the other side of Banyan Tree Bay in a small cluster of houses in the hills east of the main ferry pier. Although there was a shorter back way from her house to them, she decided to pick up a coffee first and gather the news of the day from Tony.

"Brazilian today," she said and held out the reusable cup she carried in her green canvas bag. He stirred the beans and turned on the machine that whirred into life, adding milk and a spoonful of sugar at the end without asking. Tony was a dedicated barista and took pride in knowing the individual tastes of each customer.

"What's the weather going to be like today?" Tony shook his head.

"Hot weather warning. You'd better stick to the shade. It can get very hot by afternoon." With the temperature at only twenty-four at eight in the morning Tony himself was already sweating profusely.

"I hope you don't have any work in the city today. It'll be a couple of degrees hotter there." Tony knew what Grace did for a living and had never commented on it.

"No, not in Hong Kong. But I just got a call from a friend about a missing dog on Lamma. I only hope it's not another poisoning."

"Who is it?"

"I don't know them. Neighbors of Raymond and Dawn Chan. Her name's Sylvie."

"Oh yes. I know. Tall blond French lady. Very nice. Always walks by with her dog. I think it's a terrier, a Jack Russell terrier."

"Know anything else about them?"

"Not really. Her husband's a pilot for Cathay Pacific, I think. And she runs a fitness studio at her home. Very active in dragon boat racing. A propos dragon boats, why don't you join? You're young and look very fit. The Island Five Hundred race is next week."

"Maybe. Maybe I will sometime. It's too late for this year anyway. I've seen one of the teams practicing in the harbor most evenings."

"That's the island fishermen's team. They keep their boat out by the village past the library on the way to the pavilion. But there are plenty of *gweilo* teams you could join."

"Maybe," Grace repeated. "Thanks for the coffee."

Chapter 17

It was a steep climb and her clothes were soaked with sweat when she was halfway up the hill. She climbed slowly, stopping from time to time for a sip of coffee and turning back to admire the view of the harbor and the sea beyond. It was a clear morning with none of the usual heat haze, or the haze of pollution that inescapably drifted over the island from neighboring Mainland China. Today some of the closer islands were clearly visible. Turning her head slightly left, she saw the camel-back outline that was Cheng Chau and shifting her gaze a few degrees right, saw the irregular lump that was Hei Ling Chau rising from the sea. Behind them loomed the bulk of Lantau, the largest of the two hundred-odd islands that dotted the South China Sea around Hong Kong. Visible in the background, only a few kilometers away, Lantau was almost twice the size of Hong Kong island, but being mountainous, less than two percent of the population lived there, although it provided sufficient space for the airport.

She found Raymond's house without difficulty. Dawn must have been looking out for her. The door opened and she came out to envelop Grace in a hug. A tall woman with red-rimmed eyes stood behind her. She was a handsome woman in a dancer's leotard and leggings, graceful and lithe in her movements. Today, Grace thought, she had a defeated air about her as though she knew the worst had already happened.

"You're Sylvie." Grace put out a hand, but Sylvie ignored it and hugged her as Dawn had done.

"Thank you. Thank you for coming," she said huskily, verging on tears again. Seeing how distraught Sylvie was about the missing dog, Grace tacitly assumed she was dealing with a childless woman, and the missing dog was a substitute child. Entering Dawn's living room, she saw a two-year old girl clambering onto the sofa. The resemblance was unmistakable. Dawn caught her glance from the child to Sylvie and smiled.

"Yes. Remarkable, isn't it? She's a beautiful child. Already the spitting image of her mother."

Dawn and Sylvie sat down in two cushioned armchairs, which left only the sofa for Grace. She sat at one end of the sofa, furthest from the little girl who had managed to sit up on it. As soon as Grace sat, the child scooted over and crawled into her lap. Grace was not used to little children and felt a bit uncomfortable, trying not to let the discomfort show. Neither Dawn nor Sylvie seemed to notice her discomfort. Sylvie gasped.

"Grace, you must be a natural mother. Adeline never goes to anyone." Dawn nodded.

"I've been trying for months to get her to come to me. I'm jealous. Grace! Motherhood calls." Grace blushed in embarrassment, but put her arms around Adeline anyway and the child settled comfortably on her lap sucking on a thumb, fingers of the other hand firmly entwined in Grace's hair.

"Thank you again for coming," said Sylvie. "Where do we start?"

"I know what Jack Russells look like but do you have any photographs, did he have any distinctive markings?"

"Of course, I have very much at home." Sylvie's English accent was very French. She looked uncertainly at Grace. "Could we move... next door to my 'ouse?"

"Yes, of course." Grace moved to set the child on the sofa but Adeline clung to her so she stood up with the child in her arms. Sylvie cocked her head in surprise.

"Adeline. What is the matter with you?" but the child simply shook her head and didn't budge.

"I'm alright. Don't worry," said Grace, suddenly feeling comfortable with this self-willed but compliant child in her arms. It was as though she and the child had come to an understanding and it was a good feeling. They walked next door to Sylvie's house which looked the same as Dawn's from outside, but inside was a large open-plan living room that moved seamlessly to dining-cum-kitchen and then doors that led off to other rooms at the sides. Sylvie waved them to chairs and disappeared to look for dog possessions or pictures, returning shortly with two framed photos, an album, a hard rubber dog bone and a retractable leash in a red leather case.

"This is all I have," she said apologetically. "Our dog doesn't have much. I suppose we are her possessions." She laughed nervously, as though realizing how absurd it sounded, but Grace found the statement oddly touching.

How right that was! Life was not about possessions. Life was about the people in our lives, wasn't it? Dogs knew that. So many people did not. At first sight of Sylvie's tall elegance, Grace had made a snap judgment, that she was haughty and aloof. She was mistaken. This was a beautiful woman, a beautiful human being, both inside and out, and her concern for her missing dog was not maudlin but touching.

"I can't promise anything. I'll simply sit here in silence for a while and see what images come to mind. Please feel free to do whatever you wish. You don't need to sit here, but you don't need to go away either."

"Shall I take Adeline?"

"Not if she's comfortable where she is. She doesn't bother me." As she spoke, Grace realized that she had imitated the child, and was curling a wisp of blond hair around her own forefinger. Sylvie nodded and moved to the kitchen to wash up dishes in the sink. Dawn took a magazine off the center table and began to look through it, glancing curiously from time to time at Grace and the placid child in her lap. Grace ignored her surroundings. As though understanding what was happening, Adeline remained perfectly still. Grace glanced at the framed photographs. One was a family photograph, with Sylvie, her husband Jacques, the two children; there was an older daughter, Madeleine; Adeline, and Frank. Frank was still a puppy.

Why Frank? Grace had asked. He loved frankfurters, so we called him that; Frank for short. She put the photos down and fingered the hard rubber bone. She closed her eyes and absently brought the bone to her nose. There was a healthy smell of canine saliva and a sense of the dog's hot, panting breath. She inhaled and sat back, could almost hear it now. She knew that the dog was still alive, but could not be certain so decided to say nothing to Sylvie. She bent down and buried her nose in Adeline's hair. Her hair smelt of some gentle soap with overtones of child and overriding that was the strong smell of Frank's presence. Had he slept in the child's cot?

"Sylvie, where does Adeline sleep?"

"Her room is upstairs. Why?"

"Can you show me? Show me your room, Adeline."
The child pointed up the stairs. Grace carried her up the narrow stairway, Sylvie leading the way, looking mystified.

The room was small with only a child's cot and a matching chest of drawers, a thin rug, a kelim, on the floor. Nothing else.

"There is a bathroom here." Sylvie opened the door to reveal a shower in one corner, a washbasin and a water closet. Light entered through a window. A small aircon unit was mounted on another wall where a second window should be. Grace opened the window and peered out. As in most houses here, there was a ledge above each window, giving shade to the floor below, and also providing a convenient platform to mount an external aircon unit.

"Does Adeline sleep here alone?"

"No. We wait till she falls asleep with us, then carry her up to this cot. Frank stays with her and barks to let us know if she cries or wakes up."

"Frank's gone." said Adeline.

"Where's Frank gone? Show me," Grace asked. Adeline pointed to the window.

"He jumped out of the window?" Adeline nodded, but looked uncertain. Grace opened the window and looked out again. If Frank had jumped out of here, he would have fallen two floors and either been killed or badly injured. Sylvie read her thoughts and said, "He's not anywhere in the compound. I looked everywhere." Grace handed Adeline back to her mother.

"May I sit here for a while alone?" She was not sure why she made the request, but it felt like the right thing to do. If the dog was dead, she would sit here quietly for a moment as a token of respect. Dawn had followed them up and was silently watching. She turned to leave, followed by Sylvie carrying the unprotesting child. Grace sat back on the bed and closed her eyes. The image of the two thugs from Beulah's cottage, one of them with a Burmese python head in place of a hand. She shook her head impatiently. That was not it.

Suddenly she knew beyond doubt that the two thugs were harmless, just as a Burmese python is harmless. Even on the rare occasions it attacked a human being, it was simply following its nature and there was no evil intent behind the attack. The real evil lay somewhere behind the two thugs. Now she was confusing the issue, because she was here to look for a missing dog, and this missing dog, Frank, had nothing to do with the thugs. But Beulah's dog did. She shook her head again, confused. What was going on? She was tired and very thirsty. She realized she had come out of the house for coffee and had eaten nothing that day. It was eleven in the morning. She felt faint and lay down sideways on Adeline's bed. And fell asleep.

Sylvie woke her an hour later. She had quietly crept up the stairs, peered into the room, found Grace sleeping, knelt by the bed and gently touched her arm. Grace woke up, bewildered and confused, her mind a total blank.

"Where am I?"

"You're tired. You fell asleep. Adeline is asleep too, downstairs. Come. I will make you something to eat." Grace felt foolish and looked wildly around the room.

"But I know Frank is here somewhere."

"There is nowhere to hide here. Only two rooms," said Sylvie, impatient now, a trace of skepticism creeping into her voice.

"One last look around," persisted Grace. Sylvie nodded shortly and went downstairs. Grace felt despair. Could her instinct be wrong? Nothing was certain in this nebulous land of clairvoyance except a growing conviction that Frank was alive, and that his disappearance had nothing to do with Doodle's poisoning. She was about to leave the room when she noticed the window had not been latched properly. It wouldn't close, so she opened it wide to slam it shut, when she heard a faint whisper in the wind. She opened the window and leaned out. She leaned out further and saw that, for a cat certainly, and for an agile dog, perhaps; it might be possible to jump out onto the window ledge and from there to the ground by jumping obliquely from one ledge to another. From what she knew of dogs, Jack Russells were agile dogs and great jumpers. She went downstairs swiftly, her gloom dissipated.

"Come on," she said. "Let's walk around your garden." She went outside, walking backwards to look up at Adeline's bedroom window.

"You see those window ledges?" she pointed out to a mystified Sylvie. "Frank could have jumped from there to there to there to the ground." Sylvie shrugged.

"And then?"

"And then… I heard him in your garden." Both Sylvie and Dawn, who had followed, looked skeptical. Grace ignored them and walked along the wall of the garden. There were carefully tended flower beds with red and yellow flowers, a frangipani tree, two oleanders in large pots along the wall on either side of the gate. Grace walked carefully, looking at the ground. She stopped when she came to a solid round metal plate like a large manhole cover in the ground.

"What's that?"

"That's an old, dry well. It was dangerous for the children, so Jacques had it covered with a metal plate. It's heavy. I can't lift it. The dog couldn't have opened it. Look at it! The grass around it! It hasn't been opened for years." Sylvie was in tears again, almost screaming at Grace in exasperation, on the verge of calling her names.

"Listen," said Grace. Now they all heard it, faint but furious barking.

143

"But how…?" Sylvie could not believe her ears.

An hour later, Frank was back in the house, soiled but unhurt. When they got help and lifted the heavy metal lid, they found him at the bottom of the dry well. They saw the hole he had dug, a foot below ground, in pursuit of some rodent, and then the sudden fall into the bottom of the well from where he could no longer get out. Sylvie burst into tears again; tears of happiness this time; happiness and contrition.

"Thank you. Thank you." she repeated again and again.

"I should never have doubted you." Grace laughed, relieved. Her instinct had been right and renewed her confidence that she was right about the triad thugs as well. They were not dangerous. The two men were mere pythons. They were no harm as long as she and Beulah kept out of their way. The real danger lay behind them, someone who perhaps might truss Beulah up and throw her to the pythons to feed.

Chapter 18

The next week was uneventful. Grace spent most of the week on the island reading, walking in the fine evening light, swimming in one of several secluded bays where there were hardly any other people, walking through the town, getting to know some of the tradespeople. After six months, she was beginning to learn the numbers and picking up a smattering of Cantonese phrases. She was called once by a businessman in Sheung Wan on Hong Kong island who wanted her to predict his business outlook for the coming year and offered her a lot of money for it. She had to spend half an hour on the phone explaining the difference between her skills and that of a fortune teller before turning down the offer.

She cooked porridge oats some days for breakfast and ate that with a couple of spoonfuls of Raymond's honey. She invited Dawn and Raymond over for a meal one evening and fed them rice with a Thai green curry that Estrella had cooked for her in the morning. Afterwards she served them coffee and they sat together over glasses of a fine single malt they had brought. They talked for a long time about inconsequential things, the way friends do. After they had left, Grace cleared up in the kitchen and felt much less isolated on this island. She was slowly developing a community around her, she realized.

She had friends in Dawn and Raymond, had formed a bond with Beulah, Tony and his wife, and then there was a large number of people whom she knew by sight if not by name; tradespeople whom she liked, the women in the grocery store, the man with the wispy Ho Chi Minh beard who drove his motorized cart at breakneck speed through the town. Not to forget the stone-faced man who delivered and replaced her cooking gas cylinders; he arrived within minutes of her call, with never any expression on his face, never meeting her eyes, but the speed and efficiency with which he served her were like offerings of friendship.

There were Sylvie and Adeline, whom she might also count as friends, although she had not yet met Jacques who was constantly away flying to distant places. She had run into Sylvie at the grocery store that week. Adeline had hugged her knees and Sylvie had been very warm, repeating thank you's for finding Frank.

Saturday was a big day at the Power Station Beach, the one closest to the town, overlooked by the three tall chimneys of the coal-fired power station. A quarter of the coal station's capacity had been converted to natural gas, and the chimneys rarely smoked. Whatever pollution they emitted was invisible and was minuscule compared to the amounts that drifted over from Mainland China on some days when the wind was unfavorable.

Today the normally deserted beach was transformed. It was the day of the annual Island Five Hundred dragon boat races. Tents had been put up all along the length of the beach and colorful pennants flew in front of some. Children raced up and down, in and out of the water, diving into the small waves, playing games, digging in the sand, and having the time of their lives. Meanwhile, the tents were thronged with men and women from the various teams, every tent recognizable from a distance by the distinctive uniforms of each team. Some of the contestants' T-shirts and leggings were plastered with advertisements like the overalls of Formula One drivers, and had team logos emblazoned front or back. There were teams representing bankers, international finance companies,

Merrill Lynch, Hong Kong schools, local fishing communities, various *gweilo* communities, the Hungarian Dragon Boat team, for instance, and even a team, made up mostly of finance people, from the Liechtenstein Princely Navy.

There were more than forty teams and a large number of heats before the final races, all run along a five hundred meter distance, starting from mid-bay toward the shore, along seven parallel channels marked by buoys. Competitors rested in the shade of tents between heats, listening to music, to pep talks by their team leaders, or chatting. A couple of teams did impressive aerobic exercises in the narrow line of sand between the rear of the tents and the thick line of mangroves at the edge of the beach. Grace admired the acrobatics, but if intended to discourage the opposition, the exercises were mostly a flop.

Tony had brought his coffee service to the beach that day, so she bought a cup from him and strolled along the shore, taking photos with her cell phone camera of the fourteen dragon boats lined up in the water. A maximum of seven boats competed at a time, so while each race was in progress, announcers called other teams to man the remaining boats and paddle out to the starting line for the next race. Grace was impressed by the well-organized chaos, and most impressive was that everyone present seemed to be having a good time.

Grace cheered the home team which did well in the first heat and qualified to race against five other winning teams in the fourth round. Grace shouted encouragement to her team in their distinctive blue T-shirts emblazoned with red dragons, as their boat edged into the lead nearing the five hundred meter mark. From where she stood, there was only one other boat that stood a chance of beating them, in lane one. As the boats approached the finish line, she saw that these paddlers, dressed in black, looked like a bunch of professionals, closely matched in size and build. They were paddling at a terrific pace, more than one hundred strokes per minute. The black-clad crew shot into the lead with a final spurt and they won by a third of a boat length. Grace's cheers choked in her throat when one of the men in black half stood in his seat and punched a fist in the air in triumph.

Seen up close, the dragon boats were all identical, heavily built of teakwood, slightly tapered fore and aft. They were wide enough for twenty paddlers to sit two abreast and had built-up platforms at each end. At the front, facing the paddlers sat the drummer who beat the strokes with a drum. On the rear platform was a steersman to guide the boat with a long-oared tiller. Regardless of the makeup of the crew, the steersmen and women were all from the local fishing community, the owners of the boats. The message was clear. They were happy to rent out their boats to foreigners and business people to play at dragon boat racing, but they took charge of their own boats and ensured their safety. As the black shirted crew beached their winning boat on the shore and dismounted, Grace got a close look at the man who had punched the air. He was definitely one of the two thugs from Beulah's cottage. Seconds later she spotted the second man disembark from a seat towards the rear of the boat. She edged closer to distinguish details of the uniforms. Their black half-sleeved T-shirts were beautifully designed, adorned front and back with a silver dragon. Below that were Chinese characters followed by the name of the firm in English. Ma Wood Industries. Grace quickly stepped back into the crowd, not wishing to be noticed by the two men.

She mingled among the watchers and looked out to sea. Straight ahead of her, six hundred meters offshore was the flagged starter's boat where the races began. Off to the left was a long line of motorized yachts and pleasure craft moored in the water. Most of these had swim platforms from which people were jumping off for a dip in the sea. On other boats, people sat on shaded upper deck tables and sipped drinks, watching the races from a privileged vantage point. One of the boats was a particularly large and striking motorized yacht, sleek with a gleaming black hull. Four men sat on the upper deck watching the races through binoculars. Grace examined the boat. It looked large enough to have three or four staterooms and a dozen crew members. She could count at least three in black T-shirts and white shorts who were obviously involved in handling the boat. She examined the black prow of the vessel and thought she could make out a leaping silver dragon with a name below. "I'll bet it says Ma Wood Industries," she said aloud to herself.

"Grace, come and meet Jacques," said Sylvie, interrupting her thoughts. She looked long-limbed and graceful in the island's blue and red boating uniform. Jacques was warm and as effusive in his thanks as Sylvie had been. Grace's thoughts were still on the silver dragon, so she pointed to the yacht.

"That's a beautiful boat. Any idea whose it is?" It turned out that Jacques was a boat lover, although he did not own one himself.

"I'd love to get my hands on that beauty." he said in a voice husky with emotion that Grace thought should properly be reserved for his wife.

"Ninety to one hundred feet, probably Italian built, judging by the lines, fifty to sixty tons, I'd say, anything from two to four million dollars US." Sylvie in the meantime had been called away to the women's race and

Grace laughed at the raw desire in Jacques' voice. He blushed, recognizing how he'd given himself away.

"Any idea who it might belong to?" she asked, partly to deflect his embarrassment, but mainly because she was sure it belonged to the man who employed the two thugs. She fleetingly remembered her dream of the python's head. If the python's head was harmless as she thought it was, the poison resided on that boat. She was sure of it.

The dragon boat races ended a couple of hours later with lots of people heading to the island's bars and watering holes to recap and celebrate the events of the day with copious amounts of beer. Grace didn't want to do that, so she walked the long way home and called her mother.

Chapter 19

Grace chatted with her mother for over an hour and was pleased to hear that Sarah's guest house venture was beginning to do well after nearly five lean years. The renovations were finally complete, many of the wooden bits that were being attacked by white ants had been completely renewed.

"When will I see you?" Sarah asked. Grace was touched. She sensed a mellowing since their last meeting more than a year ago. For once Sarah simply listened as Grace told her story of events of the last six months and did not make any suggestions, the kind of suggestions that always seemed to put Grace into resentful daughter mode. Maybe I've mellowed too, Grace thought. The sense of alone-ness in the world, something she sporadically felt, was curiously assuaged by the conversation with Sarah. Sarah, whom she thought of as a distant mother, whom she had always kept at arm's length, was suddenly closer than she had been in years, a good friend even. She decided to pay Sarah a visit in the near future.

"Why don't you come here to visit? You've not been to Hong Kong since your early Kuala Lumpur years with Dad. I'm sure it's changed a lot since then." Grace already knew the answer but she asked it anyway.

"Oh, I'd love to come Grace. But I've no one here to take over the running of the Tharavad Guest House. Nirmala's lovely and she looks after all the day-to-day stuff, but she'd not manage the bookings and the correspondence."

"What about the rest of your typical Syrian Christian extended family?" Sarah laughed at Grace's question.

"It still flourishes among some families. But mine is scattered all over the world. First of all, in my generation, there were only two of us, Ranjan and myself. And you know what your uncle is like. Drought or no drought, he's thoroughly Californian and never comes here. His two sons are not only American through and through, they're mired in West Coast show business and don't know anything about India or Kerala. The only way they'd come here is if they booked a holiday here."

"But there are others, aren't there? You've mentioned uncles and aunts of your childhood… their children?"

"My own mother, Amachi, always quoted a Malayalam proverb: *Adippam polae odappam.* I see the truth of it now."

"What does it mean?"

"The closest translation I can think of is: closeness depends on proximity." Grace nodded, though she knew Sarah couldn't see her.

"Yes. I think your mother's right." She hesitated a minute and then spoke the thought she had held back ever since their conversation began an hour earlier.

"But you know, even though we've lived apart for years, meeting infrequently, I feel I've grown closer to you." There was silence at the other end of the line and Grace knew that Sarah suddenly had a lump in her throat and was unable to speak just as Grace herself was. She put the phone down with a promise to go and visit Sarah in Aymanam next month. The southwest monsoon that deluged Kerala for two months every year normally began in late June or early July. It was now the end of April and Grace thought she would go and visit Sarah for four weeks from the end of May through most of June. Maybe she could persuade her mother to leave the guest house for a few days and travel a bit with her.

She rooted about listlessly in her kitchen and refrigerator, looking for something to eat. She was hungry, but didn't know what she wanted, an unusual state of mind. She found two chunks of cheese, a Spanish manchego and a New Zealand cheddar and decided to have a glass of wine. She found a white and a red in her cupboard, chose the red with its unfamiliar label, broke the seal, unscrewed the cap and poured herself a glass.

It was an unusual wine, unlike anything she had ever tasted. Unsure whether she liked it or not, she sipped some more, looked at the label again and took several more sips. Soon the glass was empty, so she poured herself another, set out the cheese and a paring knife and put two slices of wholegrain rye bread into the toaster. She read the label while waiting for the toast. It was from the west of China, a prize-winning blend of Merlot and Cabernet Sauvignon called Deep Blue from the Grace vineyards in Ningxia. According to the label, the 2009 vintage had won several awards at international competitions. With vineyards named Grace, no wonder it tastes so good, she thought. She filled her third glass and toasted herself just as the toaster popped. She sliced and diced a red pepper and cucumber and made a meal of it together with the cheese and wine.

Afterwards she put on some music and settled down to finish the Donna Leon she had started a few days earlier. The thunder of the storm in the fourth movement of Beethoven's symphony playing in the background brought her out of her immersion in Commissario Brunetti's family life.

It was only nine, too early to go to bed, too late to finish the book tonight. She thought of the sleek black cruiser and on impulse, picked up her laptop and sat down again to search for Ma Wood Industries. She found a website with pages of information in Chinese. The English version had only two short pages. The first page listed Mr.Ma's holdings. He owned swathes of former forest land in Malaysia and Indonesia that were now palm oil plantations. He also was a dealer in tropical hardwood furniture. His products all carried an FSC imprint and were apparently certified by the international forestry stewardship council. Grace had heard of the FSC. Like the 'fair trade' label, it was supposed to be an international certificate of sustainability.

In the meantime, Beethoven's musical storm had passed and the mellow tones of the fifth and final movement, described in the CD's accompanying notes as 'shepherd's song: cheerful and thankful feelings after the storm' was playing. Grace sat back in her chair, closed her eyes and let her mind wander. She saw a few shapes, like manifestations of Beethoven's sound imagery. Peasants playing in a forest, perhaps, rejoicing after the storm. The image in her mind was vague, then suddenly grew black, although the music in the background was still peaceful and pastoral, as the name of the symphony suggested. Suddenly she sat up, eyes still closed. This was a real scene, in a tropical forest, people struggling, a fight to the death...

Grace forced herself to disconnect from the scene for a moment. She was getting too excited and the image began to fade. She took a deep breath, relaxed and sat back again, eyes still closed.

Somewhere far away. A very hot, equatorial forest. The night sounds were deafening. Cicadas, a bird's nocturnal protest at an intruder, the shrill cry of a monkey, loud groaning as of an unoiled door hinges. She realized it was the sound of two tree trunks rubbing against each other as the night air shifted. The forest felt steamy and wet. The faint sound of heavy breathing, muffled curses.

An LED lamp came on suddenly. It was a small one, but its brightness was nevertheless dazzling in the dark of the forest. All the night noises stopped at once as the forest held its breath. And then, almost startling her out of her chair the powerful roar of a handheld motor saw. The LED light played on the trunk of a slender tree with a mottled gray trunk. Sawdust flew in an arc like jewels in the white light as metal teeth raced through the trunk. Then the saw was withdrawn and another cut began to take a wedge out of the trunk. There was a momentary lull in the metallic scream and the motor burbled in relative quiet while the shadowy figure examined the cuts, then began to slice through the diameter of the trunk.

Another two minutes and the job was done. The tree tottered, fell against an adjacent trunk and the motor saw was switched off. Commands were spoken by the holder of the LED light. Two additional shadowy figures sprang to obey.

Grace strained to understand the words. It was not a language she could recognize. Although she didn't speak Chinese, she had heard enough to recognize it. There was nothing familiar in this speech. But then there were several Chinese dialects she didn't know and might not recognize. She heard two words fairly clearly. It sounded like "*Ngay mai.*" She jumped up, grabbed a post-it note and pen to write the words down phonetically.

"*Ngay Mai, ngay mai,*" she repeated to herself, trying not to forget the exact sounds. She recorded the spoken words on her cell phone, thinking ruefully that image and data transfer from mental images and visions to phones was not yet a reality. She smiled at the absurdity of the thought. Then again, perhaps it was not so absurd. She remembered reading about recent experiments where a model plane had been remotely flown by a man guiding it with only electrodes clamped to his skull. If that were possible, why not her visions of reality? It was late now. She showered, changed, fell into bed and a deep, dreamless sleep.

Chapter 20

She awoke the next morning thinking of Sarah, remembering her mother with more love and filial affection than she had felt in a long time. So before even making breakfast, she turned on her computer and began to search for flights to India. All the inexpensive flights to Kerala that came up were already sold out and, although she could afford it, Grace had inherited thrift from both sides of her family and couldn't bring herself to buy a business class ticket. She rationalized, saying to herself that a business class ticket had a larger carbon footprint than economy. This was true, but the real reason for not flying business class, if she were to be honest with herself, was thrift.

After a frustrating hour of searching various websites, she found one based in absurdly distant Scandinavia that offered a cheap, convenient, direct flight to Thiruvananthapuram from Hong Kong and she booked it immediately, although Cochin would have been a more convenient airport to her mother's village. She could hire a taxi to take her the three or four hours drive to Aymanam, she decided, and this would give her a chance to see more of the countryside. She was not sure, but maybe there was a road that went along the coast and allow her to take in some of the backwaters as well as glimpse a few beaches of the Arabian Sea.

Happy that she had done this, she felt closer to Sarah, felt a surge of contentment. There was nothing much to eat at home, and she was hungry, She checked the temperature. It was around 30 degrees, so she wore a loose fitting long-sleeved shirt with comfortable baggy shorts and strolled down to the town to buy food, perhaps have breakfast at the Green Cottage and then come back to check e-mails. She had an additional reason for breakfast at the Green Cottage. They had staff from several different countries. In addition to local Cantonese, there were a couple of Filipino girls and maybe a Thai woman working there. She wanted to try out the two words she had heard in her vision last night and see if anyone might recognize them.

She stopped off at Tony's for coffee on the way as usual and tried out her phrase on him.

"*Ngay mai,* Tony," she smiled at him. He almost dropped her coffee cup.

"What does that mean? You want coffee or not?"

"So you don't recognize the phrase?" He shook his head emphatically.

"No, I don't." She picked up a cup of the day's special, a Sumatran blend, and sat on a barstool, chatting to him about the recent dragon boat races. As an afterthought, she mentioned the sleek black cruiser.

"Ma Wood Industries?" He put his head back. "The name rings a bell. Why do I remember the name now? I have to think about it." He stopped to serve another three customers in a hurry on their way to the ferry boat. "Sorry. I'll have to talk to you about it later."

She finished her coffee, shoved the empty reusable cup into the green shoulder bag that she carried everywhere. It was comfortable to carry and big enough to use as a shopping bag if she decided to buy something at one of the little shops in town. She was trying to avoid plastic, her resolve renewed every time she looked out to sea and saw the amount of synthetic debris floating in the sea. She went into the friendly, cramped space of the Green Cottage. There were many different young men and women who worked here at various times of the day, but regardless of who was behind the counter, the atmosphere was always harmonious, and Grace wondered how it was so well-managed. She ordered from the menu her favorite breakfast of eggs Benedictine. She was served two eggs poached to perfection on a light bed of green salad accompanied by toasted muffins and a squirt of some kind of delicious mustard sauce. With the taste of Tony's coffee still lingering on her tongue, she asked for water to go with her breakfast.

The young woman who bought the order smiled as she set the food down, encouraging Grace to ask.

"Excuse me. Do you know what this means? *Ngay mai.*" She was no longer sure how the word was pronounced, so she took out her cell phone and replayed the word as she had recorded it when the phrase was fresh in her memory. The girl looked mystified, shook her head with an uncertain glance at Grace, unsure of what she wanted.

"Never mind," Grace said and concentrated on her poached eggs. She looked up a minute later to see the owner standing before her table, eyes twinkling behind his black rimmed round glasses.

"You want to know something?"

"Yes, I was wondering about this phrase. What language is it?" She repeated the phrase. He shook his head.

"This isn't Cantonese. Are you sure it's not mispronounced." Grace was positive this was exactly what she heard.

"No. Sorry. Can't help you." he said. "Want to order something else?"

"No. The food's great." She mopped up the last of her egg with the muffin, paid for breakfast and walked back. Tony hailed her as she passed. He was busy, with four customers clustered in front of his coffee machines, and he craned his head to see around them.

"If you have a moment, Grace. I think I have news for you." Grace sat on one of the bar stools while he finished serving, then turned to her.

"Ma Wood Industries," he said. "I don't know anything about Mr. Ma himself except that he's very rich. There was some problem in Vietnam, two years ago, something about exporting valuable woods without a proper license or something."

"Do you know what kind of wood, and where to?"

"No. I don't know anything else. I assume the wood was going to China. That's where all raw material is going these days." Tony shrugged. "I don't know if it's any use to you, but that's all I remembered."

"You've helped me more than you know, Tony," she said sincerely. Tony's information was a tenuous lead, but she was charged with energy despite the heat and hurried home to see what she could find. She turned on her computer and searched for two hours, looking for Ma Wood Industries and Vietnam. There was nothing. She searched for stories about wood smuggling in Vietnam using many different keywords and came across a story dated a year earlier. *Valuable Wood Seized at Transvina Port.*

According to the report, the Hai Phong Port City's border forces had recently seized ten tonnes of valuable wood being transported by container to the Transvina port in Hai Phong. There were no details of the kind of the wood, or whose the shipment was. There was another story, around three years old, about the *sua* tree, with a color illustration of a graceful, slender tree with a profusion of beautiful white flowers. Apparently people in Vietnam believed that the wood of the *sua* tree was spiritually powerful and were willing to pay high prices for it. There were reportedly several "sua billionaires" in Vietnam.

Vietnamese people believe that sua trees have spiritual value. In the past, when the kings passed away, sua wood was always used for making coffins. Especially, sua trees were ground to create powder which was then sprayed inside the coffins, because people believed that this would help the dead's soul salvation. Prof Nguyen Lan Dung, a biology scientist, has affirmed that if considering the forestry value, the sua tree is now more valuable than other trees. Sua simply is a kind of tree which can provide high quality wood.

Sua trees mostly grow sparsely in natural forests, mostly on rugged limestone cliffs. Sua wood has big firm heart, which is not cracked, warped, and it always has beautiful patterns. Sua wood was once sold at 11 billion dong per cubic meter, a sky high price level. This then prompted people to hunt for sua wood, braving their lives.

Grace did a quick check on a currency exchange calculator. One billion Vietnamese dong was close to fifty thousand US dollars. Half a million dollars for a cubic meter of the wood; valuable enough for a criminal trader or poacher to kill, certainly. She had no idea what the threshold value of human life might be in Hong Kong criminal circles, but suspected it was a lot lower than one cubic meter of sua wood. The brief glimpse of illegal wood trade that she discovered in the articles fascinated her and she pulled back to the original reason for starting this research. Beulah! Something told her Beulah's life was in danger. The article about sua wood, though interesting, was not of concern now. Beulah was being threatened for something happening here on the island. She did another search for trade in rare wood, this time specifying Hong Kong's outlying islands and immediately found what she was looking for.

POACHERS BATTLE LAMMA ISLANDERS IN BATTLE FOR RARE INCENSE TREES, was the headline of an article in the South China Morning Post a few years earlier.

...according to the police it was poachers. It turns out the tree was an Aquilaria sinensis, a species sometimes known as the incense tree, and poachers in a hurry to harvest the valuable heartwood had simply cut through much of the trunk, causing it to fall.

When infected by a certain type of mould, incense trees make an aromatic resin that permeates its core, yielding what is often called agarwood. Native to southern China the fragrant wood has long been used to make incense, joss sticks, prayer beads, oil and carvings. The extracted resin, chen xiang, is also used as a traditional Chinese medicine. Indiscriminate harvesting has almost wiped out incense trees from the mainland, prompting poachers to turn to Hong Kong where stands can still be found in the wild, because local woodlands are relatively protected under the Forests and Countryside Ordinance.

Similarly threatened worldwide, Aquilaria sinensis is categorised as a vulnerable species on the red list of the International Union for the Conservation of Nature and is listed under Appendix Two of the Convention on International Trade in Endangered Species of Wild Fauna and Flora (Cites), which means its trade should be restricted.

"The poaching is very serious. With the larger trees gone, the poachers are beginning to move to the lesser trees," said a tree expert from the University of Hong Kong. The article continued: *As the resin becomes increasingly valuable - one gram of agarwood is now estimated to be worth up to HK$12,580 on the mainland market - the plunder of incense trees worsens in Hong Kong. Police records show there were 76 reported cases of tree poaching (both Buddhist pines and incense trees) in 2011 and 71 cases so far this year.*

Most reported cases have occurred in the lowland woods of Sai Kung or southern Lantau, some on an appallingly large scale. Earlier this year, Mui Wo residents discovered a stand of 1,000 incense trees

*behind Man Mo temple had been felled overnight with poachers
making away with almost the entire haul.*

*...a concerned resident who was a former member of the Sai Kung
police department worries that the poachers are more sophisticated
than people give them credit for. "The ones I've seen appear to be very
professional ... they almost appear to be ex-PLA or something like
that ... I've heard a story, which has not been confirmed, that they've
even set up a training camp on the other side of the border for tree
cutters," he says.*

*... a 20-year resident of Sai Kung who routinely walks his dogs
in areas popular with poachers, says he has had a series of brushes
with poachers he suspects are mainlanders. Last year, he surprised a
poacher, who jumped from a bush, knocked him down and ran off.
Another time he cornered one up a tree.*

*As poachers turned their attention to Lamma Island in recent
years, the handful of police officers there (only four or five are on duty
at one time) are being stretched to their limit. ...According to residents,
police suspect most of the stolen wood is smuggled to Maoming, a city
in southwest Guangdong which has become a major market for
agarwood products.*

*Police say they are aware of the target areas and have stepped up
patrols. They are also working with the AFCD to keep an eye on
potential sites. Success, however, has been limited...*

Grace paused to make a cup of tea and came back with
pen and paper to sum up what she had learned.

First. There still were stands of agarwood remaining
on the Island. The tree, *aquilaria sinensis*, was red-listed by
the IUCN, on the endangered list of the International
Union for Conservation of Nature. There was a lot of
illegal cutting of *aquilaria* trees, and others of its kind, going
on in many parts of the world. She knew of sandalwood
poachers in India. Although sandalwood trees were not
genetically related to *aquilaria*, the problems with illegal
sandalwood trade were similar to that of agarwood in Indo-

China. There had been a particularly notorious fellow called Veerappan who had controlled vast swathes of forest lands in southern India, had kidnapped police and terrorized villagers. There was the Vietnamese example of *sua* trees. And closer to home, the South China Morning Post article about Lamma Island in particular and the illegal harvesting of agarwood. All agarwood sources in Mainland China had already been logged, so poachers were now targeting Hong Kong and its outlying islands. The poachers were only coming now because there was stronger legislation in place to protect the trees; anyone caught could be penalized with fines or jail sentences ranging from weeks to a few years.

Second. There was mention in some articles of PLA interests involved. Grace found this sinister. The People's Liberation Army of Mainland China had always been spoken of as a powerful, conservative force in the country that owned and controlled large chunks of its state enterprises. According to Grace's understanding, high officers of the PLA were a law unto themselves, not really under the control of the civilian government. These swathes of semi-private enterprise were thus largely unchecked, so corruption here was even more difficult to control than elsewhere in the country.

Third. All varieties of *aquilaria* seemed to command high prices in the market. Prices quoted in the various news articles and on Wikipedia ranged from twenty to sixty US dollars per kilogram for agarwood chips, to more than seven thousand US dollars for a kilo of agarwood oil. The newspaper article on Vietnamese wood quoted the unbelievable price of thirty thousand US dollars per kilogram for top quality agar heartwood. At even half that price, it would be well worth a poacher's effort to harvest even if they had to come a long way for it.

Fourth. The various articles she had found about agarwood on Wikipedia described it as a member of the *Thymelaeceae* family, a fast-growing forest tree with habitats ranging from the foothills of the Himalayas to the rainforests of Papua New Guinea. Outside its native habitat, agarwood was best known in the Near East and Japan. *Aquilaria's* most important species were *A. agollocha, A. malaccensis* and *A. crassna. A. malaccensis* was protected worldwide under the CITES convention. A. crassna was listed as an endangered species by the Vietnamese Government. Agarwood had been used for centuries as incense, for medicinal purposes and in perfumery. Both agarwood chips and agarwood oil fetched high prices in buyers' markets.

Agarwood, *Aquilaria agallocha Roxb.*, was believed to have originated in the Indian hills of Assam. This species was synonymous with *A. malaccensis.* The major constituents of agarwood oil were sesquiterpenes, which were very difficult to synthesize, hence extremely expensive. There were currently no synthetic substitutes for high-grade incense or oil. Agarwood had been used for medicinal purposes, incense and perfumery for thousands of years. Its use continued in Ayurvedic, Tibetan and traditional East Asian medicine.

The fact that she had seen Beulah threatened by putative Ma Wood Industries' thugs from nearby Guangdong made it all the more likely that the mysterious Mr. Ma was involved in this trade. Thinking of Beulah, Grace realized she had not seen her for over a week. She had an urge to go and visit the old lady to make sure she was doing alright and at least beginning to recover from the death of her beloved Doodle.

Grace was not hungry after the breakfast at Green Cottage, so she merely made herself another cup of tea, nibbled on some crackers and helped herself to a bowl of maple syrup and walnut ice cream that she found in her freezer. She had bought it three weeks earlier from one of the shops in the village and forgotten all about it. She went out onto the terrace, but it was far too hot to sit there, even in the shade, so she went back downstairs and sat under the fan. Soon she would have to have the aircon on at night, she thought.

After finishing her impromptu lunch of crackers and ice cream, she remembered the load of washing still in the machine from the previous night. She went up again, her bare feet blistering on the hot terrace tiles, gathered the damp clothes in a basket and hung them up to dry on the line. She was sweating again by the time she came back downstairs, so turned on the aircon in her bedroom, lay down with a book and promptly fell asleep.

She awoke at three, judged by the sun that it was still too hot to go out, so she went back to her book. There was a missed call on her phone. She returned the call. It was a potential customer from Hong Kong, a woman who was to travel to England in a week and had lost her air ticket. Grace gently suggested she contact the travel agency or the website through which she had booked her ticket for a replacement. Putting the phone down, she thought how tense and anxious she might have been, had she depended only on income from this skill to make a living, wondering what sort of compromises she might have had to make without four million US dollars in her bank account. She did not know the answer to that and fortunately did not need to know.

She waited till four then changed into a pale blue half-sleeved, calf-length dress that gave her some protection from the still-fierce late afternoon sun. She set out for Beulah's cottage and was drenched with sweat within minutes. Even the birds were silent. It was a fifteen minute walk to Beulah's from her house and the hill was steep, so she walked slowly, hugging every patch of shade on the path, enjoying the occasional glimpses of sea, anticipating the glorious sweeping view from the clearing in front of the cottage.

She thought about what she had learned about incense trees last night and this morning. Of course she had always known the origins of Hong Kong's name. That was one of the first things mentioned in the guide book she had bought before arriving in the city. Heung Gong, the original Cantonese name, difficult to render accurately in English. Fragrant Harbor. In the old days, before the British had acquired the island, Hong Kong had been a relatively barren rock, its main usefulness being a waterfall that was a source of sweet water for the ships that sailed this way to or from the great trading port and magnificent walled city of Canton. At that time, Hong Kong and its two hundred surrounding islands were well wooded. There was more than enough agarwood here to meet demand. There were also extensive forests in Mainland China, Vietnam, and most of the rest of the Indo-China peninsula. It was only in the second half of the twentieth century that exploitation had picked up pace and by the beginning of the twenty-first century, as China grew into an economic powerhouse, stocks on the Mainland had been wiped out.

Heung Gong! Fragrant Harbor! Seeing Hong Kong today, the only fragrances to be found were designer perfumes in the various shopping malls. Her thoughts came to an abrupt end as she topped the rise of the hill and entered the clearing. As always her breath caught at the magnificent view. Today, there was considerable haze over the sea and some of the more distant ships were sailing as through a thin fog. Through the corner of her eye she noticed that the front door of Beulah's cottage was wide open. She whirled around in sudden panic, bounding up the few steps into the room. It was empty. The bed was made and, a poignant detail, Doodle's red leash lay on the bed, as though she were ready to take him for a walk.

"Beulah!" she called out. "Beulah. Beulah?" She called louder. There was no reply. From the edge of the clearing she heard the coo cooo cooo of the Asian Koel, a cuckoo doing justice to its name. She ran outside and round to the back, calling out the old woman's name. There was no reply again, no sign of life. She carried the one unbroken chair from the cottage, set it in a shady corner of the verandah and sat down to wait for Beulah to return from wherever she had gone. She sat for over an hour, looking blankly out to sea, not taking in the view, her mind on hold.

Her eyes glazed over and she fell into a kind of daylight trance. Grace's eyes were open, but her vision darkened and she saw a repeat of her nightmare of a week ago. Her body rose out of a night time phosphorescent sea and floated up a cliff face. Of course! The strange familiarity of the scene was explained. Although she had never been down there, it was Beulah's cliff she had seen in the dream, seen from an unfamiliar angle, from down below. There had been the sound of desperate scuffling and panting and then the vision had gone blank. She sat upright with a start and ran to the edge of the cliff to look.

She saw the rocks far below and Beulah's boat drawn up among them. Unlike the last time, the boat was not carefully covered with the blue and white tarpaulin. The tarpaulin lay crumpled a few meters from the boat, half in the water, its ends fluttering in the breeze, weighted down by a couple of rocks.

She lay down flat at the edge of the cliff and tried to see clearly. It was impossible from here. She knew she had to go down. Something told her it was imperative. The path looked very narrow, steep and unsafe in places where the ledge had crumbled to a rounded brown surface. Perhaps there were enough tufts of grass and bushes to hold on to. Impossible to see from here. She had no choice. She had to try.

Grace hitched the long strap of her green canvas bag securely over her head so that it fitted snugly under her right arm. She wished she had worn trousers instead of the blue dress, but regret was pointless now. She would manage. She stepped cautiously onto the path. It was easy going at first and she simply took one step at a time along the switchback, not looking down, concentrating only on where she placed her feet. Again, she was glad to be wearing the Skechers. Their knobbled soles were fairly secure on the mix of sand and grass.

She was halfway down when she came to the part where the ledge had crumbled, or perhaps had been deliberately destroyed. She stopped, unable to descend further and thought of going back to the cottage to wait for Beulah, but instinct told her that the hastily beached boat might provide clues to Beulah's whereabouts. From the moment weeks ago, when she had seen the old woman's grief at the death of her dog, Grace had made a spontaneous, unspoken resolution to protect the old lady from further harm. The resolution had been subliminal, and she was not conscious of it till this moment. Once the awareness dawned Grace knew she had to go on.

She looked desperately at the cliff face above for an alternate path. There was none. Above her head were two bushes that could provide handholds to help to cross the crumbling bit. She turned to face the cliff, leaning her body forward, feet as far towards the edge as she dared, and inched along the ledge until she grasped the first bush with her left hand. Ignoring the broken twigs that tore into her hand, she jumped to the left, with the handhold to steady her. She glanced down involuntarily and her heart stopped for a minute when she saw she was directly above the jumble of rocks way below, only halfway down the cliff.

She clung there for a moment, holding on with one hand, straddling the broken ledge, face pressed into the cliff face, waiting for the trembling in her knees to stop. She tested the grip of her toes on the ledge for a moment, then quickly moved her hand and her body to the left to grab the second bush before she lost balance. Once she had a firm hold, it was easy to cross the gap. The rest of the descent was simple and she soon stepped on to the rocks and from there into the soft sand. The tide was up, she could see, and the patch of sand was much narrower than she had expected. The boat was most of the way up the beach, rocked gently by waves that nudged its stern like a chivvying sheepdog. The tarpaulin was half under the boat in the sand. The rest of it was in the water, the blue and white stripes rising and subsiding with each wave.

Grace examined the boat. A net lay coiled on the floor, wet from bilge water that sloshed about with the movement of the boat. It was not like Beulah to allow so much water to collect in the boat, thought Grace. Judging by the state of the cottage, despite relative poverty, Beulah was a neat and meticulous woman. She stepped into the boat and looked into a tiny compartment in the stern. There was more fishing gear inside. Grace put a hand to check the dark interior and drew it back with a yelp of pain. Her hand, already bruised and broken in places from the bushes above, streamed with blood from two punctures in the middle of the palm. She fell back into the bilge with a scream, thinking she been bitten by a sea snake coiled within the dark space. She was frozen for a moment and then exploded into the hysterical laughter of release from fear when she noticed the fish hooks that had been stored in the compartment.

There was nothing more to be seen in the boat, so Grace decided to draw it up among the rocks and cover it with the tarpaulin as Beulah herself might have done. She slowly dragged the boat up onto the sand between two rocks, first hauling on the prow. Then she moved to the stern, lifted the rudder up out of the water, then returning to the prow to drag it further up onto a rock. She then went back into the water, trying to ignore the blue dress that was drenched and clung to her knees and thighs. It was impossible to move, so she impatiently hitched the dress up around her waist and heaved on the tarpaulin. As she heaved, the tarpaulin came out of the water. Beulah suddenly looked up at her. For the second time in half an hour, Grace fell back in fear and screamed. She sat waist deep in the water, the hem of the blue dress rising and falling around her, and screamed and screamed and screamed. There was nothing and no one to hear her except for the giant black kite that soared and wheeled overhead.

Chapter 21

"Raymond... help me."

Grace could barely speak. She didn't know how much time had passed since finding Beulah's body. She had scrambled on hands and knees to the boat where her green bag lay. She fumbled inside for her phone, wanting to call the island police but didn't know the number. The first number she found on her contact list was Raymond's. It was Dawn who answered.

"Who is this? Grace! What's the matter? Where are you?" Grace couldn't get the words out, her jaws trembled so much.

"The police?... Raymond, Raymond, come here quick." Raymond came on the line. Grace managed to tell him where she was. He didn't know exactly where Beulah lived.

"The old lady's cottage... near your beehives...." She was sure he would be able to help the police find it.

"And Raymond..." she remembered to say. "Tell them ... ...to bring ropes."

She put the phone back into the bag, threw the bag further up into the sand and entered the water again with shaking knees. She grasped Beulah by the shoulders, her fragile body made even lighter by the buoyancy of the salt water and sat down with the old lady on her lap. She gently closed the sightless eyes that stared up at her and began to stroke the wet hair with tears streaming down her face. As she wept, she wondered why she was weeping for this woman whom she hardly knew. Was it for herself? Or was it compassion for someone weak and defenseless? Beulah had not been weak. She did not want to think of her like that. Maybe, Grace thought, the tears were really for herself, her solitude and her search for something missing in her own life...

She heard the sound of motors far above her head. A voice called out something in Cantonese. And then in English.

"This is the police. Are you alright madam?" Grace did not look up, did not reply. She sat there in a daze, gently stroking the old lady's wet hair in her lap. A long while later, the same policeman touched her shoulder.

"Madam, can you tell me what happened?" Grace did not hear him, did not move. Finally it was Dawn, who climbed down the steep cliff with a rope affixed by the police to one of the trees in Beulah's cottage clearing, who caught Grace by the shoulders and hugged her, forcing her to turn away from the body.

"Grace, I'm so sorry, I'm so sorry..." she repeated. Dawn had no idea who the old lady was. Her only aim was to help Grace back up. Dawn insisted that the police lift Grace back up the cliff with a harness, while she herself clambered back with the aid of the rope.

It was ironic, Grace thought, when she reached the clearing at the top. The tree to which the rescuers had tied the rope was an *aquileria sinensis!*

Chapter 22

The formalities were over within a week. There was a court hearing to examine the cause of death. It was determined that the deceased, who lived a solitary life, had fallen to her death while descending the path. It was noted that the ledge had deteriorated considerably under the influence of weathering and therefore a metal railing would be erected there to prevent further use of the path. Beulah's was an accidental death and the case was closed.

Grace was the only one who believed that Beulah had been murdered, just as her little dog had been. Why, she did not really know, but her vision of the previous week and the day before had been appallingly clear. It was Beulah she had heard, desperately scrambling up the cliff side in the dark, pursued by someone or something. Perhaps it had something to do with Mr. Ma's interest in valuable woods. In any case, there was no way of proving her doubts, so she said nothing, merely mentioning for the record that the old lady's dog had died of paraquat poisoning a short while before her death, and that Beulah had spoken of it as being a deliberate murder.

Life went on. Grace was beginning to attract more clients in Hong Kong. In the following month she travelled on the ferry several times a week. She returned late one evening, on the seven-thirty boat. The boat was crowded with holiday-makers although it was only Wednesday and the tourist crowds usually were between Fridays and Sundays. She checked her phone calendar for public holidays and found that Buddha's birthday was being celebrated on the following Monday, the twenty-fifth of May, and this was the start of holiday crowds that would double or triple the population of the island for a week or more. She felt a large presence hovering beside her and looked up to see the tall man she thought of as the gentle giant standing in front of her. Most of the seats on the boat were full and he apologetically inclined his head to the vacant seat beside Grace where she had deposited her green bag.

"Of course," she replied, embarrassed, snatching her bag off the seat. "I'm sorry." He noted her embarrassment and smiled his apology in turn.

"If I had known it would be so crowded, I would have taken a later boat," he said.

"This week it's not going to make any difference. All boats will be crowded whatever the hour." He smiled agreement and said nothing.

"Where do you work?" Grace asked him, in sudden, blunt curiosity. She was appalled by her own question, not knowing where the impulse came from. He smiled shyly.

"I'm a wildlife photographer," he said. "But..." there was an air of confession here, "I'm forced to make a living as a construction engineer." Grace laughed.

"Your secret is safe with me. I knew you were an artist, but if photography is your secret life, I won't tell anyone." He was a serious man and misunderstood her laughter.

"No, no. I cannot make a living from photography, so I have to build things for other people." Grace could see that he was uncomfortable about her laughter, so she put out a hand and said, "Grace Lam."

"Pawel," he said. "I'm from Poland. You don't want to know my second name. Too complicated." They both laughed together at that and he suddenly relaxed, understanding that earlier she had laughed as an accomplice, and not at him.

"What kind of wildlife do you photograph and where do you go to find it?"

"You know, for my kind of work, I don't need to travel far. I only need free time, good light and a few hours."

"A few hours flying time?" she asked. He laughed.

"No. Just ten minutes walk from my house. But I need hours to photograph what I see."

She looked curious and puzzled, so he took out his cell phone and uploaded a few photos from his website. Grace had no idea what she was looking at, but the photos looked abstract and the designs were exquisite. Mostly against dark backgrounds, stunning shapes and colors, loops and whorls, nature's design in all its complexity and all its glorious simplicity. After looking hard at one image for a few seconds, she recognized it. "Why, that's the underside of a leaf," she cried in astonishment. He nodded, pleased. "Very good. Most people don't recognize it so quickly."

"But I have no idea what the others are," she confessed.

"This one is the hair on the legs of a woodland spider. That is a close up of the bark of a tree that grows near the wind turbine. You know the hill?"

"Yes," she nodded. "I walk a lot on the island. But I haven't learned to see things the way you do."

"What do you do?" he asked. She hesitated for a moment, then told him. He did not laugh, but spoke in his slow, measured manner.

"The engineering side of my brain cannot understand what you do. To me... I apologize in advance for saying this... to me this is nonsense. But the artistic side of me understands perfectly. When I look at things close up, I see so much that is not visible to the naked eye. Who knows?

Maybe it is like that with our own intellectual understanding." Grace was impressed by this reply.

"What an interesting way of looking at it. I must remember to use this analogy if I meet a skeptic."

"You know, it does not matter what people believe. If you get results, that's what matters."

How true, Grace thought, and her face clouded in momentary pain. If you get results, that's what matters. She knew in the depths of her being that Beulah had been murdered. She had no proof and so had not tried to prove it. Pawel's phrase cut her to the quick. *If you get results, that's what matters.* And she had no results. The memory of Beulah was fresh in her mind, but for the rest of the world, the old lady was a fading memory, if that. She had walked along the path to Beulah's cottage recently, and noticed that cobwebs tugged at her face as she walked. No one had come that way for days. Soon Beulah would be forgotten, the carefully tended cottage a decaying ruin. Pawel noticed her pained expression.

"Did I say something wrong?" He looked so worried that she told him the story. She told him everything. About Beulah, about the dead dog, about finding the body at the foot of the cliff, about her suspicions that the death was not an accident. Pawel was silent for so long that she thought she had lost him. Maybe he thought she was simply an overwrought female.

"You know…" he began finally in his slow manner. "…I walk everywhere on this island to take pictures. If I see a spider among the bushes, I have to go there to photograph it. If I want to take a picture of a butterfly, I have to follow where it goes until it decides to stop. And these creatures don't follow the paths we've made. You see?" Grace nodded.

"So I know this island very well. Better than many of the locals who were born here." Grace wondered what was coming. She thought he was going to shed light on the local crime scene and which village chiefs were in control of the island's underworld dealings. What he had to say was even better than she expected.

"I've been everywhere on this island, you know. I've seen all the birds and most of the varieties of snakes."

"I've heard there are really large Burmese pythons here."

"Yes. I've seen one close up. It was six meters long at least, and its body was so thick." He made a circle with the fingers of both hands.

"Weren't you afraid." He laughed. "No. Pythons don't attack someone who is too big to swallow. No, I'm not afraid of big snakes. I'm more afraid of the little ones. You know, this big." He held two forefingers thirty centimeters apart.

"This big, green and friendly, looks like a piece of plastic, like a harmless grass snake."

"And is it harmless?"

"Not at all. This is the bamboo pit viper and it's bite is much worse than a cobra's. But worst of all are the banded kraits because you don't see them. They look like dry branches on the forest floor and, unlike other snakes, don't move aside when you approach. They are very aggressive and sometimes will come to bite you even if you don't step on them."

"You convince me," said Grace. "I'm never going to photograph wildlife like you do."

"But seriously," he said. "I will take you somewhere. Come for a walk with me this weekend. I have something to show you that might interest you." Grace's curiosity was aroused.

"What is it?" she asked repeatedly. But Pawel was mysteriously silent.

"You will see," he said and when they got off the boat, agreed to meet at Tony's at nine o'clock the following Sunday morning.

Thursday to Saturday were uneventful days. Grace read, lazed at home, walked for miles along forest paths, spent a few hours learning Filipino recipes from Estrella, met Dawn twice, once for breakfast and once for a cup of coffee at her house. They were firm friends now. Sylvie was there when she visited Dawn and was quite unjealous, if that was the word, that Adeline ran to sit in Grace's lap as soon as she arrived. She awoke early on Sunday morning and waited impatiently, like Adeline might have done, for nine o'clock.

She wore sneakers and long trousers, in case Pawel took her walking through the bushes, tossed her reusable cup, wallet and a few other necessities into the green canvas bag and strode down the hill to Tony's. She was sipping her first coffee of the day, a Sumatran blend, when Pawel arrived, apologizing for being three minutes late. He had been taking photographs and lost track of time. He refused coffee but waited till she finished hers and then they set off along the path back in the direction of Grace's house.

They passed the turning to her house and kept going on the main road until he stopped at a familiar turn-off. Grace was puzzled. The steep path leading up the hill to the left was one she knew well, but she said nothing. They climbed for ten minutes. The time was nine thirty by now and they were both sweating when they walked into the clearing.

Grace still said nothing as Pawel walked up to Beulah's cottage and then skirted past it into the woods behind. He was wearing long trousers and thick-soled boots, so Grace was glad she had thought to dress similarly. He forced his way through the bushes, holding the branches before they whipped back against her face. They slogged for a few hundred meters. They were walking through thick piles of dry leaves. Grace worried about snakes, but hoped her shoes were sturdy enough to deflect a strike if she stepped on one. Pawel seemed unconcerned and went as fast as the thick undergrowth would allow. At times he stumbled and slipped over uneven ground, turning back to see if she was managing alright. Soon the bushes thinned and they stood among a copse of trees.

"Here," he said with a flourish, spreading both arms and circling to point all around them.

"What?" asked Grace, totally mystified.

"You don't recognize the trees? We are standing in the middle of at least fifty million dollars, maybe much more. Someone has planted them here. That's obvious, seeing the way they are spaced in even rows. And what is more interesting. All around these trees is a ring of Taiwan acacia. Acacia are nitrogen fixing trees. Not only do they grow fast, they convert atmospheric nitrogen into nitrates and enrich the soil around them. So these acacia trees provide ideal conditions for the incense trees to grow."

"But who did this? How old are these trees?"

"These trees are probably thirty years old. Anyone wanting them for incense would have started harvesting them ten years ago. When the trees are five, six years old they can start making incisions in the bark that will produce valuable resin but it's better to wait till the tree is twenty or more." Grace nodded in excitement.

"I know. I've been reading about the process. The best resin and agarwood oil are produced by trees that are infected with a type of fungal infection. Infection occurs naturally in the wild, but in commercial stands they drill

holes into the trunk and spray something to infect them."
Pawel nodded.

"Yes, there are several ways of doing this. But I haven't
shown you the most remarkable thing about this clearing."

"What is it?" Grace couldn't imagine anything more
exciting than discovering this secret grove.

"Here." He began to walk in a wide arc. "Do you see?"

"The incense trees end here and then the rest of the
forest begins. What about it?"

"The taiwan acacia trees have also been planted
deliberately. Look at the spacing. Two or three trees deep
all around, so anyone walking by would not know there
were incense trees in the middle. So the acacia is not only
here as a fertilizer, but also to hide the incense trees."

"Beulah." said Grace at once.

"The old lady who died?"

"Yes. She died defending these trees from poachers. Or
at least hiding her knowledge of their existence."

"How do you know?" Pawel asked.

"Do you know whose cottage it was that we passed?"

"No. I came past the cottage only once. I was chasing
an unusual butterfly called the Golden Birdwing. It flew on
and on, slowing down often but never stopping long
enough for me to make a quick close up shot. I was in the
middle of this clearing before I realized what the trees
were. I simply thought of it as somebody's plantation and
forgot all about it until your story reminded me of the
wood's value when we talked on the boat. What makes you
think the old lady's death is connected to these trees?"

"I simply know, don't ask me how. Even if the
engineer side of you doesn't, I'm sure the artist side will
understand how I know." He looked keenly at her when
she spoke, wondering if she was mocking him, but saw she
was totally serious.

"This is what I wanted to show you. I hope you aren't disappointed."

"No, I'm not disappointed. I'm so glad I spoke to you on the boat that night. The old lady who died, I got to know her the day her dog was killed. I think in a way, I became her only friend in the world after that. She didn't speak to me because she wanted to protect me. And she was killed before I could persuade her to tell me what she knew."

"So what next?" Pawel asked.

"I wish I knew. I'm leaving for India next week. To see my mother in Kerala."

"For how long?"

"For a month."

"I'll keep an eye on this grove and let you know if something happens."

"Be careful, Pawel. I don't think Mr. Ma should be underestimated."

"Don't worry. I'll think of something."

Chapter 23

Grace flew to Kerala the following week to visit her mother. She landed at the state capital's international airport on a connecting flight from Bangkok. Interestingly, the airport was called Trivandrum International, while the capital city's name had been changed from the anglicized name back to the old Malayalam name of Thiruvananthapuram. It was a generic modern airport and the biggest aircraft to land there were from the Middle East, or Gelf as Nirmala would call it.

She changed money at the airport, got several fat wads of stapled one hundred rupee notes, and hired an air-conditioned Tata Indica taxi with driver for around two thousand rupees to take her to Aymanam. She asked the driver to take her along some of the backwaters if it wasn't too much extra driving. He said the normal driving route would take four hours for the one hundred and fifty kilometers but a detour via a picturesque village called Kayamkulam might be well worth the extra two hours and additional charge of a thousand rupees. Grace agreed at once and sent Sarah a Whatsapp message when to expect her.

The detour to Kayamkulam took longer than planned along minor roads but she was not disappointed at the scenery along the way. She reached Aymanan around six in the evening, stiff from long hours sitting in the back seat of the taxi but otherwise fresh and full of energy. Sarah welcomed her with a long embrace, a reflection of the new closeness between mother and daughter after their recent telephone conversations.

"Are you hungry?"

"No. We stopped at Kayamkulam and I had a late lunch there around three."

"What did you eat?"

"A *chemeen* fry with *parathas*. Fiery, but delicious." She released Sarah, stepped back and took a look around the entrance to the *tharavad*.

"I noticed you have a new sign."

"Yes," Sarah nodded. "I decided to change the name after the renovations from Tharavad Guest House to Tharavad Homestay. I thought it sounds more... well, homely. Inviting."

"And you have new staff..." Grace saw a couple of curious faces emerge from with the house to look at her. "...and uniforms..."

"Oh yes." Sarah looked happier than Grace remembered.

"You look well mother." Sarah really did. She looked older. There were flecks of grey in the long black hair tied carelessly at the back. She was wearing a blue silk salwar with fine red thread needlework, and in place of the usual churidars, white leggings made of some clingy synthetic material. Sarah did a quick double take at the word mother. Grace had not called her that since childhood. She had always called Olivier dad, but Sarah was simply Sarah, as though to emphasize the distance between them. But now, Sarah realized, Grace had deliberately used the word mother, stumbling awkwardly on the unfamiliar syllables, trying it out on her tongue.

Sarah could see changes in Grace since their last meeting. Not only was her daughter a year older, there was an undefinable change. Features or expression? More serious? No, not really. She seemed more relaxed, much lighter than before. At the same time there was increased depth and maturity. It was like the ocean after a storm, when everything has been swept clean and skies are blue again, but still a slight swell remains in the water like the memory of a fearful hurricane past.

Sarah took all this in wordlessly, looking at her daughter with mixed emotions. Sarah herself looked vital, healthy and happy. The pinched look Grace remembered, and the constantly nagging bossy attitude that had so irked her had disappeared. Here was a confident fifty-nine year old woman who had recovered from the turmoil of Olivier's death and the subsequent decade of financial uncertainty. At the time she returned to Kerala from Malaysia and came to live in the *tharavad*, she had faced the additional burden of not really belonging to the place and of having to look after her mother. Amachi had lived two years after Sarah's return to the *tharavad*. They were trying years for Sarah. She had grown as a person, and managed brilliantly, re-learning the slow ways of life in the Kerala countryside, the small-mindedness of tradition, the social structures that underwent rapid change as thousands of people emigrated to work in the Middle East, returning with more wealth than they had ever dreamed of.

Most of these emigrants were reasonably well educated, living frugal, thrifty lives; being tolerated by the Arab communities for good service but not really a part of them. They returned home after a decade or more of hard work with large sums of money to buy land in their own small towns and villages. The first thing they did when they came home was to build a house larger and grander than their neighbors.' The result was that land prices shot up in the remotest villages of Kerala. Within the past decade, the value of Sarah's inheritance had more than quintupled in value. Sarah held on to the property through the lean years, barely breaking even with her fledgling guesthouse venture. In 2010, shortly after Amachi's death, one of the rich Gelf returnees had made Sarah an offer for a small parcel of land at the perimeter of her extensive property. The parcel was divided from the main property by a commonly used path and was of no use to Sarah, but was ideal for a small shop. The offer was far above the already inflated market price, financed with Gelf money, an offer she could not refuse. Sarah had sold the land and used the money to complete all the renovations that the house needed. The house was completely refurbished, the woodwork gleaming and polished, the newly laid red roofing tiles glinting in the sun, the floors redone with polished black marble as in the oldest grand houses in the area.

There was a new swimming pool, ten guest rooms, four new staff to help Nirmala in the kitchen and half a dozen others to tend to the pool, the grounds, room service, the laundry and the dining room. The staff all wore simple uniforms of pale red linen with "Tharavad" monogrammed on their shirt pockets. The kitchen staff all wore white smocks or lab coats and chef's hats; all except Nirmala who had tossed her head at the suggestion and mouthed an indignant "Oh pinnae!" which was the Malayalam equivalent of sticking a finger in Sarah's eye. Sarah wisely did not insist.

Recently she had hired a young master chef, a graduate from a fine Cochi Catering school and this ambitious young man had introduced a range of daring new experimental dishes. Some of them were absolute disasters, like the fried buttermilk avocado he had served in the dining room one day. Fortunately Sarah had seen and tasted it before it was served. It was taken right back to the kitchen and never passed between the lips of a single guest.

But Sarah encouraged experimentation, so that he produced a string of successful innovative dishes like jackfruit lasagna and his signature dish of coconut sautéed fish in Drambuie sauce. The *tharavad* was becoming a local hot spot and affluent people from towns and villages nearby had started coming for weekend stays because of the quality of the food.

Grace was pleased. She could see her mother was busy from morning to night, but it was a fairly stress-free kind of busy-ness now and in between all her responsibilities, Sarah had plenty of time to herself. There was also Ninan, a distant cousin of Sarah's, recently returned from a successful stint in North America. Ninan had run his own software accounting business in Texas, earned enough money to put his kids through college there, and then returned to India once they were independent. Ninan had good business sense, was looking for something useful to do, and started helping Sarah manage her enterprise. He was not personally ambitious, having earned more than enough in his two decades abroad, but glad for something to do. Sarah had no problem handing over care of the *tharavad* to him if she needed to go away for a few days. Grace saw all this and was glad.

There was also a shift in the ethnic composition of the workforce in the last decade. As economic conditions improved in the southern states, more job seekers emigrated from the north. So Sarah's staff was a polyglot mix of Gurkha speaking Nepalis, Assamese Christian houseboys, two delicate-looking but hard-working girls from Manipur who spoke, what else, Manipuri. One of the cooks was from Calcutta and had brought with her the art of making divine Bengali milk sweets.

The only staff member who seemed not to have grown with the enterprise was Nirmala. Nirmala, who had been the mainstay of Amachi's support, who had catered to all Sarah's needs in the first couple of years, who had loyally served the family for most of her life, who had been solely responsible for looking after the house for nearly twenty years before Sarah arrived, was now a bit of a square peg in a round hole. Sarah had given her the responsibility of supervising the girls who did the housekeeping. Nirmala drove them mercilessly, especially the two Manipuri girls who were good workers really, but Nirmala did not understand their English, the only language they had in common. They were trying hard to learn Malayalam, but she didn't understand their mangled use of this language either. Nirmala was so critical that she drove the two girls to tears. It did not help that the Manipuri girls were both very light-skinned and were therefore automatically considered beautiful by the locals, while Nirmala's own dark-skinned, robust good looks went unappreciated. Things came to a head when both the girls came to Sarah to hand in their notice. Sarah knew they desperately needed the jobs to support families back home, so she refused to accept their resignations, quietly rebuking Nirmala, asking her to restrain her impulsive, scolding tongue and be more gentle with the junior staff.

As a result, Nirmala now walked around with a chip on her shoulder, feeling slighted and undervalued after all the years of faithful service. She thought Sarah was ungrateful and often told her in no uncertain terms how indignant Amachi would be if she were still alive. Nirmala was therefore the only fly in Sarah's *tharavad* ointment, but Sarah kept her on. There was no question of Nirmala's loyalty, and there was no question of Nirmala working anywhere else unless she herself opted to leave.

It was a great relief for Sarah, then, when Grace arrived. Nirmala was affectionate, greeting her with great warmth, telling her, "Gracie *molae*, you should have come home long before." Grace was curiously touched by Nirmala's use of the word 'home.' She had never thought of Sarah's house as her home, but maybe it was a kind of second home, strange thing to say for someone who did not have a first home of her own anywhere except, perhaps, she was slowly creating her own community on an island in the South China Sea.

On the first evening, after the initial half hour spent with Sarah, Nirmala took charge of Grace and showed her everything that was new in the *tharavad*. She was bursting with possessive pride. The way she talked, it was as though all the changes were her accomplishment alone. She showed the new 'gobar gas' plant, the large anaerobic digester that had been built behind the kitchen where the old one used to be. She showed her how all the plant and animal waste produced by the chickens, two cows, two buffaloes, the kitchen and all the dry leaves that were swept from the yard went into the digester where it fermented and produced gas for the kitchen. She showed her the high quality compost that was used in the extensive kitchen gardens. What remained was given free to the people who farmed the land behind the house, so they had started bringing their cuttings and other plant detritus as additional feedstock for the digester.

"And here," she took her along a narrow path and pointed to a small outhouse at the far edge of the property, "is someone who's waiting to see you."

Mystified, Grace followed her to the front door of the thatch covered brick cottage. A familiar figure reclined on a chair, bare-bodied, feet up, resting on the extendable arms of the chair. He was old, but sprang to his feet as he saw Nirmala approach. Grace had a sense of déjà vu as he turned his head back to the darker interior of the cottage and called out to Beena-mol to bring a shirt.

Beena emerged, carrying what seemed to be the same faded shirt she had brought for her father when Grace first saw her six years ago. She saw Grace, gave a shout of surprise, running up to clasp her face with both hands while her father stood beaming in the background, wringing his hands with delight. Grace went up to him and bent to touch his feet in an impulsive gesture of humility as she had once seen Beena do. This was the first time in her life that Grace had made this gesture, and the *vaidyan* was as shocked as Grace herself was.

"*Ayo, ayo, molae! Venda, venda,*" he said, grasping her shoulders quickly to prevent it. But he was affected by the gesture and repeated the word Nirmala had used that had touched Grace on arrival, the word home. Grace's eyes moistened involuntarily and suddenly she knew that, even if she didn't belong here, the feeling of rootlessness that had dogged her existence since her father's death had disappeared.

She was glad to hear that Sarah had allowed the *vaidyan* to live for free on her property after his retirement from active practice. She had even paid for the building of his modest cottage. Beena had trained as an Ayurvedic physician in the intervening six years and was just beginning her own practice. She also offered traditional Ayurvedic treatments to the guests of the Tharavad. This had become so popular that she was now employed two assistants who lived nearby and were on call if any of the guests needed an appointment.

Grace stayed with Sarah for a month. The days flew by. Sarah was able to leave the running of the Tharavad in Ninan's capable hands and took Grace out to the *kayal*. They lived for several days on a motorized houseboat, taking it for rides on the beautiful backwaters, as the mood took them, mooring at sites that took their fancy.

Three days later they drove by car for several hours along winding roads through the Western Ghats to a lake where they toured in a private boat among the islands created by the Periyar dam. This was hilly country, densely forested, and the backed up waters of the dam had created a mid-sized lake dotted with dozens of islands, large and small, creating a natural wildlife reserve. There were reputedly tigers on some of those islands. Tigers are good swimmers and can travel from one island to the next, sometimes one or two kilometers distant, in search of prey.

They didn't see any tigers, but there were solitary nilghai or blue bulls, and gaur. Plenty of deer came down to the water to drink. They saw herds of elephants, extended families that played in the water and also were capable of swimming from island to island. It was magical to silently glide along in an electric motor launch at dusk and Grace thought that not all of man's creations were bad, it was simply greed that drove people to want more than they need and destroy the earth in the process.

This was the first real holiday that either of them had had. For Sarah, her first holiday since Olivier's death twelve years earlier; for Grace her first since that gap year of travel as a twenty seven year-old, nearly six years ago. Sarah had struggled in the intervening years, not much given to expressions of grief or loss, but quietly coping. Grief had not so much affected her words, but rather the intervals between them. Sarah was marked by her silences so that, as a younger woman, Grace had thought of her mother as unfeeling; so unlike the warm, expressive father she had loved and lost. Sarah had understood Grace's reaction, had felt a mother's pain at her daughter's alienation, but not known how to change things. She had neither known how to change herself nor Grace's perception of her. Now everything between them had changed of its own accord it seemed. It was simply the healing of time, Sarah thought as she looked at her daughter's peaceful face.

Grace's features had softened beyond recognition as she sat in the boat and looked out with delight at the thickly wooded hills gliding silently past. For the first time in her life, she was comfortable being with her mother. She realized that she had finally stopped missing her father. Olivier would always be a part of her, but as a beloved memory rather than as a hole in her side.

Grace suddenly understood the meaning of an Inuit saying that she had encountered in the course of her travels. An old man, looking up at the night sky had said, "Perhaps they are not stars but openings in heaven where the love of our lost ones pours through and shines down upon us to let us know they are happy." Sitting in the boat with her mother six years later, she knew exactly what he had meant.

Grace looked at her mother sitting in the shade of the awning of the motor launch and thought how well Sarah looked. She was a woman at peace with herself, despite the verbal violence of Nirmala's frequent explosions. Sarah had fallen into the comfortable routine of a life that had enough challenges to keep her on her toes, but at the same time allowed independence and freedom from want. And Sarah was giving back to the world in many little ways, Grace noted, an example she herself should follow when she was back on the island where she had made her home.

As the launch completed its two hour tour around the many islands of the lake, Grace asked, "All those years, when I was working for Rotterdam Oil and began to find places for them to drill, I was earning a lot of money. You know that, don't you?" Sarah looked at her in surprise.

"Yes. I knew that. Of course I did. You mentioned something of that in your emails to me. I had no idea how much, but I only know it was more than you needed. I was happy for you."

"Mmmm. It was more than I needed... much more...." She spread out her hands questioningly.

"How come you never asked me for money?" Unexpectedly, Sarah laughed.

"I almost did, several times... in the first two years especially, when Amachi was alive and I didn't have as much time to devote to the *tharavad*. But I knew you were busy finding your feet in a new profession, working very hard to prove yourself. I also knew that land prices were exploding over here, and so I could always sell a bit of the property if I needed to make ends meet. Why do you ask?" Grace shook her head.

"It only occurred to me now. I knew you didn't have much, but I was too busy with my own concerns to even ask. I feel bad about it now."

"Well, you needn't. The *tharavad* is doing well; even after all staff salaries are paid, I still have more than enough left over for anything I need... your mother's a very affluent woman now, worth several crores of rupees."

"How much is that?" Grace wanted to know. Sarah compressed her lips in thought.

"Mmmm. Seven, eight crores.... eighty million rupees, that's something more than a million, a million and a half... in US dollars. Perhaps more. Prices are rising, and I don't know how salaried people can ever manage to own homes unless they inherit property like I did. Life is unfair... that's why I make sure to pay the staff much more than the going wage. Nirmala doesn't understand. She's old school, and thinks I'm foolish to spoil the younger employees. Of course, I pay Nirmala higher wages too, but she lives on the premises and has no use for money beyond the occasional fresh set of clothes." Grace laughed.

"I can see that. She's as stubborn as a mule, but I like her."

"She likes you too... you know that." Grace nodded.

"God knows," Sarah continued. "I love her to death and I'll never be able to repay my debt to her, but sometimes Nirmala's inflexibility drives me nuts. It's been so much easier for me, you know, in the few days since you've arrived." After a thoughtful silence, Sarah caught her daughter's eyes.

"You know... when I die, this property comes to you, don't you?" Grace looked uncomfortable.

"Mother! You're good for several decades yet. And you're managing wonderfully. I could never replace you. And besides, I have more than enough for myself. More than the *tharavad* is worth, actually." Sarah's eyes widened in surprise at that, but as the boat was approaching the jetty, she prepared to get off and did not say anything further.

The month was over much earlier than Grace wanted. She was relaxed and rested, much happier in her mother's company than ever before in her life. Whatever feelings of guilt she had brought with her for neglecting Sarah or not helping her out financially had been completely dispelled by her mother's attitude. She also remembered Sarah's words to her in the boat on Periyar lake. The *tharavad* was a going concern, a valuable property, and it was hers if she wanted it. She did not want it, really, but had not told her mother that. At the age of thirty-three, Grace did not really know what she wanted to do. She knew she no longer wished to use her talent to help oil firms find more oil. Her experiences in the Niger Delta had convinced her of that.

Chapter 24

Her home on the island was dark when she arrived. The house was damp with the typical un-lived-in feel of an empty place, but the air smelt fresh, not musty at all. She put some water on for tea, opened the fridge to put in the carton of milk she had bought on the walk home, and found that Estrella had left some covered dishes there. She uncovered them to find rice and what looked like a meat dish with thick brown gravy. Having eaten on the plane, she was not hungry, but Estrella's thoughtful gesture was like another little brick in the edifice of home. She had thought often of Sarah's offer, made as they sat in the launch on the Periyar lake. Did she want to settle down in Kerala and manage a prospering business in the backwaters? A prospect that would have sounded attractive to most people left her unmoved. She was not yet at a point where she could make such long-term decisions.

She slept well that night in her own bed. Although it had been a delightful month's holiday in Kerala, and wonderful to establish such rapport with her mother, a good night's sleep in her own bed was another little brick to support her independence.

Although time changes did not really bother her, she used jet lag as an excuse to sleep late the next morning. In actual fact, she did not know why she slept twelve hours instead of the normal seven or eight. In any case, she decided not to make her own breakfast but to wander down to the village instead. She searched for, and found, her trusty green canvas bag that had been folded and put away in a cupboard by Estrella. She noticed with faint regret that the bag now looked stained and shabby, and the long shoulder strap was beginning to fray at the edges. The thought of looking for a replacement in a shopping mall was unappealing. On second thought, she decided to wait for the annual island market fair when people brought hand-made goods from all the other outlying islands before buying.

She wandered down the main street of the village, making a mental note of things she needed to buy on the way back, and was received with a "Good morning, my dear," by Tony. She perched on one of the high bar stools facing the coffee machine and chatted with him for a while.

He told her of an unusually severe storm that had threatened Hong Kong two weeks earlier, but then changed course and battered the Philippines instead before rattling off further north towards the China coast. Grace told him about her trip to the backwaters of Kerala and meeting her mother again.

"Why doesn't she come here?" he asked.

"I know," Grace replied with a sudden touch of guilt. "Maybe because I've never invited her. But she'd never have the time anyway, busy as she is running her hotel."

"You never know," said Tony. She was on the verge of telling him her old news about Beulah's secret grove of incense trees, but stopped herself. It was not that she didn't trust him. She trusted him implicitly. He was discreet and would never divulge anything to harm another. But these conversations were always in a public place and there was no telling who might overhear from an adjacent room. So she decided to keep the news to herself.

She bought a load of groceries to stock her fridge. Eggs, milk, bread, frozen meat, a few small wedges of various cheeses, olives, oatmeal, rice, breakfast tea bags, herbal teas, sugar, biscuits and a few packets of crackers. The bag was getting heavy to carry now, although she still needed fresh vegetables, so she walked back to her place to unload everything. It was close to twelve and the sun, directly overhead, was very hot; at least thirty-two or thirty-three and high humidity, she reckoned. Time for a quick shower, a cold lunch of Estrella's homemade bounty, and then maybe she'd enjoy a book in the air conditioned comfort of her bedroom followed by a short siesta. The prospect was so inviting her mouth almost watered at the thought, but Beulah's face disconcertingly popped into her mind at just that moment. She was suddenly back, sitting waist deep in the water, while the waves lapped around Beulah's body, splashing her gaunt face while Grace stroked her hair and wept.

Grace was completely shaken by the searing clarity of the sudden image. Certainly she had not forgotten Beulah, but she had hardly thought of the old lady and the incense trees during her month in Kerala. Of course she had mentioned the story to her mother during their time together. Sarah had looked faintly troubled, put an arm around her daughter's shoulder and murmured, "Be careful, Grace." Afterwards no more had been said. But now, the image popped up in her brain with absolutely no warning and she was taken aback. There was no question of lunch and a siesta now. She had to go to Beulah's cottage.

Grace put on a flowing loose white shirt made of thin seersucker cotton and a light pair of three-quarter pants with her open strapped walking sandals. She was covered with sweat by the time she had reached the main path across the island three minutes from her home. She climbed the steep slope to Beulah's with a heavy tread, feet moving reluctantly as the heat sapped energy and fluids from her body, wondering why she was doing this. She knew why as soon as she reached the clearing. The incense tree by the cliff which had been used as an anchor by the police when they rescued her… the incense tree was gone. All that was left was a stump, whose light pink coloring reminded her of the scarred end of an amputee's limb. The cottage door was closed. She went closer and saw a new lock on the door. She walked round to the side window and stood on tiptoe, trying to see into the dark interior.

"Hoi!" Grace jumped back, startled.

A young man advanced towards her, arms waving furiously. He seemed to have materialized from thin air. Of course! He had come up the winding path from the sea.

"What you doing here?" Grace was suddenly equally furious.

"What are *you* doing here? This is private property." The young man looked puzzled.

"Yes, my private property."

"Did Beulah give it to you? Are you a relative of hers?"

"Beulah? Who is Beulah?"

"The old lady who lived here. Beulah."

"Beulah? Beulah? Ahhh! Bo Lai!" Slowly recognition dawned. The young man had an open face, honest eyes with a touch of humor in them, Grace decided. As she watched, those eyes began to crinkle at the corners. Although well-built and muscular, he no longer looked threatening.

"Beulah! Bo Lai! Lai Bo," he said to himself again. "I think you speak of my grandmother, Lai Bo" he said, openly smiling now. "Lai Bo. Bo Lai. Beulah. Are you a friend?"

"Yes. I'm Grace." She held out a hand. He took it, laughing hard now.

"Sorry. I only know my grandmother's Chinese name. Lai Bo. Beulah!" he repeated, shaking his head and laughing harder.

"Sorry. I don't know why. It sounds funny." Grace was laughing herself. Beulah! Such an unusual name for an old Chinese fisherwoman. With the name Lai Bo, Beulah's personality had altered for her completely. Shakespeare was wrong and the ancient Egyptians were right. There is much to a name. In Vedic cosmology, the Universe was created by the vibrations from the first primeval sound. Om. Perhaps one's true identity was locked up in the syllables of one's original name.

In which case, who was she? Grace? Grace Lam, Grace Lam, Grace Lam. She rolled her own name on her tongue while the young man laughed. She felt entirely comfortable with her own name, she decided, and would not change it. But Beulah! The old lady suddenly came into character with the name Bo Lai. Bo Lai! Lai Bo! This was the courageous old woman who had stood up to protect what she loved. The young man had stopped laughing and suddenly looking serious, nodded.

"Grace? You're the one who found my grandmother's body. You were her friend."

"I was not much of a friend, was I?" He heard the sad doubt in her voice and raised both hands in protest.

"You were her friend. She told someone in Yuen Long village and then the headman told me when she died. The people in that village like you because you helped my grandmother."

Grace was unbelievably touched. It was like hearing another stone of the edifice, a large one this time, thudding into place; maybe she was making a home here. She must learn Cantonese, she decided, if this island was where her home was going to be. She had a moment of doubt. If this young man was who he professed to be, how much did he know of Beulah's secret?

"Do you know how your grandmother died?" The young man, whose name he said was Wenbo, looked troubled.

"She fell?" It was a question-statement, and did not hide the doubt in his voice.

"The police and the court decided that she fell," Grace said. He looked at her for a long moment, weighing her up.

"But you don't believe it. Why?" Grace shrugged, looking helpless.

"I wish I knew. I was hoping you might have an answer."

"The village headman knows something, but he won't tell. He simply asked me to come and live here. This house should not stay empty, he said."

"Why did you cut the incense tree at the edge of the clearing?"

"The headman told me to."

"Why?"

"I don't know. I asked him why, and he said something about experience. Old proverb."

"Experience? What proverb?"

"Yes, a proverb," Wenbo nodded. "Headman said, experience is a comb that nature gives you when you grow bald. Now go and cut that tree. Nothing more. So I obeyed."

"What is his connection to your grandmother?"

"He helped her after grandfather died. He helped her get the land on which this cottage stands. He even helped her build it." Grace nodded thoughtfully. There might be several secrets hidden here. If so, she was interested in uncovering only one; the one that involved trees, not personal relationships.

"How old was your grandfather when he died?" Grace asked. Wenbo was puzzled by her question.

"My father was very young when his father died. Why?"

"Nothing. Just a thought… When can I meet this headman?"

"I will have to ask him."

"Maybe the next time you see him…" Grace was thinking it might take a few days.

"I'll ask him now…" He took a black mobile phone from his pocket and made a call, speaking rapid Cantonese. He put a hand over the mouth piece.

"He wants to know why…" Grace thought quickly, didn't want to give him an excuse to fob her off.

"Tell him I have some news about Beulah's death," she lied. Wenbo spoke into the phone some more.

"Okay, he says I should take you to him right now."

Grace was pleasantly surprised and dismayed at the same time. She hadn't eaten all day, only drunk a cup of coffee. It was now two in the afternoon, her throat was parched and she could hardly talk. Her clothes stuck uncomfortably to the small of her back and she felt more trickles of sweat run down her spine. But there was never a right time in this kind of weather.

"Let's go, then," she said.

The walk was not that bad. Grace asked questions and Wenbo replied in monosyllables. He was wearing rubber flip flops but seemed to have no problem skipping down steep bits of the path. When they reached the main path at the bottom of the hill, he flipflopped so rapidly she had to take long quick strides to keep up. They turned to the right off the main street and on a small concrete bridge across a swampy section of the path to a cluster of houses. A grey haired man stood in the concrete front yard of one of the houses and waved. The severity of the concrete yard was relieved by a row of large flower pots, each of which contained flowering plants, freshly watered and carefully tended. It seemed he did not speak English, for he nodded affably at Grace, motioning her to one of three chairs set out in the shade of a large Chinese banyan. He had a rapid-fire exchange in Cantonese with Wenbo. Grace did not understand a word, so she sat down and looked at the view while she waited. The bunch of houses overlooked the swampy area they had crossed, but to her surprise what dominated the view was the opposite hillside with a large flowering bauhinia bush, a small tree really, covered with purple flowers. Seen from here, the swamp itself was covered with white flowers that looked like arum lilies.

It was cool and pleasant in the shade. A pedestal fan positioned in a corner over a large flat metal tray of water blew cool air at them and she enjoyed the rest, wondering if she could ask for a glass of water. The two men stopped talking and Grace looked at the headman expectantly. He sat down and smiled at her while Wenbo disappeared into the interior of the house. He read the question in her eyes and replied with raised hands pointed at the door where Wenbo had entered. He soon returned holding three cans of ice-cold fizzy drinks that Grace normally might have spurned, but today she almost gasped with relief. Wenbo handed a can to each of them. Grace flipped the tab open, taking a long gulp as a cold stream of bubbles exploded in her mouth on the way down.

"You wanted to ask grandfather something?" Wenbo said. "He will talk to you." The headman smiled again, a picture of wordless affability. His gray hair was closely cropped over a round head and his front teeth were discolored, but he looked fit and healthy, in a close fitting, half-sleeved T-shirt and loose three-quarter length black pants. His feet were bare and he had no tattoos as far as she could see that might connect him to triads or the underworld. Grace had been thinking furiously on the way down about what she could ask without prying into personal details that did not concern her. She had decided to start with questions about the death of Doodle.

"Beulah seemed convinced that someone killed her dog on purpose. Do you know why?" Grace noted that he involuntarily smiled at the name, as Wenbo had done. To them the old lady had not been Beulah really.

"I mean Lai Bo," she said, correcting herself. The headman raised a hand as though to ward off apology, then answered, looking at Wenbo.

"My sister told me that too, but did not tell me why."

"Do you think she was correct?"

"Most of the time the world does not care what we think." Grace waited for Wenbo to translate more. It seemed the headman had replied with two sentences, and Wenbo had translated only one. She looked enquiringly at Wenbo who remained silent.

"But I care what you think," said Grace. "I do not think of Beulah as a foolish old woman. I think she was very wise, and I cared about her opinion, as I believe you do." The old man hesitated for a long time before replying, choosing his words with care.

"Sometimes bad people get angry for very little things. I think dog barked at them when they came up the path."

"Why would they come up the path instead of landing at one of the piers if they came by boat?"

"I don't know."

"So do you think Beulah, sorry, Lai Bo, was protecting something? Did the men want something from her. Did they come searching for something?"

"They come from far away. The men… I think they are not from here… from…"

"From Mainland China?" He made a mixed gesture, half shrug, what does it matter? half head shake, do not know for sure.

"From far away," he repeated. "Not from Hong Kong." Grace could see this interview was not going to get her any further unless she could find a way to establish trust and break the circularity of the conversation. First of all, she had to be sure that the headman was someone she herself could trust. Obviously, if Wenbo was right and the headman had helped Beulah start a new life after her husband's death, he had been on her side. But money nearly always changes things, changes people.

"After Lai Bo's tragic death, I went for a walk," Grace said conversationally. Puzzled, Wenbo translated. Grace was instantly sure Wenbo had no idea which way she was going. She was watching both of them to assess their reactions. The headman's face was impassive when Wenbo translated, although by now Grace was certain he did not really need a translator.

"I went for a long walk… through the jungle… behind Lai Bo's cottage." The headman's face remained as impassive as before, but there was a sudden, deeper stillness to his immobility that made it a certainty. Grace now was sure he knew about the valuable stand of incense trees hidden by the acacias. And now the headman knew that she knew. The old man was silent for a long while, then looked enquiringly at her, waiting for her to speak again.

"Do you know what I found?" she asked provocatively. He simply shrugged and waited to hear.

"I found it is not healthy to go there. The acacia trees grow too close together and the undergrowth is too thick.

There is the danger of stepping on a banded krait resting among the dry leaves." The old man smiled faintly and nodded.

"Yes. Poisonous snakes can be dangerous. That is why no one has gone there for many years. That is why I asked Wenbo to go and live in Lai Bo's cottage."

"It is very lonely in her cottage," said Grace. "So even though Wenbo is a young man, perhaps he should have a dog for company." The old man nodded thoughtfully while Wenbo looked thoroughly mystified by the fact that he was translating a conversation about himself for them. But he translated anyway and did not ask why.

She spoke to the headman for a further five minutes, Wenbo translating, but by the time she left, Grace was certain of four things. Firstly, the headman really had not needed a translator. He had understood her well enough. Perhaps his passive knowledge was much better than his spoken English, or he was easily embarrassed by mistakes. In any case, it had been tactically wise for him to have a translator. He had had more time to formulate his responses and also to observe her as she talked and listened. Second, Grace was certain now that he was a potential ally, or at the least, was not responsible in any way for Beulah's murder.

Third, both Beulah and Doodle had been murdered, and their deaths had something to do with the trees. The fourth point was one that she had picked up on, not from anything spoken, but from several faint but unmistakable similarities in the body language of the two men. The way they walked, certain small movements, the way they sat. There was a story here whose details she would never know. That story was not important. Something that had happened between Lai Bo and the headman five or more decades ago. Those had been anxious, troubled times, and a young widow would have been in need of a male protector. Or perhaps there was a real love story here; a story whose truth could never come out in the open.

The story itself was not important to Grace, but its implications were. If Wenbo was, as she suspected, really the village headman's grandson, then it was doubly certain that the headman was protecting Beulah's secret grove and would keep a watchful eye over the young man.

Chapter 25

It was past four o'clock by the time Grace returned home. She was starved and thirsty. She drank a liter of water, opened a can of beer and ate Estrella's food cold, straight from the fridge, too impatient to warm it up. She sat down to drink the beer and felt sleepy immediately after, remembering her foregone siesta. She dropped onto the bed for a half hour nap. When she awoke, it was five the next morning and still dark. She remembered vivid dreams. Beulah had appeared in them as Lai Bo, a beautiful young Cantonese woman six decades younger, in a country ravaged by war and revolution. Survival was a struggle made doubly difficult by marriage to a drunken sluggard who beat her at every turn. And then an unlikely savior had appeared in the guise of her husband's younger drinking companion. His name was Yu Lin, an 'old soul' they said, despite his drunken ways. He had stopped his friend from beating Lai Bo on several occasions, and after this they began to exchange the secret looks of love, invisible to the outside world, but instantly recognized by both. Somewhere, sometime, in those troubled years, Wenbo's father had been conceived and been born as the drunkard's son.

Grace woke in her darkened bedroom and remembered the dream story in every detail. The floods of panicked refugees fleeing from a China racked by Mao's revolutionary zeal. The furtive dashes for the border, any border, out of the chaos caused by random upheavals, after sudden denunciations, arrests, trashing of personal possessions, after the looting of treasures, after the desecration of centuries of tradition and history. Everything ancient and old thrown out as rubbish, the good with the bad; bound feet together with accumulated wisdom, books, old pottery, priceless vases. Across Hong Kong's border with China, desperate refugees threw themselves into the water, on anything that would float and carry the weight of a fleeing body or two; coracles, country boats, junks, sampans, bundles of coconut husks. They paddled or floated or prayed or sank or swam and hoped for wind and current to take them to the relative safety and comfort of British-administered Hong Kong. Some of the refugees came ashore onto an unknown, thickly wooded island, scrambling up steep slopes rising from the shore. Starving as they were, they killed and ate anything that moved, cutting down trees for cooking fires.

When they found some of the trees were incense trees, they harvested more of the wood for the island's markets, and later moved to the neighboring island as illegal refugees and squatters in the tenements mushrooming in the hills around Hong Kong. Some of the desperate refugees who landed on the island, among other Hong Kong territories, were desperate enough to rob and kill people living in isolated cottages far from the villages. Lai Bo was a young mother with a little son in a solitary cottage at the edge of the shore and when she was widowed, no eyebrows were raised when a young Yu Lin moved in to protect her and look after the little boy.

Grace lay in bed and listened to the birds waking up in the trees around her. The dream was very clear, and replayed like a film in her mind. There was no need to enquire whether the images were true or not. They fitted in with what she had observed so far, and the real truth was a technicality that did not matter. This story was morally true and would provide an operational frame of reference to keep her mission on track. Her mission? She realized that sometime in the night, together with the dream, something had coalesced in her mind. The determination to bring the murderers of Beulah and Doodle to justice. Yes, even Doodle, whom she had only known as a canine corpse in her arms, even Doodle's murder would be avenged. In Grace's book, the little mongrel had as much right to justice as Beulah did.

But were the images thrown up by her dream true? The truth did not matter to Grace any longer. In the years of her youthful desire to improve the world, to right wrongs, to ensure justice, she had time and again come face to face with all the ambiguities of the human condition. During her years in the Niger Delta, prospecting for Rotterdam Oil, she had repeatedly come face to face with what economists call the 'resource curse.' She had seen that a region endowed with immense natural wealth slipped into worse poverty than before that wealth was discovered. Some of it was the natural profiteering instinct of a global enterprise like Rotterdam Oil. They were in business to make money and they made no pretense about it. But there was also the petty greed of powerful people within poor communities, people who were willing to barter the well-being of their own communities for the sake of private gain. She had seen that there were always local elites who trampled on the rights of their own compatriots and did not care as long as their own pockets were lined with a portion of the oil company's profits. It was all this that had moved her to stop working for Rotterdam Oil, to plead to her friend Hans van Houten that she had lost the ability to divine the presence of oil in the ground and leave the firm. Yes, Hans van Houten had become a mentor and friend. She still kept in touch with his wife and daughter and considered them part of her extended family. In fact, when she resigned from Rotterdam Oil, they had urged her to stay with them for a while and either reconsider her decision or mark time in comfort while deciding what to do with her life.

No. It did not matter what the truth was. There was a certain *menschliche* correctness to the images in her mind, quite in keeping with her assessments of character. She was sure she could and would work with Yu Lin to find the trail that led to the killers. She was also quite certain that the physical deeds, the murders, had been done by Mr. Ma's two thugs or others like them, but their guilt was a mere technicality. She wished to bring Mr. Ma himself, or whoever was behind the thugs, to justice and, with all her capacity for visions and seeing beneath the surface of things, the new powers that she gradually felt growing within her, she knew she needed allies; she could not do this alone.

Grace got out of bed, did a few morning stretching exercises on the terrace to welcome the dawn, then went downstairs and made herself a cup of tea with two slices of toast and butter. She felt too lazy to make filter coffee and did not feel like drinking instant coffee, of which she had a couple of sachets left. A large hornet buzzed into the room through the open French windows to the balcony. She maneuvered a while carefully with an old newspaper until she was able to nudge it outside again, then drew the sliding screen doors shut and ate her toast, looking for the dove that called every morning, hidden in the tree opposite. She knew from Pawel that the bird was probably an Emerald Dove, a shy, elegant bird whose cry was just like that of its homelier cousin, the common spotted dove. Apparently many of them lived on the island but were hardly ever seen.

She finished her tea and toast with the last of
Raymond's honey, then went in to shower, changing into a
light pair of trousers and a long-sleeved seersucker shirt.
She still had some vegetable shopping to do. Perhaps she
would cook something today or prepare a fresh salad for
the evening. And she looked forward to finishing the half-
read Donna Leon. As always, armed with the now shabby
canvas shoulder bag and the re-usable coffee cup, she
headed for Tony's, the first stop of her shopping trip.

She was down in the village, about to turn right
towards Tony's bar in the direction of the main pier when
she heard the loud banging of drums, clashing cymbals and
several other discordant wind instruments from the left,
from the direction of the little temple. It was a temple to
Tin Hau, the Goddess of the Sea. In traditional times, when
the people of the island lived from fishing, Tin Hau had
been the most important deity on the island, and the annual
festival to Tin Hau was celebrated with much enthusiasm.
A large crowd had gathered to watch the celebration. A red
dragon danced in front of the temple. The young man
carrying the dragon's head on his shoulders was sometimes
visible as he leapt high in the air and the dragon shook its
fearsome colored appendages. An unfortunate second
dancer had a less eye-catching role at the lion's rear end;
restricted to a painful half-crouch, he nevertheless had to
match the lion head's impressive dance, furiously wagging a
hand held whisk that was the tail. Both dancers were
quickly exhausted and other young men took over,
changing places so adroitly there was hardly a break in the
dancing.

After a while, the dance ended and visitors crowded to
the door of the temple, carrying bundles of incense sticks
and large offerings made of colorful paper. They paid brief
homage to Tin Hau at the door of the temple and planted

the lighted incense sticks in the deep sand basin at the entrance. They then took their offerings of wealth, in the form of paper money, colorful red and gold houses, toy cars and other desirable objects for the afterlife, all made of paper and sold at rows of small temporary stalls lining the path. They took these offerings and burnt them in a brick-lined, covered fireplace that was carefully tended by a village volunteer. After this there was a short display by some of the young people of the village who wore white T-shirts with the green-printed logo of their martial arts training group. They individually demonstrated vigorous punches, kicks and body movements in turn, with each display earning applause from friends in the audience. Grace noted that it was an older man, who normally drove one of the small village vehicles, the one with the Ho Chi Minh beard, transporting goods for people along the narrow paths, who earned the most applause.

There was a playground opposite the temple. A high bamboo structure had been built to give the entire large playground a temporary ceiling, and in this large hall there were nightly performances of Chinese opera to coincide with the Tin Hau festival. It was obvious from the way people greeted each other that many of the attendees were locals who lived elsewhere, in Hong Kong, mainland China or much further abroad, and had returned here on the occasion of the festival to meet relatives and friends. Grace recognized the Canadian accent of a Chinese woman watching the dragon dance and chatted to her.

"Yes," the Canadian visitor told her. "My family is from here, but I've lived in Vancouver most of my life. Tin Hau is one of the most important deities in Hong Kong. There are seventy or more Tin Hau temples in all of Hong Kong."

"A Goddess of the Sea makes sense in a fishing community," Grace remarked.

"Yes," said the woman. "The legend goes back to the Song dynasty in China. In Fujian province lived a girl who was an excellent swimmer and often swam far out to sea. She was called 'silent girl' because she did not cry when she was born. One day there was a storm at sea when her father and four brothers were out fishing. Silent Girl meditated and rescued them in her dream. After that she climbed a mountain and went to heaven."

"Does Tin Hau mean silent girl, then?"

"No. This girl lived in Fujian province in the tenth century and is known as Mazu, or Mother-Ancestor. The Hong Kong name means 'Empress of Heaven.'"

"I see," said Grace, who really did not see, but took this not-knowing in her stride, since there were always local variations of deities' stories. She was used to this from India, where Sarah had told her several stories from the Ramayana and Mahabharata, but while travelling in the country she kept hearing endless local variations of the same stories.

"And the dragon dance?"

"Actually, there are two dragon dances," the helpful Canadian woman told her. "A red dragon and a green dragon."

"I saw only one."

"The other one will appear shortly."

"Red and green, like yin and yang." Grace nodded knowingly.

"Not at all. It's another legend," laughed the woman. "Once in heaven, Mazu had two guardian generals, who fell in love with her. They're traditionally represented by the two dragons; a red dragon with one horn, and a green dragon with two."

"I see only one."

"The other one will be along shortly. You can bet on it," the Canadian said confidently. "I grew up here. This place has changed a lot, but some things never change!"

Sure enough, another dragon appeared ten minutes later, a long, green one, followed by a raucous procession, many of them carrying enormous smoking incense sticks. Several *gweilos* were part of this procession, obviously long-term residents who had gone native and were thoroughly enjoying their part in the festivities. Clearly, whatever the truth of triads and gangsters living here, this was a relatively crime-free and harmonious island society, and Grace was glad to be even remotely a part of it.

Grace had moved a little away from the temple, back towards Tony's coffee shop and the ferry pier. The green dragon passed her at a narrow point of the path with shops on either side. As the colorful dragon's head passed her, it suddenly made a giant bound in the air, coming down right beside her, shaking its head fiercely. Grace was pressed back against the wall of a shop, unable to move further, hemmed in by the crowd in front and behind her. The dragon's ruffles shook fiercely in her face and Grace shrank back in alarm. A couple of *gweilos* in the procession laughed at her fear, not realizing that she had seen the snake tattoo on the dancer's hand. Grace ignored the laughing crowd and fought her way out of the narrow passage past the dragon's head and made a beeline for the pier.

"Good morning, Grace," Tony greeted her as she passed, but she did not stop to acknowledge him. Another two minutes half-running she came past the fish restaurants to a stretch of path with a clear view of the pier and slowed down. As she suspected, the sleek black cruiser lay low-slung in the harbor, dominating the near side of the pier. Several tourists crowded on the pier, admiring the boat, but beyond the beautiful lines, there was little to be seen behind the smoked glass that hid the interior.

Grace walked slowly to the pier, stood alongside the boat. There was a name painted on the side. Lucky Jade and a serial number with four eights in a row. 8888. Eight was considered the luckiest Chinese number, and symbolized money. Obviously the boat's owner had plenty of it. She drew her mobile phone out of the green bag and took a photo. Then she deliberately stepped back, hoping someone was watching from behind the smoked glass and took a leisurely photograph of the length of the boat. A man wearing white ducks in the upper deck cabin waved a hand to say she should stop, but she ignored him and took several more. A gangplank slid smoothly out from the ship to the pier. The man in white now stood on the gangplank, smiling and inviting her to board. Grace walked on immediately, determined not to show fear. She tried to look cold and haughty as she boarded, and was obviously successful, for the sailor's smile faded abruptly to be replaced by a stony gaze. But there was a hint of respect in it. Grace did not speak. Simply waited.

He opened the door to a luxurious air-conditioned saloon, softly lit, tastefully furnished with matching beige leather sofas and armchairs. Seen from the inside, the smoked glass was perfectly transparent. The sailor bowed his head and indicated a seat. She ignored him and remained standing in the center of the room, trying to look perfectly at ease. He gave a little shrug and disappeared through a door.

"Miss Lam. Miss Grace Lam," said a soft voice. Grace turned. He was very short, very pale, and had firm, regular features in a rounded face. His nose was flat, but his black eyes were almost Caucasian, and Grace wondered whether he was like her, of mixed parentage, or had had the fat removed from his eyelids. Grace was perfectly content with her own unmistakably slanted eyes and would never think of changing them, but she knew that a procedure called blepharoplasty was popular in some parts of China.

"You know my name."

"Yes. Mr. Ma makes it his business to know anything that affects his business." Grace was puzzled by his use of the third person, certain this was the elusive Mr. Ma himself, the source of the poison.

"And I affect your business?" asked Grace incredulously. Mr. Ma seated himself in an armchair and inclined his head to Grace, indicating another. She sat down and looked at him expectantly.

"Grace Lam," he recited. "Thirty-three years old, spinster, father deceased 2003, Olivier Lam. Mother, Sarah Lam, née Chacko, currently residing at Aymanam, Kerala, runs a successful business, Tharavad Guest House. You worked four years and eleven months for Rotterdam Oil, earning a total of five million, eight hundred and ninety-five thousand US dollars in that time. You resigned, even though your employer wanted you to stay. What made you do that?"

Grace said nothing, too shocked to speak. This was not what she had expected. She had expected a gangster, someone crude and threatening. There was something almost likeable about this man's gentle face and refined manner. When Grace didn't speak, he went on.

"Now here you are on this outlying island, living a simple existence, earning hardly any money. I can see more success ahead of you. You have undoubted talent, but you will never earn the kind of money you did at Rotterdam Oil. Why are you here?"

"Burnout. Quite common in the field." Mr. Ma raised two deprecating hands, palms outward.

"Please! If it was burnout, Hans van Houten would have given you paid leave of absence for as long as you wished." Grace could not hide her astonishment. How could he know what had been said in a conversation in the privacy of Hans's Rotterdam office? She suddenly felt very vulnerable, as Mr. Ma probably intended, and realized he was merely toying with her, enjoying his power. All at once, she recalled the image of Beulah walking with a dead mongrel cradled in her arms. And then Beulah's own lifeless body in her own lap. Enough of these games of wealth and power! She rose to her feet.

"Lai Bo was my friend," she said simply. "I believe she was killed, although the police report says otherwise. I want her killer or killers brought to justice."

"Is that all you want?" He spoke so softly she thought she had imagined the words. Grace nodded, but did not speak. For now, she thought. For now. The interview at an end, Mr. Ma inclined his head again. The sailor materialized at her side as if by magic and respectfully escorted her to the door.

Chapter 26

The Sea Superior had just docked at the ferry pier and was disgorging its passengers as Grace strode down the teak walkway with its polished chromium railings.

"Grace!" Dawn and Raymond were coming off the ferry with Sylvie and Jacques following. They looked at her in astonishment as she emerged from the black cruiser. Jacques' astonishment was laced with more than a tinge of envy.

"How did you manage that? Do you know the owner?" Grace shook her head.

"Let's get away from here. How about a coffee somewhere?" Adeline trotted up and held on to Grace's hand, forcing her to slow down. Grace was really glad to see her five friends, but wished it hadn't happened right in front of Mr. Ma's boat.

"Come. Let's get away from here," she repeated. Dawn sensed Grace's urgency and shushed Raymond's emerging question.

"You heard her. Let's all go sit down somewhere; the Green Cottage, maybe."

The Green Cottage was full when they got there, so Grace agreed to accompany them up the hill to Dawn's house and fill them in about her encounter with Mr. Ma.

There was more space in the Leroys' living room, so they went there, led by Adeline, while Dawn and Raymond hurried to fetch food and drink for a spontaneous potluck lunch. Sylvie and Raymond were the cooks of the two families, so they retired to the kitchen end of the large open room, while Dawn joined Grace on the sofa, Adeline firmly esconced in Grace's lap, thumb in mouth, fingers of the other hand curling Grace's straight hair. Jacques was dying of curiosity about the cruiser.

"So tell me Grace, how do you know this man? What is the boat like? Did you see all of it?"

"Sorry, Jacques. I hardly saw anything of the boat. I was only there for twenty minutes to talk to Mr. Ma and only remember being in a luxurious salon, about twice the size of this space here." Jacques was obviously disappointed by the answer, so he busied himself getting glasses and cold water for them to drink. Dawn was the only one who seemed to have an inkling of what Grace was up to, having seen her visceral outpouring of grief at Beulah's death.

"Grace," she said gently. "Are you in some kind of trouble?" There was silence in the room. Raymond and Sylvie, busy in the kitchen, stopped what they were doing. Jacques set some glasses on the table and stared.

"Why should she be in trouble?" he asked.

"Because." said Dawn.

"Yes, because…?" Jacques was skeptical.

"Because I know Grace was troubled over the death of a dog. And because I saw how she mourned the death of a lonely old woman."

"What has that got to do with a rich man and his boat?" asked Jacques who was obviously still obsessing about the cruiser. Grace looked round seriously. Raymond and Sylvie moved out of the kitchen and stood closer, oblivious to the knives in their hands, concerned by the gravity of her manner.

"You have become… all of you… are… dear friends. You have helped me make this a home…"

"You found Frank for us, and Adeline is totally in love with you," Sylvie interjected, her accent even more French than usual. Grace smiled and nodded.

"There's a pot of gold on this island," she said slowly, looking round at each one in turn. "A dog and an old woman were killed because they came in the way of people looking for it. Knowing that it exists is bad enough, but to know its location can be fatal. These people will kill, I know it. That is why I haven't told you anything."

"How big is this pot of gold?" Raymond wanted to know.

"I can't say for sure. I heard an estimate of fifty million dollars, US. After reading a bit more on the internet, I think it could be twice that... I have no real way of knowing."

"So, you heard an estimate... which means someone else knows," Dawn noted shrewdly. "Someone on this island?"

Grace smiled at her. The remark was typical Dawn. She was direct, compassionate, witty, missed very little, and Grace thought this woman was quickly becoming her closest friend. Grace stood up, displacing Adeline from her lap, suddenly restless and uncomfortable. It was an awkward situation, so she decided to be frank.

"I can tell you about it, but two people have died trying to protect this secret. The fewer people know, the better. Do you want to know?"

"No," said Dawn and Sylvie together, immediately. Jacques was doubtful, curious, but he joined the other two. "No."

"Can we at least know what it's about? That way I can stop my mind spinning about uselessly, speculating." This was Raymond. He looked around at the others in apology. "Sorry… I can't help it." Grace was suddenly relieved.

"I can tell you that. It's a grove of precious incense trees, well hidden, growing on this island."

"Of course," said Raymond. "Heung Gong! Fragrant Harbor. Agarwood trees." Jacques' eyes widened.

"The cruiser! Ma Wood Industries. He's after it." Jacques looked very worried. "And you went to see him? Are you crazy? He knows of you now?"

"I followed my instinct and went to warn him off this island. He already knew everything about me. About my mother, about my work for Rotterdam Oil, about my father's death, the rest of my career… everything."

"Well, in that case, he has private detectives and also knows we are friends," said Sylvie, looking at her small daughter. "We're all vulnerable, even Adeline. Wouldn't it be better for us to know more, so that we are more aware of the possibilities… of danger, I mean…kidnapping."

"No," said Raymond immediately. "We know enough for now. It might be dangerous to know more."

"I think we all need a drink," Sylvie suddenly interjected, looking at her husband. "Especially you, Grace, who has been in the lion's den, so to speak."

"And what a den…" muttered Jacques, still eating his heart out with envy about the cruiser as he moved to do his wife's bidding.

Grace was suddenly moved to tears by the varied reactions of her friends. These five people were special, she realized. Although worried by the news, not a single one of the adults had shown concern for themselves, but rather for each other, herself included; Sylvie worried most of all, naturally, about Adeline. She suddenly felt lighter. An invisible cloud lifted from her heart; a cloud that she had forgotten resided there, the nagging sense of loneliness that sometimes assailed her in solitary moments; the sense that most other young women her age were married, with families to look after, while she herself chose to live a single existence in pursuit of an unknown goal, waiting for the flowering of elusive talents that had been half-promised by a few muttered phrases in broken English by an Ayurvedic physician a thousand miles away and half a decade earlier.

Chapter 27

The following week she was busy with a visitor. Gordon came to Hong Kong on a business trip and after two days work in the city, moved over to spend an extended weekend with her on the island. Gordon was unmarried, but they were good friends, just that and nothing more. Grace had known for years there was a girl-friend in the background somewhere in England, but had never met her. Over the years she came to know more.

Her name was Marjorie and she was Jamaican. Gordon was absolutely devoted to her, but she had a congenital heart condition and could not travel. She was on a waiting list for a suitable transplant donor. Gordon loved to travel and, despite devotion to Marjorie, was obviously delighted to get away from London and doubly glad to catch up with Grace.

She took Gordon to Macau one day, saying, 'you have to see this show.' They took in a performance in the purpose-built arena of the House of Dancing Water and afterwards Grace was pleased because Gordon shook his head and said. "What was that!" in admiring disbelief of what he'd seen; ninety minutes of acrobatics and breathtaking feats that seemed to explore the limits of human ability; all this in an arena where mid-sized lakes appeared and disappeared in a matter of seconds.

Although ferries ran between Macau and Hong Kong twenty four hours a day, the show ended late so they decided to stay overnight in one of Macau's oversized casino hotels rather than risk missing the last midnight ferry from Hong Kong to the island. Being thrifty, they shared a room and slept beside each other like siblings. Later, when Dawn came to know of her stay in Macau, she had asked, " Wasn't it expensive to take two rooms for just a few hours?"

"No, it wasn't," Grace explained. "Casino hotel rooms are cheap. They want you to stay and gamble. Besides, we shared a room." Dawn raised her eyebrows, but said nothing.

"It was nothing like that," Grace protested. "Nothing like that at all. He's one of my oldest friends and I enjoyed meeting him again."

"I didn't mean to pry," Dawn apologized. "It's just that… Raymond and I have talked about you…"

"Oh?"

"You're such a lovely woman, Grace. Really! Now, don't protest. This is not flattery. Sometimes… sometimes we wonder why you're alone and Gordon seems like such a nice man. We were hoping…" Grace walked over and hugged her friend.

"God knows, Dawn, I'm no vestal virgin. I do feel alone at times. It's been much better after getting to know you both. But Gordon has a girlfriend he's devoted to… no, there's nothing between us except friendship. I've known him since we were children."

There had been a flurry of telephone calls to Grace's mobile number in the week Gordon was visiting. Most of them were requests to help locate precious lost objects, and Grace had set up a series of appointments in Hong Kong for the following Monday. She was up early, stopping for a coffee on the way to the ferry when Tony said, "I have some news for you. I remember you asked me about Ma Wood Industries." Grace was intrigued, but there was only five minutes till the eight o'clock ferry and her first appointment in the city was at nine.

"Is it urgent? Can you tell me tomorrow?"

"Of course it can. Just something I heard. See you tomorrow." Tony waved her away.

She had three clients that day, two in the morning, both in the Causeway Bay area of the city, and one in the afternoon on Hollywood Road in Soho. The morning's visits were a mixed bag. The first was to an apartment on the thirty-first floor of an ugly high rise building near Times Square. She took the metro to Causeway Bay, walked to Times Square and rode up a creaking lift, and wondered at the size of the apartment she entered. It was at least three times the size of the normal cramped city apartment, lavishly furnished with outsized wooden furniture. To Grace's untutored eye, the pieces looked very old and valuable. Her host, Mr. Thomas Wong, saw her glancing at a chair and was immediately voluble.

"Chippendale style," he said, patting the chair, proudly. "American colonial period, around 1800." He then informed her at length about the cabinet maker who had made the pieces. Apparently Thomas Horton's cabinets fetched extremely high prices in the US and these particular drawing room pieces were the only ones in Asia. Mr. Wong sounded as if he could talk about antique furniture for hours. His eyes lit up as he spoke, and only stopped when Grace asked with feigned timidity if she could have another chair to sit on. He stopped short in surprise then burst into affable laughter.

"Miss Lam. Please sit. Sit down anywhere you like. These pieces are all here to be admired and also to be used."

Grace managed to steer him to the purpose of her visit, which was to try and locate a missing document; his father's original handwritten will that bequeathed all the furniture to him. After initially accepting the terms of the will, Mr. Wong's brother James had come to know that the original will had disappeared and was now contesting the bequest, saying that without a will, the valuable pieces should be divided equally between the two brothers.

"How did it happen?"

"Well, you see, my father was very ill… on his deathbed, here in this house. I looked after him after my mother died. James was a loving son, came to see our father every day. One day I showed him the handwritten will, about how our father wished to see his assets shared and that I should have all the furniture because of this large apartment. He agreed completely. There was no problem between us. One day, soon after our father's death, I happened to mention that I had misplaced the will. Couldn't find it. The next day, he brings this complaint that I'm cheating him of the inheritance and he should have half of this furniture. It would break my father's heart to see this collection divided."

Grace asked a number of questions. When did he die? How many people were in the house when he died? Was James in the house? Where had he kept the will?

"That's the problem," Thomas confessed. "It was such a stressful time. I normally file all important papers away, but I have no recollection of doing that after showing it to James."

"Might he have taken it?"

"Before this incident, I would have sworn not. But now I'm not so sure."

"Try and recall the moment after James read the will, did he hand it back to you or put it down on the table?" Thomas Wong screwed his face up in an agony of recall.

"I honestly couldn't say for sure, but I think he put it down on the table, right here."

"Assuming he put it down on the table, and it was forgotten there, might someone, your wife or a maid, have tidied it away without knowing its importance."

"My wife would definitely have known its importance. But…"

"But?"

"…we have a maid who comes to clean. Maybe she put it away somewhere." Grace noticed a Chippendale style writing table in one corner of the room; the kind whose slanted writing surface sometimes has a hollow storage space beneath it. Thomas Wong caught her glance.

"That one's called a Davenport desk. They're small, you see, so they can be easily transported. They were designed for military use…" Thomas was getting carried away again, talking about furniture.

"What about the compartment under the writing surface? Have you checked there?"

"Nonsense! I never open it. It's always locked." Grace went over to the desk to see for herself. There was a keyhole and no key in the lock. She idly traced a forefinger on the underside of the lid and pushed up.

"It's not locked now," she said, as the lid came up, revealing a couple of plastic folders within. Thomas Wong jumped to his feet in disbelief.

"What? How… Who could have…" He snatched the folders from her, glanced inside, then looked up in a wordless gesture of thanks.

"Miss Lam… I… you've helped…" His eyes filled with sudden tears and he fumbled for a tissue.

Grace's second visit of the day was equally successful within a short time. She had allocated two hours for this visit, which was to help a widow find a lost diamond ring. Grace found the ring in five minutes, again by simply asking questions, without the help of any intuitive insights. When the woman said she had last worn the ring five weeks ago, Grace remembered that there had been a cold spell that week.

"Do you wear gloves?" she asked.

"Only when it's very cold," the woman replied.

"Show me where you keep them." Grace inspected the draw which held several scarves and two pairs of cotton and silk gloves. She pressed down on the gloves, felt a lump in one of them, and drew out the missing ring from inside. It was such an easy find that she tried to refuse payment. The grateful client insisted, however, thrusting two thousand dollars into her hand.

The second visit was so short that Grace had an hour and a half before her third appointment, with an antique dealer on Hollywood Road. She walked down the road till she came to Possession Street and stepped into a Vietnamese eatery she knew of. It was full. There was a small queue outside the door, always a good sign, but the queue seemed to be moving fast, so she waited to be seated. Five minutes later, she was sitting down to a serving of delicious Vietnamese spring rolls on a bed of delectable edible greens, washed down with a refreshing glass of watercress honey.

The last case of the day was particularly interesting. An antique dealer had bought a collection of things from a recently demolished village house. Among the old furniture, pottery and artifacts was a landscape painting in the classical Chinese style. The antique dealer had catalogued it as a work from the late Qing dynasty, around 1850, by a famous artist from Yangzhou. However, two weeks ago, an elderly man had walked in, claiming the piece was his brushwork, done six decades earlier. He had been forced to hide it during the late nineteen sixties because of the turmoil of the cultural revolution. If it was a genuine Qing dynasty work, the painting was potentially worth several million Hong Kong dollars. The elderly painter produced an almost identical twin of the antique dealer's painting as proof of his skills. On hearing about the case on the telephone, Grace had conditionally accepted to mediate in this matter, more out of curiosity rather than conviction that she could help resolve the issue.

"Why not use carbon dating?" was her first question on entering the antique shop. The antique dealer was a suave, dark-suited Hong Konger named Hule with quick answers to all her queries.

"Not in this case. Not accurate enough. Remember Elmyr de Hory? The international art forger? His fake Modiglianis are available on eBay, listed as forgeries, and still command good prices. He managed to fool the world's greatest art houses for decades."

"Don't they have more sophisticated tests now?"

"Yes, but still, there's an element of doubt. Miss Lam, look at the painting, meet this man, talk to him. Perhaps you can tell me if he is who he says he is." He quickly raised both hands before she spoke.

"I know. I know. You warned me. No guarantees. However, I've heard about you from a friend, and I want your opinion."

Grace spent the rest of the day on the case. She asked to be alone in a room with the painting and nothing else. The vibes from all the other antiques in the crowded space were driving her crazy. After some telephoning Mr. Yule found a room in an adjacent office that had been completely stripped awaiting refurbishment. He left her alone in the bare room with unpainted concrete walls, a solitary chair and the painting. Grace brooded in the spartan surroundings till late in the evening, walking around, examining the painting from all sides, sitting still for long periods with eyes closed. The only images that came to mind were of Mr. Ma talking softly in his boat. He frightened her, she realized, with his soft voice and the threat implied by his extensive knowledge of her life. She shook her head and tried to focus on the painting, but her thoughts kept drifting. She was annoyed with herself, and this further disturbed her receptivity to outside influences. She left Yule's office at seven that evening, promising to return the next day for another try. Maybe she should would have better luck after a good night's rest.

She stopped for coffee the next morning on her way to the eight o'clock ferry.

"What I wanted to tell you ...," Tony said, seamlessly continuing the conversation of the previous day. "...you had asked about Ma Wood Industries…"

"Yes," said Grace eagerly. She had been thinking so much about the painting in the night that she had temporarily forgotten Mr. Ma. "Do you know anything about him."

"No. I know nothing about Mr. Ma," said Tony, handing her a cup of Sumatra blend, his special flavor of the month. "But you know that large house for sale in Mo Tat Wan?"

"No. I've not heard."

"Yes, well there's a house for sale in Mo Tat Wan village for eighteen million dollars. More than six thousand square feet with its own private jetty and a separate guest house. The only way to get there is from the water. I can't think who would want to buy such a place. Who would want that kind of isolation?"

"Someone with lots of money, and doesn't want people to see what they're up to, perhaps."

"I suppose so," said Tony shaking his head in wonder. "It takes all kinds... I heard yesterday that Ma Wood Industries is thinking of buying it. I assume as a guest house or holiday home for its employees." Grace took a sip of coffee and looked at her watch.

"Thanks for letting me know, Tony. I've got to go for the boat now. Cheers."

She went back to the solitary room next to the antique store and spent hours with the painting, examining it from different angles, sitting quietly and allowing the mood of the landscape to work on her. She talked to the elderly artist for nearly two hours in the afternoon, with the antique dealer translating for her. It was late in the evening when she finally turned to Mr. Hule.

"I'm sorry," she said. "I don't have the faintest clue about this. I'm afraid my instincts, or sixth sense, or whatever, are completely asleep on this one."

"Miss Lam. Try, please try. You can't let me down like this." Grace had encountered this before. Clients who took her failure as a personal affront. Mr. Hule was one of those. He went on trying to persuade her to give an opinion, pleading and threatening by turn. For some reason, his trader's mind, accustomed to suspicion, had convinced him that Grace knew more about the painting than she was letting on, for nefarious reasons of her own. His manner turned from cajoling to bullying and threatening.

"I'm sorry Mr. Yule. But I warned you. There was no guarantee, and there's no charge." She picked up her by now shabby green canvas bag and swept out of the dealership, angry with herself for having wasted the extra day of effort. She should have listened to her instincts and said no in the first place. Perhaps it was a warning. She had allowed ego to make the choice. She would not let that happen again.

Chapter 28

Grace felt a bit low the next day and kept to herself. Estrella came for her two-hour clean up, as cheerful as usual. This lifted Grace's spirits a bit. She ate a vegetable stew with fine vermicelli noodles that Estrella cooked for her in typical whirlwind fashion and then sat down with a book she had bought the previous week. She read a few chapters and was considering a late siesta when the phone rang. It was Dawn and she sounded very serious.

"What's the matter?" There was a slight hesitation at the other end.

"Oh, Raymond and I were wondering if we could drop by later in the evening, bringing our dinner with us."

"Of course. What a lovely surprise! See you around seven then."

Grace was even more surprised when Sylvie and Jacques turned up too, with Adeline all dressed for bed and packed into a comfortable stroller with wheels big enough to negotiate the island's occasional steep flights of steps.

"Hello. This is an even nicer surprise," said Grace, a bit flustered, since she had only four of everything; placemats, glasses and cutlery. Sylvie came up the front steps and hugged her warmly.

"Don't worry about us. I'm French. I've bought everything we need for food."

"She's brought enough to feed an army," said Dawn. "Fortunately, I'm a one-woman army!" Adeline took her usual proprietary place in Grace's lap, sucking her thumb, and promptly fell asleep. When she was fast asleep, Sylvie carried her to Grace's bedroom, while Dawn unpacked the food onto the dining table. Raymond carried a dining chair to the living room and sat with arms folded over the backrest, looking very serious. Grace sat still, knowing something was coming, but with no idea what. All four of her guests were looking at her expectantly, including Dawn who had just returned from laying the table.

"Shall we eat or shall we talk first?" asked Dawn.

"I just have to know what's going on," Grace exploded, unable to contain herself. Dawn and Raymond looked at each other doubtfully. It was Raymond who spoke.

"A young man died today on our island."

"Wenbo?" The name shot out of her mouth. Grace knew the truth as soon as she asked the question, did not need to see Raymond's nod of confirmation. She stood up, agitated, restless. How could her instincts have let her down so badly? First with the painting and now this murder? She was shaken. There was no question in her mind that it was murder. Grace rose to her feet.

"I've got to go and see Yu Lin." Raymond held up a hand.

"Best wait till tomorrow. I'll come with you. Might be useful to have an interpreter."

"What kind of an accident was it?" Grace asked grimly.

"No one knows for sure. I only heard it was an accident in a fishing boat."

"Who told you?"

"I went to buy chicken from the frozen food store and overheard two customers talking. Such a tragedy. Such a nice young man. I couldn't help listening while waiting to be served, but then one of them said, 'so soon after Lai Bo's death.' So then I interrupted the conversation to ask. Lai Bo's grandson? They said, do you know him?'

"You heard nothing else? What kind of accident?" Raymond shook his head.

"I didn't want to ask any more. They were already giving me curious looks."

"I wish I'd taken Yu Lin's telephone number," Grace fretted. "I always assumed I could reach him through Wenbo." Dawn drew close and put an arm around her shoulder.

"Don't blame yourself, dear. There's nothing you could have done. You couldn't have known."

"I'm not sure," said Grace miserably. "I had dreams a week ago, of illegal logging somewhere, in a thick forest, pitch dark, one LED lamp and two men working with a power saw, cutting down trees, I don't know what kind of trees, and then a phrase…"

"What phrase?" asked Raymond. Grace struggled to remember, but could not, so she searched her cell phone for the recording she had made the morning after the dream.

"*Ngay Mai. Ngay mai…*"

"What does it mean?" Raymond asked. "It's not Cantonese for sure."

"I don't know. I couldn't even see the people who were cutting, but it was obviously illegal. They felled five or six trees, and then the phrase… I asked around the next day, but no one seemed to know."

"Did you try Facebook?" Dawn asked. "You could post it on the Island Resident's Facebook page and ask." Grace looked doubtful, but said, "I'll try." She posted the query right then from her mobile phone.

"Let's eat now," she said.

Sylvie had brought a classic boeuf bourguignon as her contribution to dinner. Grace offered the leftovers of Estrella's cooking and Dawn had a large number of cheeses and three different kinds of crackers and bread from the local bakery. No one protested greatly when Grace suggested opening a bottle of fine Bordeaux that she had been saving for a special occasion. And after the first one they opened another simply because it was there. Jacques was beginning to pour wine from the second bottle when Grace's mobile phone pinged. It was a Facebook message from someone with a Chinese name on the Island Community website.

'*Ngay Mai*. Could be Vietnamese. My wife is from Vietnam and she says in her language it means 'tomorrow.' Grace nodded, as though the word were meant for her personally.

"Yes, tomorrow…" and looked at Raymond, who nodded.

"Yes, tomorrow I'll come with you to see Yu Lin."

Chapter 29

Grace slept soundly that night after they left, but she awoke early in the morning with a startlingly clear memory of a dream. It was an exact repeat of the dream a week ago, just as brief and unrevealing as the previous one. But she understood more this time, because it was a second viewing and because she now had a geographic context. This was Vietnam, she decided, and the man who said '*ngay mai,*' was not a native speaker. Somehow, the way the word rolled around on the man's tongue made it sound foreign. On the other hand, the other shadowy figures doing the cutting, she could hear a soft patter of indistinguishable words, but again instinct told her these were Vietnamese minions, doing the bidding of a Cantonese or Chinese employer.

She got out of bed, made herself a cup of strong coffee in the hope that it would sharpen her thinking and sat down to trawl the internet for background. She searched for 'illegal logging Vietnam' and found, to her surprise, an article about forestry that said forty-four percent of the country had wood cover, although only one percent of this was primary forest. She also found that an agarwood species, *aquileria crassna* was registered as endangered by the Vietnamese government. Presumably the best specimens of this variety yielded the same high quality oils as the Hong Kong incense trees did, and fetched similar astronomic prices.

There were other reports of illegal logging in Laos. In Cambodia and neighboring Thailand there was yet another species of valuable tree whose stands were being illegally decimated, this time for the recreational pleasure of youth in Europe and America. And where the youth of Europe and America went, the children of western-educated elites worldwide followed in droves. This news was a real eye-opener to her.

Grace had often been to parties during her college days in England where many of her acquaintances, and a few of her friends, had taken Ecstasy. Their euphoric reactions to the drug had stopped her from trying it, but at the same time Grace had regarded Ecstasy as a relatively harmless recreational drug. Now she pieced together a great deal of evidence from disparate sources that showed her people could die or face injury at both ends of the trade.

At the consumer end were frequent reports about addiction, fatal overdoses, and a range of other symptoms. In addition, there was always the risk of adulteration by suppliers trying to fatten profit margins. Grace had always seen the misuse of drugs as a law-and-order problem in affluent societies. Now her search for Lai Bo's killers brought her to the cusp of a problem for underprivileged people in the poorest countries of the world, as their natural wealth was plundered for quick profit.

In the Cardamom Mountains of Cambodia was a tree known by several different names in English; Selasian Wood, Saffrol Laurel or Martaban Camphor Wood. The tree, identified by its botanical name *cinnamonum parthenoxylon*, was being extensively and illegally harvested here, close to the Thailand border. These forests were among the largest remaining stands of intact tropical forest in Southeast Asia. Ironically, these forests had flourished and been preserved because of Cambodia's civil war and its aftermath. The remnants of the hated Khmer Rouge had taken refuge in these forests, and so the area remained largely pristine.

Grace read an article entitled *How to Make Ecstasy*. The recipe went into fine detail on a pharmaceutical industry website, with bland remarks indicating the criminal portions of the process. "It all starts with the sassafras plant. The bark of its roots, or sometimes its fruits, are taken and oil is extracted from it. This gives you safrole, a colorless or slightly black oil, the primary precursor for all manufacture of MDMA. Safrole... (has to be) bought from black market sources at very high prices. Even solvents (are) not available without question, and some ingredients require(d) a poisons license."

She even found an award-winning documentary on YouTube showing a group of Cambodian forest rangers hunting down illicit safrole distilleries. The documentary was called "Forest of Ecstasy" and gave the impression that the people running this trade were criminal elements from Vietnam. According to the documentary, Cambodian peasants who performed all the hard labor of harvesting, building distilleries and then carrying out the safrole oil earned just about two US dollars a day. Grace was convinced that Ma Wood Industries was a major player financing this illegal logging. It had to be someone with influence and money enough to buy off key members of Cambodia's ruling kleptocracy. The film also stressed that the illicit loggers were well armed, often much better than the forest rangers. Grace was sure that Mr. Ma was either a high-ranking member of the People's Liberation Army, or had good contacts within. Mr. Ma had a lot more to answer for than the deaths of Lai Bo and Wenbo.

She breakfasted on buttered toast and Marmite, a taste acquired during her schooldays in England, before going down to Tony's at nine to meet Raymond. Tony had heard of Wenbo's accidental death, but knew no other details, so she walked with Raymond to Yu Lin's house.

The front door was shut but Yu Lin opened as soon as they knocked. His face was impassive, his close cropped grey hair and grizzled beard showing no signs of strain. Only his eyes showed the depth of his grief, all the worse perhaps, because he could never acknowledge that Wenbo was his grandson. Grace didn't know what to say, so she folded her hands in a gesture of prayer and bowed her head to him. He acknowledged the gesture with a light hand on her shoulder and ushered them in. They sat facing each other on the three chairs that had stood in the courtyard on her previous visit with Wenbo.

"I am sorry to hear of the death of Lai Bo's grandson." Raymond translated. Yu Lin nodded silently, head bowed to hide his grief.

"I want to go and live in the cottage, with your permission." Grace's request was like a sharp knife that cut through the tendons of his grief. His head whipped up, eyes black, wide, moist. A slight shake of his head. No.

"I must."

"Why?"

"A promise I made." To herself. To Beulah. Mr. Ma terrified her, but she would face up to her fear. Instinct pushed her, an inner voice she could not ignore. She must take care. Protect herself. She knew. Not sure how, but she would find a way. Raymond, translating, protested inwardly. There would be time later. With Dawn to help him dissuade her. To object to Grace's foolish plan.

"Too many accidents. I cannot allow you." said Yu Lin.

"I will know before they come," said Grace, with a confidence she did not feel.

"You did not see what happened to Wenbo."

"I know. I was distracted by other work in the city. It won't happen again." He looked at her for a long time, scanning her face, reading her grief that mirrored his own. Finally he nodded. To him, it was important to protect Lai Bo's secret. A secret that was perhaps his own as well. To Grace, it was important to avenge Beulah's death, and Wenbo's. She would find a way to stop Mr. Ma. Grace sighed with relief when Yu Lin nodded, but felt at the same time as though a suicide wish had been granted.

After the visit to the headman's house, Raymond invited Grace up to lunch.

"Dawn's expecting you," he said. Dawn asked no questions when they arrived. She served lunch immediately, a bowl of pasta with homemade tomato sauce garnished with fresh basil leaves from her kitchen garden. Raymond sprinkled his helping liberally with grated parmesan and spoke, sauce dribbling from his chin.

"She wants to go and live in that house." This was to Dawn, who understood immediately what he was talking about. She looked enquiringly at Grace, who nodded. To Raymond's surprise, Dawn said nothing. He paused with forkful of spaghetti poised incredulous in mid-air.

"And you think it's a good idea?"

"Of course not." said Dawn.

"You've not said anything."

"What I think isn't important. I want to know what Grace thinks."

"I know it sounds crazy…" Grace began.

"You bet," said Raymond. Dawn raised a hand to stop him.

"I know it sounds crazy…" she repeated. "I have to go and live in that cottage, otherwise I won't know what Mr. Ma will do." Dawn nodded.

"In a counter-intuitive way, I might be safer staying there," Grace added. Dawn nodded again.

"I'll come and stay with you." The sudden wave of relief made Grace realize how much she'd dreaded her own decision.

"I can't allow it. I won't." Even as Raymond spoke, he knew that, short of physical force, he could do nothing to stop his wife.

"I can't allow you to do that Dawn." Grace added her voice to Raymond's. "It's too dangerous."

"Nonsense! Risky? You're telling me about risk? I made a living for three years, voluntarily throwing myself off mountains. I've more lives than a cat, else I wouldn't be here."

"Well, in that case…" said Raymond. Dawn looked at him, fully expecting an outburst.

"…in that case, maybe it's time to bring my engineering expertise out of retirement."

"What about the police?" Dawn asked. Grace dismissed the idea immediately.

"No. Mr. Ma is so well connected, he probably has paid informers everywhere, including the police. So by notifying the island police we'll simply be tipping our hand."

"I must agree with that." said Raymond reluctantly. "I fear Grace is right." Raymond rose from the table, muttering, 'if you can't beat 'em…' Dawn grinned.

"Where are you going?"

"See you at the cottage later," Raymond said as he left the room.

Raymond examined the contents of his long-unused tool box in the cramped storage space. It contained mostly fine tools for working with electronic components, but there was a large pair of heavy duty pliers. He made a shopping list, then went down to the village electrical and water works shop carrying the tool kit. He bought a new lock, two of the largest screwdrivers he could find, duct tape, insulation tape and several other small screws, tacks and nails. Then he went up to Beulah's deserted shack, broke open Wenbo's shiny new lock and set to work.

Dawn and Grace trudged up the hill carrying backpacks and trundling small suitcases with a change of clothes, food for their dinner and breakfast, as well as a couple of bottles of wine and beer. Their reasoning; if they were going to camp out, they might as well be comfortable and enjoy themselves. Raymond was still at work, looking quite tired by the time they arrived.

"What have you been up to?" Dawn asked. He proudly explained.

Later that evening Grace phoned Pawel to tell him about Wenbo's death and that she was staying in the cottage overnight. He was very concerned and offered to come and spend the night up there instead of her, but Grace reassured him she had Dawn for company.

"Promise you'll call if you need help. I can be there in fifteen minutes." Grace promised.

As Grace hoped, her dreams returned when she moved to the cottage. The dreams were nothing like she expected, though. No visions of illicit agarwood harvests or clues about tattooed men.

A boy, fat, pasty faced, dressed in thick blue serge shirt and matching trousers. He squirms in terror before a tall Chinese man in a high-collared black Mandarin coat. The man holds a leather strap in his hand and nods to the boy. The boy whimpers, covers his head and face with his arms. A soft order, repeated twice, and the boy turns his back with a little moan. The black strap descends repeatedly. The man's head turns and Grace sees long black uncut hair, tied in a pigtail that reaches to the middle of his back.

The boy no longer moans. He is unconscious. The cheap blue clothing slowly turns dark as blood oozes into them from his back and flanks.

Grace sat up in Beulah's bed. Dawn, stretched out on an air mattress on the floor beside her, snored softly. The pedestal fan that Raymond had carried up for them whirred unseen in a dark corner of the room. Grace quietly opened the cottage door and looked into the moonlit clearing, hearing only nature's quiet night whispers. She thought of what she had seen. Why was the boy whipped, and by whom? She walked to the edge of the clearing, looked down at the pale zigzag of the path down the cliff, saw Beulah fall on a dark night as she tried to escape from Mr. Ma's thugs. How did Wenbo die? An accident in a fishing boat out at sea, just out of sight of land, Yu Lin had told her. He got entangled in his own fishing net when he dived overboard to free the fouled outboard propeller of his grandmother's fishing boat. Strange he would jump overboard when he could have swung the propeller up out of the water to free it. The police presumed the net had snagged on a rock somewhere. Wenbo's dying struggles had freed the net and trapped him. Grace felt a hand on her shoulder and her heart skipped a beat.

"Grace!" It was Dawn at her side. "Is something the matter? I had such a fright. I woke up and you weren't there." Dawn looked like a pale angel in a diaphanous nightgown in the faint moonlight. Grace told her about the dream.

"I can't connect it to Beulah or her grandson." Dawn stood at the edge of the cliff and looked down. The tide was up but the small arc of sand was still visible.

"This is how they'd extract the timber of course," Dawn said conversationally. "They'd harvest the trees, throw them off the cliff and pick the floating logs from the water. Brilliant! All they have to do is get rid of us first."

"Yes," said Grace. "We know this, but sadly Wenbo didn't. That's Yu Lin's secret burden. He blames himself for not telling his grandson."

"His grandson?"

"That's his second secret," said Grace. Dawn put an arm around her shoulder.

"Come on. Let's try and get some sleep."

Chapter 30

Dawn and Grace slept every night in Beulah's cottage for two weeks. To her consternation Grace slept dreamlessly. The nights were getting hotter and they both regretted the absence of an aircon unit. Fortunately most nights there was a cool breeze blowing in from the sea, but on still nights the fan simply stirred the listless heated air and did little to relieve the sticky damp.

They both slept badly on such still nights and were glad to return to their respective homes, turning on the air conditioning immediately for welcome relief. Raymond offered several times to relieve them but Grace always refused, believing that, if anything dangerous were to happen, she would be warned by a premonition. The lack of dreams was beginning to trouble her, although she did not admit it to her friends. Sylvie invited them to lunch very often. Grace was glad to spend time with them, eating sumptuous French and Vietnamese cuisine.

"How did you learn to make all these dishes," she asked, overawed after another flawless serving of *banh xeo*, a crispy crepe bulging with pork, shrimp and vegetables.

"I grew up in France with all this," Sylvie explained. "Vietnamese is a part of French cuisine now."

"I didn't know that."

"Yes, you see, when it comes to food, the French have no racial prejudices. I also like to make a good curry…"

"You'll have to try the restaurant in my mother's guest house, then."

Pawel called, after they had been living in the cottage for a week. "I've been thinking…" he said in his typical measured voice. "I would like to come to the cottage and install something, if I may…" Grace was puzzled, silent. "…for your own safety," he explained.

"Oh, yes, yes of course. But Raymond has already set up motion sensors out by the cliff and along the pathway. We activate them at night before we go to sleep and floodlights come on when something moves."

"And how does it work?"

"Very well. The lights go on several times a night. I had no idea there was so much night life on this island," Grace laughed. "All kinds of small animals and birds." Pavel nodded.

"There are two different kinds of owls here, Scopes and the fish owl, both active at night. And," he added, the smile in his voice almost visible, "if you see an eagle owl, call me at once. I haven't seen one yet. They are very rare."

"I hear animals too." Grace added.

"Yes, there are feral pigs. A farmer's domestic pigs that escaped and went wild…" Pawel was thoughtful, silent for a minute.

"Maybe it's not good for the lights to go on for every small animal that passes. I have an idea. I will talk to Raymond first."

Pawel came back two mornings later, just as Grace and Dawn were going back to their homes after another night in Beulah's cottage. He was carrying a huge backpack, an armload of two by fours and digging equipment.

"I have taken the day off," he explained with a shy smile.

"What have you got in there?" Grace asked, curious.

"In the construction business, there is always need for explosives," he said enigmatically. "I will tell you this evening what I have done. I have explained to Raymond already and he will help me later."

He was still there when they returned to the cottage at dusk. He bent his tall frame to wash his muddy hands outdoors with a bucket of water. He looked very pleased with his day's work.

"What have you done?" they asked. He straightened. "Much better than I thought," he beamed, and proceeded to show them.

Dawn and Grace slept better after that. Their lives became a routine of nights spent at Beulah's flat and days living their normal lives at home. Apart from Pawel, Raymond, Sylvie, Jacques and Yu Lin, no one knew that Dawn and Grace spent their nights at the cottage. As days passed and Grace's anxiety subsided, she began to dream again. It was usually the same dream, deep in the gloom of some tropical forest; the typical deafening noise of insects. Then dead silence at the sound of footsteps. The intermittent buzz of an electric saw.

With each repetition of the dream, Grace began to understand more of what she was seeing. They couldn't use more powerful motor saws because of the noise, so had to rely on smaller, portable electric ones. Two saws, stopping in turn as the cutting teeth overheated. There were two more men, making the felling cut with a long crosscut handsaw. They worked fast and were good at their work, repeatedly inserting a felling wedge before the weight of the tree pinched their saw blade. The work began in the evening and went on late into the night. Grace assumed that these people worked at other jobs during the day. They did not speak, but because of the phrase she had heard the very first time, weeks ago, assumed the trees were being felled somewhere in Vietnam. She was also sure the men were employed by Ma Wood Industries. She knew these people were merely his minions, so tried to focus her dreams on Mr. Ma, but it was as though Mr. Ma was shielded from her dreams by his wealth and the one-way smoked glass of his cruiser.

Estrella came to clean Grace's flat one day, looking distressed.

"What's the matter?" Grace asked.

"I've been looking for another job, ma'am. Haven't got anything yet."

"But why?"

"My employer's moving to Singapore."

"If you need a place to stay, you can move in here," Grace offered.

"Thank you ma'am. But if my employer moves away, I have to go back to the Philippines."

"Don't you have a residence permit?"

"It's connected to the job. If my employer leaves, I have to leave."

"I see. How long have you worked here?"

"Seven years in Hong Kong and three years on this island."

"But you have automatic permanent residency rights after seven years! That's what they told me at immigration."

"For you, ma'am. Not for domestic workers," said Estrella apologetically, as though she were to blame for the law. Cushioned by her wealth, Grace had been granted a one-year residence visa on presentation of her bank balance, with the promise of annual renewals on application thereafter for seven years, when she became eligible for permanent residency.

"This is distressing news. Estrella, I have no idea how long I'm going to live here, but would you like to work for me?" Estrella beamed.

Grace spent the next two days on the third floor of the Immigration Tower in Wan Chai, learning the intricacies of life as a domestic helper in an affluent country. Domestic workers had limited rights, she learned, and their restrictive work visas only allowed them to work for one employer. Any change of employment meant that they had to leave the country and re-enter only when a new visa had been issued. This bias ensured that employers had enormous power over their helpers' lives. Grace was appalled at the way the labor laws were stacked against the domestic workers, with the result that they had no easy means of help when they were abused in the workplace, where employers had 'home advantage.'

Grace had of course seen other examples of laws that discriminate in favor of the rich and affluent in many countries. In the case of her former employer, Rotterdam Oil, she had had first hand knowledge of how the giant corporation legally avoided taxes in most countries they operated. They incorporated national branches of Rotterdam Oil around the world as individual companies in obscure places, island tax havens, for example. In these small nations, even a one percent tax on the turnover of a large corporation amounted to a huge windfall for the nation, not to mention its elites.

Until now, the problems faced by domestic workers in countries like Hong Kong and Singapore had been only newspaper items, but now she saw the true face of it. One more battle to fight, she thought, but this is not for me, not now. For now, I will give this one young woman secure employment and a home.

The formalities were quickly done. Grace filled out several forms, guaranteeing a modest monthly wage of a few thousand Hong Kong dollars plus food and lodging. She decided that Estrella could have the spare bedroom, and if Sarah ever decided to come and stay she would have to share Grace's own double bed. As for other friends like Gordon or his mother Susan, she would simply book alternative accommodation for them elsewhere on the island.

Estrella's visa arrived in the post ten days later, after processing through the government's efficient machinery. Grace sent Estrella on a day trip to Macau. This was Estrella's first time there after ten years in Hong Kong, so she was delighted to go. The day trip was sufficient to cover the formality of departure and reentry with a new visa, so Estrella's official employment with Grace began after her return from Macau, although she had moved in three days earlier.

In moments alone, Grace wondered again about her role in life. She had been on this island for eight months now, and was slowly acquiring the trappings of semi-permanence. Her rented house was filling up with little odds and ends collected on walks through the island, clothes she bought on infrequent trips to Hong Kong, a few brass pots and wood carvings, mementoes from her frequent trips to the Niger Delta of Nigeria a lifetime ago, two rosewood and teak wood inlaid tables, gifts from Sarah, Olivier's little mahogany work desk, the only thing of his she owned. Maybe this was the substance of her life and it was foolish to think she was marking time while waiting for her talent, her real mission in life, to emerge.

In her five years with Rotterdam Oil, she had made frequent trips to the Niger Delta. Initially she had felt there was some greater purpose in her presence there. The oil fields of the Niger Delta were located in more than five hundred fragmented sandstone pockets, which meant there was a lot of drilling to be done. RotOil's geologists did a great job of pinpointing where the oil and gas reserves lay, so that one in two drilling attempts struck oil. But Grace's own strike rate had been close to one in one. That meant, practically ten out of ten spots where she recommended drilling struck oil. This saved the company a great deal of expense. Thanks to Hans van Houten, the promised percentage of outlay for successful strikes was increased and flowed into her account as the oil flowed into RotOil's barrels.

Only a handful of people within RotOil knew what she really did for the company and how much she earned. To the company's geologists in the field, Grace was an employee with a touchy-feely title and task. To them she was a social scientist studying the impact of oil wealth on local communities. Her job was ostensibly to liaise with the local authorities and warn the company of local grievances or potential conflicts of interest. Grace had thrown herself into this bogus role whole-heartedly. She had seen that the aftermath of the Biafran war of succession still played an important part in the psyches and perceptions of the people in the area, especially the older ones. She was able to sense the resentment some of the people in this area felt; resentment not directed at the foreign company extracting this natural resource from under their feet, but caused by the perception that the predominantly Muslim population of the north and northwest benefitted disproportionately from their oil wealth.

Grace travelled the Delta's small villages and towns with an interpreter, using her special connection with Hans van Houten to plead for more investment in local infrastructures. Hans did try. Small amounts were spent in some cases, but cash injections from abroad were useless without reliable local partners. In any case, the intellectual climate within the company was dominated by hard-hatted engineers and petroleum geologists, practical technocrats. These men, the overwhelming majority were men, had no use for public relations and emotionally charged ownership issues that were internal Nigerian matters. They preferred hard-nosed, uncomplicated dealings with Nigerian lawmakers who operated, in the years of military dictatorship, with no political oversight and were a law unto themselves.

Three years visiting the Niger Delta had convinced Grace she no longer wanted to be part of this enterprise, but Hans had persuaded to stay. She stayed for another two years out of a sense of loyalty and affection for him and his family. Now, seeing how absurdly grateful Estrella was for the little thing Grace had done, she wondered at her own discontent. She discussed it with Sarah during a late morning phone call.

Here is Estrella, Grace explained, separated from husband and children in a foreign country. She has to make do with twice weekly phone calls, participating in their lives like a kind of benign ghost. How does she do it? How does she stay so positive and cheerful? Am I ungrateful that I can't be satisfied with my privileged position? Sarah was sympathetic to her dilemma, unable to provide answers.

"I don't know much about the human condition Grace. All I can say is, after Olivier died, I felt lost and alone. Utterly alone. I couldn't connect with you. And then, over the years, I've been so busy, first looking after Amachi, and now the running of this place. I'm content with life now. I'm grateful for what I've had, for what I have now. I'm grateful you're you, my daughter. I'm proud of you and your accomplishments. I love this little corner of the world, despite its many frustrations and limitations. And you? If you tell me you're vaguely dissatisfied, then I see myself in you, as I was at your age."

"I wish," said Grace, "I wish I could bootstrap myself to wisdom. To stop feeling the way I do."

"These are attitudes," Sarah told her. "Simply regard them as such. Attitudes are like clothes, easily changed. It's a matter of practice. And choice. Choice and practice."

Grace felt better after the conversation. At the other end, Sarah put the phone down, quietly content. She noted this was the first time Grace had asked, as an adult, for her mother's advice.

Dawn and Grace continued their routine as the weeks passed. Sometimes they laughed about it.

"We're becoming like an old married couple."

Raymond was growing tired of nights on his own, but didn't complain. Sylvie said she missed Dawn's company, especially as Jacques was so often away and wondered if she should accompany them with Adeline some nights.

"Absolutely not," said Grace firmly.

The dreams began again at the end of July. They were not frightening in the least, merely puzzling.

She saw a repeat of the pasty faced Chinese boy being whipped by the black coated mandarin with his waist-length pigtail. This continued in a sequence for several nights and Grace realized she was seeing something that had occurred repeatedly over weeks and months, or perhaps years. She had no idea of the geographic context of the scene. There was always the same vague background, uniformly gray. It could have been a scene from an earlier century in the courtyard of a traditional Chinese house in a *hutong*, or else it could be taking place in the slums of a modern city.

She saw scenes of civil unrest in a Chinese city. People wore Mao suits. Many young people marched in the streets. Some of the young people wore colored rags around their heads with red characters painted on them. Many elderly people were beaten and punched and kicked by the young men. There were young girls too, kicking and shouting just as loudly as the boys. This was clearly the Cultural Revolution, and it was the country's intelligentsia, meaning anyone who owned books, anyone who could read and write, being targeted. Grace thought she recognized one of the older men singled out for punishment. It was the tall mandarin, no longer in a high-collared black coat. His head had been shaved. His trousers were in tatters and his torso was bare. Much of the collective fury and invective seemed directed at him, organized by a lean, wiry youth chanting slogans into a megaphone.

There was one macabre scene where the youth made the older men run in single file. Following an order shouted through his megaphone, Grace saw each man awkwardly bend and grasp between the legs of the man in front. They ran like this, gasping and stumbling while children pelted them with muck and jeered. Anyone who lost his grip on the penis of the man in front was assaulted with whips. The men screamed with agony as each bent runner tightened his hold on the crotch of the man in front in order to escape the whipping. Grace woke, nauseated, certain she knew who the wiry youth was.

She will win who knows when to fight and who the enemy, thought Grace in grim parody of Sun Tzu. Mr. Ma had terrified her on his boat with his soft voice and his knowledge about her. As the dreams continued and her knowledge of the boy's life grew, her fear began to drain like water from an unplugged cistern. She no longer feared

Ma. Neither did she hate him. *Hate only weakens the hater.* But stop him she would. She would make sure that his criminal despoliation of the world for quick personal gain was stopped.

Dawn and Raymond had reserved a summer holiday for the entire month of August. This had been done the week before they first met Grace in April. They had booked flights to and hotels in Turkey and Greece. Dawn was reluctant to leave Grace alone in Beulah's cottage and talked about cancelling the holiday. Raymond had looked forward to the Mediterranean holiday, but hid his disappointment and tried to cancel the online bookings. When Grace came to know they would only get a fifty percent refund for cancellation, she put a foot down.

"I absolutely insist you go." she said. "I'll be alright. If it'll reassure you, I'll find someone to spend the nights with me."

"Who?" Dawn wanted to know.

"I don't know yet. Estrella, maybe. She's asked several times if she can come with me. Or Yu Lin."

"Estrella's a sweet girl, but you need someone like me with you," said Dawn, and insisted on cancelling the trip, but Grace would not hear of it. Dawn and Raymond came to say goodbye before they went on holiday. Dawn hugged her long and hard. Raymond kissed her, patting her shoulder.

"Be safe, you hear." Dawn looked misty eyed and miserable as they left. Grace tried to laugh her out of it, but choked on her laughter, she was so touched. Pawel came to see her up at the cottage the night after they left.

"Dawn asked me to look in on you. They are so worried about going away."

"I insisted," Grace told him.

"I know how stubborn you are," Pawel smiled to soften the remark. "So here's what I suggest for your additional safety..." He repeated his instructions of a month ago, explaining again the technical details of what he and Raymond had put in place in case of nocturnal intruders.

"Of course," he said, with a characteristic shrug. "The best security measure is not to stay here..."

"Don't worry," said Grace with a self-assurance she did not feel.

Chapter 31

August came and went. It was lonely staying in the cottage nights without Dawn. It rained frequently and heavily throughout the month. July and August were the two traditional typhoon months on the South China coast. This year there were only a few squalls. The first typhoon of the season announced itself at the end of August. Grace had come alone, late in the evening as usual to the cottage. It was heavily overcast. Her mobile phone pinged and Grace read a 'black rain' warning for Hong Kong and surrounding islands. This was bad, but did not really trouble her. It only meant that everyone stayed indoors and all offices would remain closed as long as it continued. On a coast that was frequently lashed by typhoons, Hong Kong had long since learnt to batten all hatches and shut down when the weather dictated. The Met Office kept an eye on the weather and broadcast coded messages for thunderstorms and typhoons.

A black rain was the most severe rainfall warning, meaning that over seventy millimeters of rain fell per hour. This was the equivalent of someone continuously pouring buckets of water on your head, and resulted in extensive flash floods and severe landslides. Anything not firmly anchored was washed down hillsides. A few years ago, a little boy had been swept into the harbor on his way to school and the body had never been found. Since then, everyone, school children, office workers, shop keepers, all stayed indoors where they were, either at home, in schools, offices or in a shelter, until the warning passed. Grace realized she had obviously missed the two earlier alerts, amber and red, prior to the black. Just as well. She was safe now in the cottage.

The rain began and all light was blotted up by the thick black clouds. Up in the clearing on top of the steep hill the rain was fiercer than anything Grace had experienced in her life. Bolts of lightning struck alarmingly close, followed by deafening thunderclaps. She thought she heard a thump on the door and saw the handle move. Luckily it was bolted from within. She looked around desperately for a weapon, and found a rolling pin. She held it upraised and put a ear to the door. It sounded like a female voice, so she unbolted the door, prepared to strike. A bedraggled woman in black slithered into the room, bringing a deluge of noise and rain with her. It was Dawn. Grace put a shoulder to the door, bolting it again.

"I hope you had a better holiday than this!" Dawn began to laugh hysterically.

"I tell you, I've never seen anything like it. The path up here was a river; rocks, leaves, twigs, mud. Sometimes the water came up to my knees and I thought I'd never make it."

"Didn't you hear the black rain warning?" Grace chided. "You could have been hurt."

"I am hurt," said Dawn ruefully. "What kind of a welcome is this. We got back an hour ago and I thought I'd come to see you."

"I'm sorry." Grace knelt down beside the puddle that was Dawn and embraced her friend. "I'm sorry. And it's so good to see you here. Come and get dry."

All Dawn's clothes had been soaked by the rain. She wailed when she found her mobile phone, carefully wrapped in sodden clothes, no longer worked.

"Raymond will worry. He didn't want me to come out, but I promised to call as soon as I reached."

"Here, take mine."

Half an hour later, Grace fed her soup, having given her a change of clothes and called Raymond to reassure him that Dawn had arrived.

"Now tell me about your holiday," she said, pouring glasses of brandy to celebrate Dawn's return. They talked till midnight. The downpour had died down to a mild patter of raindrops when they went to bed. The floor of the cottage was soaked from the rain that had come in when she opened the door for Dawn, so they both shared Beulah's single bed. Dawn promptly fell asleep, but Grace squirmed, trying to find a restful position. She slept fitfully and was awakened by stillness. Not noise, but the complete absence of noise. The rain had stopped and it was as though the world itself was dead. And then she heard it. A faint squelch. It seemed to be right outside the door. Oh shit! she thought. Her early warning inner radar had failed again. If someone was so close, Pawel's safety precautions were of no use now. They had been designed to stop intruders at the perimeter.

She tried to shake Dawn awake, but she was sleeping literally like a log. The cottage had a second weakness they had also discussed. It only had side windows. Nothing in front. She had no way to see who or what was there without opening the door.

"Oh shit, oh shit," she thought to herself, rolling off the bed on all fours to the floor. Instinct told her not to open the front door. She grabbed the remote control that Pawel had left for her, panicking, unable to see in the dark the different buttons he had shown. She crept to the rear door, cautiously opening it a crack. Pitch dark outside. She could not see.

"Unconcentrate, Grace! Unconcentrate!" she admonished herself. A thought came to her mind from nowhere, although she had flown over SunTzu's work only once in her life.

In every situation, seek your advantage. Her advantage: she could not see. Therefore she would not be seen.

She crept outside, feeling mud and sodden leaves beneath her bare feet. The leaves helped deaden her footfalls as she crept round to the side of the cottage. She could make out the lesser darkness of the clearing and hoped she could stick her head out low round the side to see who or what was at the front door. She crept along the side, face almost to the ground, and peeped at the front porch. There was a massive dark shape there, huge as a bear. She had no idea what it was. As she watched, the shape expanded, split into two. Two men.

The two shapes exploded into action before she could react. The front door caved under their joint assault with a splintering crash and they disappeared from sight. She stood up to peer through the side window. One of them had a penlight torch. They shone it on the bed, grabbed Dawn and dragged her, dazed and unresisting, out through the front door. A quick flashlight check of the cottage to make sure there was no one else and then together they dragged her to the edge of the cliff.

Grace desperately tried to remember Pawel's words. Several charges. Buried two by fours. At the edge of the cliff. At the edge of the clearing. By the path. Left button, right button. Center, red button. She tried to see, but could distinguish neither colors nor positions of buttons in the dark. She held the remote in the palm of her left hand and felt with three fingers of the right. Here they were. Left, center, right. God help her if she were wrong. Please. Please. Don't let anything happen to Dawn!

She could not see, dammit, the spot where the charges were fixed. She sprinted towards the soft dragging sounds, straining her eyes to see. Dawn was struggling now, resisting. Oh God, they were almost at the edge of the cliff, ready to throw her over, and where were the charges? She pressed. Wrong button! The ground in front of her heaved. A spray of mud and dirt stung her face. The buried two by fours shot out of the rain-softened earth and landed heavily beside the two men. The faint phosphorescence of the sea outlined their frozen erect figures. She knew where the other two charges were laid. They didn't. No matter that the explosions would not hurt them. They would be distracted.

Use the advantage of surprise, Grace. She pressed the other two buttons; one, two.

Two more explosions. To them, it might have seemed as though grenades were being lobbed at them. They could not explain the explosions. They did not hear Grace. She picked up a heavy two by four, swung it like a club at a man's head. Dawn began to struggle again just as he fell. The second man kicked Dawn viciously in the ribs, and began to move toward Grace, grabbing hold of the two by four and twisting. He was too strong for her. It was almost out of her grasp, so instead of struggling to hold it, Grace drove her legs forward. He wasn't expecting that. He stepped backwards, flailed with both arms for a moment, releasing the plank, and was lost to sight.

"Dawn, Dawn!" Grace in panic, knelt by her friend, felt her face, a mass of fabric stuffed in her mouth. She drew it out, as Dawn began to gasp and gag.

"Thank heaven! Are you alright?" She felt Dawn's nod of affirmation. Still holding the fabric in her hand, she touched the fallen man who was beginning to stir. She grabbed both arms and quickly pushed them behind his back, rolling him over onto his stomach. She twisted the fabric into a length and knotted it around his wrists as tightly as she could, placed a muddy two by four plank on his back, pinning both his arms, then stood on it. She could think of no other way to control him he if he came back to his senses and strength.

"Dawn, can you get up?" she called urgently. Dawn managed a strangled yes.

"Get my cell phone and call Pawel, Raymond and the police."

Pawel arrived first, armed with a torch and a big wrench. He shone the torch around the clearing, took in the scene and relieved Grace. The man groaned as Pawel's great weight came to rest on the plank. Grace, relieved, went to look after Dawn, who had bruises all over her body and was hobbling badly.

"I think I've hurt my knee. One of my old ski injuries," she said. "I'll be ok in a few days."

The island police came roaring up, lights flashing. There were two of them. One of them on a four-wheeled quadricycle; the other in a car with a narrow wheelbase suitable for the island's small paths. Raymond arrived soon after with Yu Lin. After calling the police, he had quickly called the headman, correctly assuming that Yu Lin would be the right person to deal with the police.

Rather than interrogate the prisoner in custody, the police seemed to be more concerned with questions about the smell of explosives that hung in the air. Grace and Dawn professed total ignorance. Obviously something that the thieves had planted here, suggested Yu Lin. Why trouble the victims about something the attackers had done?

In the first of light of dawn, the police looked around and scratched their heads in puzzlement at the gouged earth, the two by fours and bits of wire that littered the clearing. Fortunately Pawel noticed the detonator that Grace had dropped, casually bent to pick it up, then wandered over to the cliff edge to look at the inert body lying far below. He idly picked up a rock and threw it out to sea, sending the remote with it.

For the second time in six months, the police attached a long rope to a tree at the top of the clearing and sent a man to investigate the fallen body. Grace looked down with faint regret for the death she had caused. It would be poetic justice, she thought, if the man lying among the rocks below were the one who had pushed Beulah to her death. Small justice. Greater justice would have to wait till Mr. Ma was brought to book.

That morning, after the police had taken Mr. Ma's thug into custody and left, Raymond had asked Yu Lin what would happen with the cottage. Dawn would not be able to come to the cottage for at least two weeks till her injury healed and Grace should not stay alone after this. Yu Lin agreed.

"I have someone else," he said.

"Oh, good. Who is it?"

"A grand-nephew." he said.

"Another one?" asked Grace. Yu Lin laughed a mischievous laugh.

"Yes, and this time, he knows who his grandfather is."

Grace laughed with him, glad to see that he was beginning to heal after the loss of Lai Bo and Wenbo.

Three days later Grace walked into Dawn's house for dinner late one evening. Such a relief not to have to spend another night in Beulah's cottage, beautiful though its location! She had thoroughly enjoyed the past three nights in her own bed. If anything, Estrella, who hated sleeping alone in the house, was even happier to have Grace back.

Raymond was cooking tonight. Dawn sat on the sofa with her right leg, thickly bandaged at the knee, stretched out in front of her. Sylvie was there as well. Jacques was away again, and Adeline was asleep in her own bedroom, watched over by Frank and a young babysitter.

Sylvie stood up and embraced Grace with great warmth. Grace bent over Dawn and kissed the top of her head. Raymond wandered over to Grace, ruffled her hair paternally and gave her a great big hug.

"All's well that ends well, my dear," he said. Grace said nothing. Dawn cocked her head and smiled slowly.

"It's not over yet, is it?"

Grace nodded after a long silence, reluctant to acknowledge to herself what she already knew; the truth of Dawn's words. She had been suppressing it for three days.

"Yu Lin told me it's safe now for his nephew to be there..." Raymond was flustered.

"Yes," said Grace.

"Yes, but..." Dawn insisted.

Grace looked at Dawn, loving this woman who had become best friend and sister to her in the short space of four months.

"It's not over as long as Ma Wood Industries is still dealing in rare wood and wood oils. Tony confirmed yesterday that Mr. Ma has bought the large villa on Mo Tat Wan for eighteen million dollars Hong Kong. To me it looks like a small investment made by a rich man who hopes to make fifty to a hundred million dollars, US, from an illegal harvest on this island.

"And in other parts of Asia, the harvesting is still going on... in Vietnam, in Cambodia and Thailand, close to their common border."

"You can't solve all the problems of the world, Grace," said Raymond gently.

"I know. I don't expect to. I've spent the past five years looking… searching for my role.. in life. It might sound pretentious…"

"Not at all," Dawn and Raymond spoke together. Grace smiled.

"…but I know I have a role, some kind of a task to accomplish. And you know, I've been searching among people like you, my friends and family, for signs, for indications, to try and find out what that role might be."

"And…" prompted Sylvie, intrigued.

"…and… my role was pointed out to me a month ago by someone… to my face. I wasn't listening, because I wasn't expecting that kind of a message from that kind of person."

"From whom? Adeline?" Sylvie couldn't contain her curiosity, and she was only half joking about her daughter. Grace did not laugh.

"I really spent some time thinking if Adeline's inexplicable affection for me was some kind of a message…"

"Of course it is," exclaimed Sylvie. "Anyone can see you're a born mother. You like to take care of people. No wonder children love you."

"Not all children, though. Only Adeline. She's an exception. So that's not it… although I don't rule out motherhood." Grace smiled again as Sylvie settled back with a pout.

"So who did the message come from?" asked Raymond, impatient now.

"From Mr. Ma himself. I'm sure he didn't mean it that way. But if ever the universe sent me a message, it was that conversation on his boat where Ma told me the story of my own life. Why else would a perfect stranger bother to find out about my life in such detail? If he wasn't worried that I would somehow interfere in his plans? Somehow, someday…"

"So what does this mean in practical terms?" asked Dawn, always the one who brought discussions back to the here and now.

"This means… that I'll be going away for some time. A few weeks, maybe months."

"Oh, where to?" Dawn's manner was elaborately casual.

"I've had dreams about the Cardamom Mountains for some time. In Cambodia, close to the Thai border."

"Literally dreaming?" asked Dawn. Grace nodded and shrugged; outwardly a gesture of resignation, inwardly an acceptance of what she knew she had to do.

"Yes. Literally," said Grace.

"Well, then. You have to follow your dreams, don't you?"

"Yes."

"When do you think you'll leave?" Dawn's manner was even more casual.

"I thought maybe in a week or two."

"Oh no, the doctor said you'll have to give my knee at least three weeks to heal."

"What?"

"I'm going with you."

"No."

"Yes."

"No."

"Yes." Grace burst into laughter at Dawn's emphatically reiterated yes.

"Yes," she said. "If you insist."

"And what about me?" Raymond interjected.

"What about you? You can come along if you like."

"And my bees?" Raymond exploded. "Who's going to look after my bees?"

Dawn looked at Raymond in consternation, then noticed the beginnings of a smile. She arched her torso over the backrest of the sofa and raised her arms overhead, hugging him.

"Let the birds looks after your bees for a while, darling," she murmured.

END OF BOOK ONE

THE TREES OF TA PROHM

(Grace in the South China Sea: Book Two)

The man held an amber vial of oily liquid in his hand, obviously proffering it for sale. He was tall, with Indo-Chinese features and close-cropped hair.

"How much?" asked the soft-spoken man. He was small, with Chinese features and Caucasian eyes. Grace recognized him instantly. It was Mr. Ma.

"How much you give?" asked the tall man.

"One hundred American dollars." The tall man wagged a finger in contemptuous refusal in the smaller man's face.

"This costs more than ten thousand dollars, American. I will give it to you for five thousand."

"Yes. Because you stole it. I will give you two." Mr. Ma's hand moved and he deftly caught the vial as the taller man crumpled to the floor.

Grace woke with a start and stared blankly at the wall of the hotel room in Siem Reap. Had this happened already, or was she seeing something that was to happen in the near future?

If ever there was a country in the second half of the twentieth century so blessed by geography but cursed by history, Cambodia was it. The thought occurred to Grace as she walked through the landmine museum on the outskirts of Siem Reap.

It hadn't always been so. From the ninth to the fourteenth century the Khmer Empire had been a Great

Power, in a capitalized, geopolitical sense of the word.

It was a small museum, started by one man. Dawn was visibly moved as she walked slowly around the small space, reading the small print on the exhibits with intense concentration. From time to time she wiped her eyes to suppress upwelling emotion. Grace felt the corners of her own eyes moisten in sympathetic reaction and put a hand on Dawn's shoulder. Dawn shook her head without looking up.

"Domino theory!" she exclaimed.

"What?"

"When were you born?" Dawn asked.

"1982. Why?"

"I was born in 1967. When I was growing up, a lot of my father's conversation around the dining table was about the justification of the Vietnam War. And my father believed in the domino theory."

"What was that?" Grace had never heard of it.

"It was a theory on which American foreign policy was based in the 1950s and 60s, and my father was a staunch supporter although, Canada, thank heaven, largely stayed out of the Vietnam war."

The land mine museum was housed in a non-descript building a few kilometers from the magnificent ruins of Ta Prohm. Even though Grace had visited the ruins years earlier, and Dawn knew what she would see at one of the most photographed sites in the world, they were both moved to silence by the intertwining of works by the hand of man and the magnificent trees of the encroaching jungle.

It was as though the invading trees had sanctified what was otherwise an abandoned holy place and imbued it with renewed spirituality.

Such was the aura of the ruins that they felt its spiritual power despite the large hordes of noisy tourists who clambered atop stones with the inevitable selfie sticks clutched in their grasp, ignoring the feeble protests of the uniformed monument guides who tried to restrain them.

Still steeped in the aura of the ruins, they were accosted by a fierce urchin girl with unkempt hair who was selling picture postcards they didn't want. They waved her away, but she looked them in the eye and didn't move.

"Where you from?" she asked Grace.

"Mmmm. Hong Kong," said Grace after some hesitation. She really did not know where she was from.

"Yat, yee, sahm, sahp, ng,…"

"Actually, I'm from India," Grace laughed, refusing the postcards.

"Ek, do, theen, panch, char…."

They gave up the unequal contest then, each buying two sets of picture postcards from the girl before she could begin to count in French for Dawn.

Afterwards they drove back to Siem Riep in their tuk-tuk. On the way, their tuk-tuk driver, who had told them his name was Steve, asked if they wanted to stop and see the landmine museum. "Very interesting," he assured them. "All tourists stop here."

Neither Grace nor Dawn wished to stop where all tourists did, but the improbably named Steve looked so eager that they decided to humor him. They were primarily not here as tourists, but to learn about the country before exploring the forests near the Thai border to the south, so they said yes.

ABOUT THE AUTHOR

Aviott John lived for two years on an island in the South China Sea. Previously he worked for four decades in Austria as a librarian, science writer and publicist. He now divides his time between Austria and India with hopes of building a sustainable, off-grid enterprise in the Thar desert. Read more on his blog at aviott.org

Made in the USA
Charleston, SC
21 November 2015